DRAMATIC MURDER

DRAMATIC MURDER

A Lost Christmas
Murder Mystery

Elizabeth Anthony

with an introduction by
MARTIN EDWARDS

This edition published 2024 by
The British Library
96 Euston Road
London NW1 2DB

Dramatic Murder was first published in Britain in
1948 by Hodder and Stoughton Ltd, London.

Introduction © 2024 Martin Edwards
Volume Copyright © The British Library Board
Dramatic Murder © 1948 The Estate of Elizabeth Anthony

Cataloguing in Publication Data
A catalogue record for this book is available from the British Library

ISBN 978 0 7123 5556 8
eISBN 978 0 7123 6813 1

Original cover image: *Shop Early* by Freda Beard, 1927.
Image © London Metropolitan Archives (City of London).

Text design and typesetting by Tetragon, London
Printed in England by CPI Group (UK) Ltd, Croydon, CRO 4YY

CONTENTS

The author (right) with her daughter, Elisabeth, to whom this book was dedicated.
Photograph courtesy of the estate of the author.

INTRODUCTION

Dramatic Murder is an entertaining novel originally published by Hodder in 1948, and the first mystery by an interesting but little-known author who used the pen-name Elizabeth Anthony for her regrettably infrequent ventures into crime fiction.

Of all the many hundreds of mystery novels which begin at Christmas-time, few have quite such a vivid opening situation. Doctor Harley and his passenger, a journalist called Katherine Mickey, are travelling through the snow in Scotland, en route for a Christmas party on Possett Island. The setting is Possett Castle, which is evocatively characterized:

> Its turrets and crenellated battlements were witchlike, reminding Katherine of an illustration to an old book of *Grimm's Fairy Tales*. Although every window was brilliantly lit, there was something cold and forbidding about the exterior, and as they approached the entrance she became aware of a peculiar throbbing which seemed to reverberate through the air.
>
> "That's the generator, miss," Benson explained.

Harley and Katherine have been invited to a Christmas party by the renowned playwright and broadcaster Dimpson McCabe—always known as Dimpsie—but the castle seems strangely deserted. They go to his studio and are confronted by a large Christmas tree:

It was planted in a green wooden tub, its topmost branches reached up to the ceiling, and it was hung with coloured geegaws and trinkets of every description. Hearts, flowers, tiny umbrellas, miniature pianos and a dozen other objects were fashioned in blown-glass of blue, parrot-green, scarlet, yellow and flame. There were tiny vases, covered with silver or gold netting, all kinds of animals, and fantastic birds with long silken tails which were perched precariously among the greenery. Festoons of silver were draped lavishly from branch to branch and long strands of tinfoil, resembling icicles, gave a frosty, fairy-light effect. At the base of the tree parcels were piled up indiscriminately, their coloured wrappings providing a kaleidoscope pattern. Tiny coloured electric bulbs were clipped on to the branches, but they were not alight.

Quite a sight. But there is more.

From between the branches Dimpson McCabe's face peered whitely at them, his eyes stared owlishly through thick spectacles; one hand, pushed through the tinsel draperies, pointed a long finger at them.

Katherine screams. Because their host is dead.

The seasoned mystery reader will immediately assume that Dimpsie is the victim of foul play, but at first the authorities seem willing to accept that his death was, in Harley's words, "a clear case of accidental death... he must have been trying to remove one of the little bulbs from the flex... The end of the flex was plugged into the wall—into the power... he had cut the flex and the wire was bare on each side where the bulb had been attached. Why he didn't turn off the current before doing this I simply can't imagine…" Unfortunately, his feet were wet: "He must have been out in the snow… I don't know why he should have gone out in his slippers, but I'm afraid that's what caused his death… a chance in a million…"

We are duly introduced to Dimpsie's other guests, several of whom are, like their late host, involved in the theatre world; there's also a big game hunter, one of those characters not uncommon in classic crime novels, but nowhere to be found in contemporary mysteries. When Katherine considers the members of the party, she concludes that "most of them stood to gain by keeping him alive." But as the Christmas puzzle turns into a theatrical whodunit, Dimpsie proves to be merely the first victim of a determined killer who is "rotten to the core". Suspicion shifts from one person to another as the official detective work is undertaken by a low-key Scotland Yard man called Smith. A London theatre provides a suitably dramatic backdrop for the finale.

So who was Elizabeth Anthony? Very little information is available about her online and I'm grateful to her grandson Noel Hulsman and family friend Peter Stickney for sharing some background details about this talented and cultured woman. She was born Barbara Frances Courlander in Kilburn in 1906 and married a writer called Howard Rubien; Morgan A. Wallace, who has written an informative online article about her, suggests that her husband was also an actor, known as Howard Nelson Rubien, who appeared in films including *Death in Venice*. The couple had a daughter, Elisabeth, to whom *Dramatic Murder* is dedicated.

A year before this book appeared, Barbara Rubien had produced under her own name a non-genre novel, described by Hodder as "a sensitively written story of a woman who indeed drowned her honour in a shallow cup and sold her reputation for a song. Miss Barbara Rubien has already written plays and contributed material to several revues. With *The Cup and the Song* she makes her debut as a novelist of unusual promise."

No more novels appeared under her real name, but she used the name Elizabeth Anthony when collaborating with the composer Vivien Lambelet on the song "Wayfarer", which appeared on the soundtrack of the popular 1949 film *The Glass Mountain*. The following year, Elizabeth Anthony the crime writer returned with *Made for Murder*, about a woman who wins a large amount of money only for her luck to run out when she encounters a homicidal conman. With this, her brief career as a novelist came to an end, although seven years later she contributed a short story, "Seventh Murder of Henry's Father", to *Ellery Queen's Mystery Magazine*. And that seems to have been that, as far as her writing was concerned, although she lived until 1996. Peter Stickney tells me that she was a dog lover who patented a dog mat which earned her royalties before her daughter passed the rights to the RSPCA.

Unfortunately, Howard Rubien left the marriage when their daughter was only two and it may well be that the demands of parenting meant that Barbara had to sacrifice her writing ambitions. I gather from Noel Hulsman that she was entrepreneurial, and ran an antiques shop on High Street, Steyning, Sussex, as well as buying and selling houses, which was her main source of income. Quite apart from the demands of these activities, it's possible that, like so many other capable writers before and since, she became disheartened by a lack of success. Perhaps she felt overshadowed by the crime writing achievements of the dedicatee of *Made for Murder*, "my sister-in-crime Shelley Smith". Shelley Smith was the pseudonym of Nancy Hermione Courlander (1912–98), who was briefly married to Stephen Bodington. Nancy achieved considerable success during a long career as a published novelist from 1942 to 1978 and returned the compliment by dedicating a couple of her fourteen books to Barbara. She too lived in Steyning for many years.

Both sisters were authors of conspicuous ability but have long faded from view. Interest in Shelley Smith's books was revived when Julian Symons reintroduced her wonderfully enjoyable *An Afternoon to Kill* in a reprint edition and it would be good to think that this reprint will help to rescue the work of another good writer from the obscurity into which it has fallen.

MARTIN EDWARDS
www.martinedwardsbooks.com

A NOTE FROM THE PUBLISHER

The original novels and short stories reprinted in the British Library Crime Classics series were written and published in a period ranging, for the most part, from the 1890s to the 1960s. There are many elements of these stories which continue to entertain modern readers; however, in some cases there are also uses of language, instances of stereotyping and some attitudes expressed by narrators or characters which may not be endorsed by the publishing standards of today. We acknowledge therefore that some elements in the works selected for reprinting may continue to make uncomfortable reading for some of our audience. With this series British Library Publishing aims to offer a new readership a chance to read some of the rare books of the British Library's collections in an affordable paperback format, to enjoy their merits and to look back into the world of the twentieth century as portrayed by its writers. It is not possible to separate these stories from the history of their writing and therefore the following novel is presented as it was originally published with one edit to the text and minor edits made for consistency of style and sense. We welcome feedback from our readers, which can be sent to the following address:

British Library Publishing
The British Library
96 Euston Road
London, NW1 2DB
United Kingdom

DRAMATIC MURDER

FOR
ELISABETH
WITH LOVE

I

FOR WHOM THE BELL TOLLS

I

THE FINE SNOW THAT HAD BEEN FALLING SINCE THEY LEFT Edinburgh was thickening, and the sky was black with large powdered flakes. They collected on the windscreen, and the wiper, pushing them aside, groaned protestingly. The car sped onwards, eating up the road which stretched like a long, white ribbon, bordered by fir trees that were jet-black in the half light. At the side of the road a signpost pointed the way down a narrow cutting between the trees; painted in black and red it had a sinister appearance and the words POSSETT ISLAND stood out bleakly. Doctor Harley swung the car off the road and it skidded slightly on the soft snow. His passenger blinked.

"Heavens!" she said, "I've been asleep."

"Don't I know it!"

"Oh!" she was apologetic. "You should have woken me... I'm dreadfully sorry..."

"That's all right," he assured her. "I had plenty to think about. Cigarette?"

"Thanks. Are we there?"

Doctor Harley switched on the headlights; it was dark in the little wood. The golden beams reached out, turning the road through the trees to a golden pathway, and in contrast the surrounding trees and bushes were shaded blue and purple.

Katherine Mickey lit her cigarette, and pulled the hood of her coat over her head.

"You must be frozen," she said to the doctor.

He grinned. "Not too bad," he said. "What about you?"

"I shan't be terribly sorry to arrive. I hope Dimpsie's got plenty of hot drinks waiting for us."

"I think we can count on that, don't you?"

In front of them the ground sloped gently to where the Loch stretched out a frozen surface. Several hundred yards away it was just possible to see the Island which, in the gathering darkness flecked with powdered snow-flakes, seemed to be just a cluster of trees. At the edge of the Loch a small cabin showed lighted windows. Doctor Harley sounded the horn, and a figure hurried out to them.

"It's Benson, sir," a man's voice said. "Is that Doctor Harley?"

"That's right, Benson," said the doctor, "and Miss Mickey is with me."

"Will you drive straight over, sir?" Benson said, "the surface is gravelled, and the ice is more than a foot thick—it's perfectly safe." He stepped on to the running-board as he spoke. "It's only a few hundred yards, sir, and just follow the slope on the other side."

Doctor Harley drove slowly on to the ice. The gravel crunched under the weight of the car, but the ice did not crack. It was not until they had driven up the slope, and on to the level ground, however, that they were able to catch a glimpse of their destination. As they got out of the car they noticed that the snow had stopped falling, and Possett Castle stood out sharply against the dark blue sky. It was built of grey stone, which looked black in the evening light, and its turrets and crenellated battlements were witchlike, reminding Katherine of an illustration to an old book of *Grimm's Fairy Tales*.

Although every window was brilliantly lit, there was something cold and forbidding about the exterior, and as they approached the entrance she became aware of a peculiar throbbing which seemed to reverberate through the air.

"That's the generator, miss," Benson explained. "We've got our own electric plant now."

Katherine looked up at the Castle. "Of course, it's very rich and grand," she said, "but I believe I'd settle for something cosy in the High Street."

Doctor Harley laughed. "Dimpsie would be terribly insulted if he heard you," he said. "It's very attractive inside." He pointed to a wing that had obviously been added recently. "That's the famous studio," he said. It was the only portion of the castle in total darkness.

Benson came up behind them with the baggage. "I'll bring the cases in, sir," he said, "and Elspeth will take them upstairs for you."

Lights were shining from the hall, and the front door stood slightly open.

"It's very quiet," Doctor Harley said. "Where is everybody, Benson?"

"I couldn't say, sir, I'm sure." He put the suit-cases down, and hurried away through a door at the end of the hall.

Katherine and the doctor looked at each other blankly. Katherine chuckled. "Just like Dimpsie," she said. "He's probably going to pop out at us from somewhere… let's fool him."

She opened the first door to hand—it was a cloak-room. Hats and coats hung from pegs, some skis were propped in a corner, and on the floor were little puddles of water, and a pair of snow-boots.

One by one they peeped into every room leading off the hall, only to find them all empty. At the last door the doctor paused.

"If I remember rightly," he said, "this should be the studio. Dimpsie was rather fussy about it last time I was here… didn't like one to go barging in… but still, he can't expect us to hang about in the hall waiting for him to turn up."

"I don't know," Katherine said, her voice hushed in the silence, "I can't say I think much of his idea of a joke. It's so queer to leave us like this in an empty house. Where is everybody?"

"There's Benson," said the doctor, "—I suppose he's in the kitchen somewhere; and the maid Elspeth, wherever she is… the house isn't really empty."

"I don't like it," Katherine said, and shivered.

"Well, we needn't whisper," he said, trying to make her laugh.

"I never realized we were," she said gravely.

He opened the studio door. The lights were on here, as they had been in all the other rooms. Black velvet curtains filled an entire wall, covering enormous plate-glass windows. On the right, facing the curtains, was a fireplace in which burnt a tremendous log fire. A grand piano stood in a corner, the keyboard backing into the centre of the room, and at the end, facing the door, stood the Christmas Tree. It was planted in a green wooden tub, its topmost branches reached up to the ceiling, and it was hung with coloured gewgaws and trinkets of every description. Hearts, flowers, tiny umbrellas, miniature pianos and a dozen other objects were fashioned in blown-glass of blue, parrot-green, scarlet, yellow and flame. There were tiny vases, covered with silver or gold netting, all kinds of animals, and fantastic birds with long silken tails which were perched precariously among the greenery. Festoons of silver were draped lavishly from branch to branch and long strands of tinfoil, resembling icicles, gave a frosty, fairy-like effect. At the base of the tree parcels were piled up indiscriminately, their coloured wrappings providing a kaleido-scope pattern. Tiny coloured electric light bulbs were clipped on to the branches, but these were not alight. Evidently they were to be saved for the party.

Doctor Harley and Katherine walked over to the fire and stood warming themselves.

"What a glorious tree!" Katherine said, gazing at it. "Dimpsie will be hopping mad when he knows we've seen it."

"No doubt he will," said Doctor Harley. "But I'd like to see his face if he'd come three hundred miles and found no one to greet him on his arrival."

"It's this awful silence that gets me," Katherine said. "It's so uncanny. I can't understand where everyone is! After all, what's he done with all the other guests? It's so creepy, don't you think so? If someone doesn't come in soon I shall go and rout out that man in the kitchen. He'll just have to go and find—" She was walking over to the tree as she spoke, and she broke off suddenly and stood staring in front of her. "Dimpsie! You devil! Come out at once! You scared the wits out of me!"

Silence hung in the room; tangible, eerie. The air was close from the heat of the fire. Katherine felt the sweat break out on her forehead.

"Dimpsie!" she gave a nervous giggle. "Do come out!" She turned to the doctor. "Isn't he a beast!"

Doctor Harley looked blank. "Where is he? I don't see anyone."

Katherine pointed a shaking forefinger at the tree. "Look!"

From between the branches Dimpson McCabe's face peered whitely at them, his eyes stared owlishly through thick spectacles; one hand, pushed through the tinsel draperies, pointed a long finger at them.

"Dimpsie!" Katherine, losing control for a second, screamed. A high-pitched, thin sound that echoed weirdly from the wires of the open piano.

"Wait a minute!" the doctor spoke with authority. He crossed the room and went round the back of the tree. Dimpsie, a length of silken flex held tightly in each hand, stood close up against the tree, his face hidden in the branches, his body outstretched. He was quite dead.

II

Doctor Harley looked at the girl standing by the fire. She had her back to him, and her voice, when she spoke was throaty and thick.

"Is he dead?"

"I'm afraid he is," the doctor said.

"Oh!" she gave a little cry. "But now—what happened?"

Doctor Harley walked heavily over to the fire. He put his arm round Katherine's shoulders, and spoke very gently.

"I don't think it can have been anyone's fault. Poor old Dimpsie—I think he must have been trying to fix the lights for the tree…"

"Did he have a heart attack, then?"

"No." The doctor paused; it was not easy to explain in cold blood. "I'm afraid, Katherine, it looks as if he—he got a shock."

"My God! Electrocuted!" The tears welled up in her eyes and rolled down her cheeks. "Poor Dimpsie! Poor old thing!"

"We'll have to get the police," Doctor Harley said, "and nothing must be touched here. Let's go and find Benson…" He led her out of the room, and locked the door behind them, slipping the key into his pocket. "Benson!" he called. "Benson!"

The man came hurrying out of the kitchen. He was wearing a white coat—a chef's cap on his head.

"Benson, there's been an accident," the doctor said. "Can you get hold of the police? Are you on the phone here?"

"No, sir, we haven't a phone. But I've got my motor bike handy—I can go at once…" He stood still, a worried frown between his heavy eyebrows. "Excuse me, sir, it's not Mr. McCabe, I hope?"

"I'm afraid it is, Benson. And it's pretty bad, too; just as bad as it can be. Unfortunately, I was too late to be able to help. Mr. McCabe must have been trying to fix the lights on the tree. By the way, I take it you didn't know he was in the studio?"

"No, sir. I thought everyone was gone off to the woods. Mr. McCabe said something about a game they was to play there... I wasn't to tell you—it was to be a surprise—"

"Did they all go?"

"Yes, sir. That is, all except Mr. Walters. He went into Drumbrunnock to get some tobacco and cigarettes." He glanced uneasily at the studio door. "Is Mr. McCabe in there, sir?"

The doctor frowned. "Yes, Benson. Now look here, has your wife arrived yet?"

Benson shook his head. "She'll be here any moment now, sir. Had I better tell her what's happened?"

"Yes, I suppose you had; I hope she won't be very upset. If she can come over and hold the fort—some people may be needing a hot drink, you know. I'd like you to get over to Drumbrunnock as quickly as possible. Have you any idea how long it will take you?"

"Not more than twenty minutes, sir. I can be there and back within the hour."

"Very well, then. Be just as quick as you can, Benson. And—I suppose the other guests will be coming in, soon?"

"I'll ring, sir." Benson crossed the hall and opened the front door. At the right of the porch a length of rope dangled to within a foot of the ground. Seizing this in both hands, Benson tugged vigorously. Somewhere far above them a bell tolled out into the night air; a cold, mournful, clanging note that resounded frighteningly in the darkness. Katherine and the doctor stood in the porch and waited... waited and listened to the doleful bell ringing out across the Loch.

Presently, over the vast, snow-covered expanse of lawn, and beyond, where the tall fir-trees stretched their black branches into the dark bowl that was the sky, little figures came running out of the wood; hurrying over the snow, back to the house where Dimpsie lay dead.

To Katherine, the next few hours were indescribably confused. Doctor Harley's announcement had come as a terrible shock to Dimpsie's guests; they had all begun to talk at once, asking innumerable questions, and this, combined with the roar of Benson's motor cycle, the clanging of the fire-bell, and the arrival of the Police Inspector, had combined to give her a splitting headache. But at last Inspector Smith had departed, and the guests had retired to their own rooms. Katherine and the doctor sat by the fire in the lounge; they were not speaking, they were both engrossed in their thoughts. It was still difficult for Katherine to believe that she would never again see her old friend; never again see that benevolent, plump face that reminded her so irresistibly of a baby owlet; never again hear that slow drawl that could utter such devastating remarks in such sugary tones. Dimpsie had been so alive—so vital—so full of being. And yet—he had died almost instantaneously.

As the only journalist present, she had felt obliged to take advantage of her position. Dimpsie's death was news. And Dimpsie would have been the first to insist on the exploitation of every possible angle. Somewhere, deep down inside her, Katherine thought that perhaps he might be glad that it was she who would be the first to tell the world of his death. "I'll tell the world!" Dimpsie's own pet phrase. As "The Tatler" Dimpsie *had* told the world; he had broadcast regularly every Sunday evening. And, one way and another, he had told the world a good deal. It had been said that a few words of praise by "The Tatler" and a book might become a best-seller, a play could be a success over-night. He had been known to mention a book which had flopped badly, and had so spoken of it that by the end of a week it had sold fifty thousand copies. Katherine wondered how much this power had affected Dimpsie. She had heard him discussed with kindness—and with venom. It was inevitable that such a man should have made enemies, but few who knew him well could have failed to love him. Katherine, remembering him since childhood days, felt her loss to be irreparable. And now, sitting quietly by the fire, relaxed at last, after the exhausting experiences of the past few hours, Katherine wondered just what magic touch Dimpsie had used to make himself as powerful and as sought after as he undoubtedly had been.

"It's a funny thing," Doctor Harley said, as if he could read her thoughts, "there are people who would have given anything to be invited here for a week-end."

"I know. Dimpsie often talked about turning the Island into a club… I wonder what will happen to the place now?"

The doctor shrugged. "Who can tell?" He lit another cigarette and stared into the fire. He was remembering how Benson had disclaimed all knowledge of McCabe's whereabouts. Surely, he thought, someone must have known Dimpsie's plans. The door opened and Henry Walters, Dimpsie's secretary, walked softly up to the fireplace. He rested his arms along the back of the sofa, and leaned over, looking down on Katherine as she lay with her legs up, stretched out full-length on the cushions.

"I've been talking to Gallia," he said. "Poor darling, she's in an awful state. I was wondering…" he smiled dubiously at Katherine.

"Do you mean you want me to go up to her?" she asked. "I will, of course, if you think it will do any good."

"She's in bed now," Walters said. "Mrs. Benson took her a hot drink. But you know how temperamental these Russians are, and

Gallia has wept on my shoulder until I feel positively damp." He laughed ruefully.

Katherine swung her legs on to the floor. "All right," she said, "but this isn't going to be a party. Doctor Harley, if I'm not down in a quarter of an hour, please come and fetch me!"

"I certainly will," he said firmly.

She went slowly over to the door, and they could hear the tap-tap of her high heels on the stone floor outside. Henry Walters sat down in Katherine's place.

"This is a dreadful business," he began.

The doctor frowned. The insincerity of the words jarred badly. "I can't imagine how it came about," he said severely.

Walters gave an infinitesimal shrug. "Dimpsie would insist on decorating the tree himself. The studio had been kept locked for days... no one was allowed inside. And the curtains had been drawn to prevent peeking. I begged him to let me help, but he wouldn't hear of it. And, of course, he didn't know a thing about electricity."

"Really?" Doctor Harley raised his eyebrows.

"Not that there was anything to know. But he wanted to fix the lamps on the tree... the fairy lights, you know. I simply can't imagine what can have gone wrong!"

The doctor was silent.

"There'll be an inquest, I suppose?"

"I'm afraid that's inevitable," Doctor Harley said.

"Oh dear! Does that mean they'll *all* have to attend?" Henry Walters looked worried.

"I shouldn't think so. You, of course, as McCabe's secretary, and Miss Mickey and myself... I do not think it will be necessary for the others to be there."

"What did the Inspector think?" Henry Walters asked tentatively.

"I couldn't say," said Doctor Harley. "No doubt the Sheriff will find it all quite in order. All I can tell you is that McCabe was electrocuted... it's up to the Inspector to find out if there was anything wrong with the set up... or if someone had fooled about with the lighting."

"You don't mean—" Walters looked unhappily at the doctor.

"I don't mean anything. I'm merely saying that it's the duty of the Inspector to find out if there was anything wrong. He will then put the result of his findings to the Sheriff, who will direct the inquest."

"It all sounds dreadfully sinister," Henry Walters said glumly. "You're not suggesting there was anything... well..." He did not finish the sentence.

"I'm not suggesting anything at all," said Doctor Harley, getting up from his chair. "And now, if you'll excuse me, I'll be turning in. Good night to you, Walters," he nodded briefly to the secretary, and went up to his room.

Henry Walters remained sitting by the fire.

"Not suggesting anything," he muttered to himself, "not suggesting anything. Hell!" He got up and hurled a cushion savagely to the ground. Then, standing with his back to the door, he leaned his arms on the mantelpiece and gazed thoughtfully into the fire.

III

Gallia Karmanskaya dabbed at her eyes with a chiffon handkerchief. "All this crying," she thought, "I shall be a sight to-morrow." And then, remembering that to-morrow it would no longer matter how she looked, she wept afresh. A tap on the door roused her, however, and she called "Come in" quaveringly. Katherine smiled at her from the doorway.

"Ah! Kate, my darling! You have come to cheer me up? That is kind of you!" Gallia patted the bed with a beringed hand that was surprisingly slim. "Come and sit here, my little one!"

Katherine took the stool that was in front of the dressing-table and brought it to the side of the bed. The bed itself was crumpled and untidy; on the quilted chintz cover, which Gallia had not troubled to remove, were strewn cigarettes, a box of chocolates, a looking-glass, powder-box and a lipstick. At the foot, on a folded rug, a little Pekingese lay sleeping. Gallia was wearing a transparent pink chiffon nightdress which did not attempt to conceal her very voluptuous charms; round her head she had draped a soft, shetland wool scarf. An electric heater was turned full on, and the atmosphere was close and heavily perfumed. As Katherine approached the bed the little dog awoke, and jumped up, barking loudly.

"Ting-a-Ling!" said Gallia reproachfully, "that's a bad dog... barking at Katherine like that. Apologize at once!" She looked sternly at him, and the Peke sat up meekly, his paws hanging dolefully, his muzzle quivering.

"Oh, he's sweet!" Katherine said. "What a darling! I've never seen him do that before."

"It was a new trick!" Gallia explained. "I taught him specially for Christmas... I wanted him to do it for Dimpsie..." Her eyes filled with tears again. The Peke licked her hand, and she stroked him lovingly. "There! good boy!" she tried to smile. "Kate! you will think I am very silly, I am afraid."

"Of course not, why should I? We all loved Dimpsie... I know how you must feel." Katherine felt a little embarrassed.

"But for me it was different..." Gallia passed the cigarette-case to Katherine and then took one herself. "You see, for me Dimpsie was more than just a friend... he meant so much to me..."

"I know," murmured Katherine.

"Yes? He had spoken to you of me, then?"

"Well—I guessed you were to be here for Christmas, of course."

"Of course." Gallia blew a cloud of smoke which hung in the heavy air. Katherine began to feel faint; she unbuttoned the neck of her sweater. "You are too hot?" Gallia said. "Me, I feel the cold very much!" She wrapped the scarf cosily about her head. "Yes, it was for me that poor Dimpsie has had all those big fires. He knew that I feel the cold so much in this big, stone castle."

"He liked to make everyone comfortable," Katherine agreed.

"But me—me—specially me," Gallia insisted. "You see, little one, we were to be married... we were going to tell this at Christmas to everybody." She tried to smile bravely, but it was a watery attempt, and Katherine felt an absurd pricking behind her own lids. She did not know what to reply to Gallia's confidence.

"I had no idea—" she said at last.

"No? We kept our secret well, Dimpsie and I! But, little one, you are not surprised, I think."

"Well..." Katherine hesitated. "I knew Dimpsie was very fond of you—but he did not tell me any more than that."

"Fond of me!" Gallia laughed. "He adored me, little one. In all my life I have had a lot of men to love me—but never one more than Dimpsie." She blew her nose with the wisp of chiffon. "Poor darling! We shall find out what really happened, and then—then it is I, Gallia Karmanskaya, who will avenge him." She looked fiercely at Katherine and the little dog began to bark again. "Be quiet, Ting-a-Ling!" she ordered.

"You were not with Dimpsie at all this afternoon?" Katherine asked.

For a moment Gallia hesitated. "No. No—I was in the woods. Dimpsie made me promise to go in the woods. He wanted to prepare a surprise."

"Who were you with, then?" Katherine asked idly.

"With? why—with everybody," Gallia said. "With Frederica—and Glen, and Henry—Walters, you know. Holly and Mr. Brown were behind—I did not see them all the time."

"Wasn't Jeffery with you?"

"Oh yes—Jeffery was with us, too. All were in the woods together... we were playing at hide-and-seek, you see." She sighed heavily. "If only I had known—"

"Poor Gallia!" Katherine sympathized. "So you never saw him after lunch—you went off in the woods with the others."

"Yes, yes! I was in the woods with the others."

"And was Ting with you?"

"No! Ting stayed up here. I do not want to take him in the woods, he might be lost in among all those big trees. The woods are no place for little Ting-a-Ling!"

"You're right" Katherine suppressed a yawn. "Do forgive me— I've had rather a long day, I think I'll have to get some sleep."

"Poor little one! Yes, you must go! It is I who am so unkind to keep you up when you are nearly half sleeping."

"Can I get you anything before I go?" asked Katherine.

"Little one! You are so thoughtful for me! If you will be so kind to pass me the tray over there? so!" She sat up in bed, the tray on her lap. "Now—on the writing-table you will find a packet of cards... yes?"

Katherine went over to the writing-table. On it was a heterogeneous mass of letters, papers, scarves, gloves, a pair of silk stockings rolled into a ball, and two handbags, their contents spilled out over the jumbled mass. Searching among the papers, she could not help noticing an open letter in Dimpsie's characteristic bold handwriting. "My dear," it began, "it is only fair to tell you..." but before she had time to more than glance at it, Gallia was by her side, her bare feet noiseless on the thick carpet. Whisking the letter away she scrabbled to the bottom of the rubbish and produced a pack of cards.

"There!" she said triumphantly, "you see I am able to find my way in all this pickle, eh?" She pinched Katherine's cheek affectionately.

"Don't catch cold!"

"No. I take the cards to bed… I play a little Patience, perhaps—or perhaps the cards tell the future for me… who knows?"

She sat on the edge of the bed, watching Katherine as she went to the door. Katherine said good night again and went out into the corridor. The air was cool and refreshing after the heat in Gallia's bedroom. Doctor Harley was at the top of the stairs, and she put her finger to her lips.

"Okay?" he asked, his eyebrows raised.

She nodded. "I left her about to play Patience. I don't think we need worry—she was pretty upset—" She stopped abruptly. Perhaps it would be better not to betray Gallia's confidence.

"Oh well," the doctor said, "if she can get interested in Patience I think we can safely leave her to sleep in peace. You'd better get along to bed. You look worn out!" He smiled quizzically at her, and she felt a rush of affection for this dumpy, plain little man who had been so kind to her. She had a sudden impression that he would have liked to kiss her, but instead he took her hand in both of his. "Now, don't worry," he said, "and try not to do too much thinking," He walked down the corridor with her and watched her go into her room. "You'll be all right now?" he asked.

"Of course. Good night, Doctor Harley, you've been very kind." She opened the door of her room. The bed had been turned down, and a fire burned invitingly in the grate. The room smelled fresh and the scent of flowers was in the air. On the dressing-table a copper bowl of chrysanthemums gave a note of colour. Katherine did not remember having noticed them before, but perhaps, she thought, she had been too upset, then, to notice anything.

A comfortable armchair was drawn up to the fire, and by it stood a small table. On this was a tray holding sandwiches, a thermos flask and a small bowl of fruit. Katherine stood in front of the fire; she had kicked off her shoes, and the soft, sheepskin rug was warm and silky. She unscrewed the flask and sniffed at the contents: Ovaltine. Suddenly she realized how tired and hungry she was. She undid her dress and reached for a hanger from the closet; quickly she undressed, slipped on a pair of pyjamas, and a navy-blue quilted silk dressing-gown. Then, at last, she sank down into the armchair. She would enjoy the Ovaltine and a sandwich before getting into bed. She stretched out her toes to the fire, blessing whoever had thought of making it for her. She looked round the room appreciatively; at the pink chintz curtains and matching spread, the attractive, old-fashioned wallpaper, and the draped dressing-table, with its mirror placed exactly in the right light. How well Dimpsie had arranged everything! How thoughtful he had always been for the comfort of his guests! Well—Doctor Harley had warned her against dwelling on the past; resolutely, she put all thoughts of Dimpsie out of her mind. She sipped the Ovaltine slowly. It was so cosy by the fire, it was a pity to have to leave it… with an effort she put out her hand and switched out the light. She would doze for a few seconds… the warmth of the fire… so cosy… just a second or two… she felt herself slipping away into that delicious half-world between sleeping and waking. A faint noise seemed to come from the door, but she did not hear it. Again the faintest sound seemed to creep across the room—but the sleeper by the fire did not stir. The door handle began to turn—very gently and with infinite care. The door opened a fraction, and the light from the corridor struck Katherine as she slept. With a start she was awake… on her feet.

"What is it?" she said. "Who's there? What do you want?"

"It's only me," said a voice. "Jeffery. May I come in?"

Katherine relaxed into the armchair again. "What is it? Wouldn't to-morrow do?" She switched the lamp on again.

Jeffery Gibson crept into the room. He was a young man of about twenty years old. Fair-haired and blue-eyed, tall and slim. He was wearing a camel hair dressing-gown, his hair was rumpled, and a bath towel hung over his arm. His feet were thrust into woolly slippers. "I had to come now," he said. "Don't be cross, Katherine. I just *had* to talk to you…"

Katherine could not keep a note of exhaustion out of her voice. "Well?" she said. "What is it that won't keep?"

Jeffery looked contrite. "I'm dreadfully sorry to bother you," he began, "I'd forgotten you'd had that dreadful journey. You must be worn out." He glanced uncertainly at the door. "It's just—you see—nobody's told me anything… I don't really know what has happened to poor old Dimpsie—if I could just know that—" he paused and looked at her miserably.

"But Doctor Harley told everybody," Katherine said. "When you all came back from the woods. I don't know more than that myself, Jeffery."

"I didn't get in in time to hear what he said," Jeffery explained shyly, "and I couldn't very well ask him, then. I thought it better to wait and see if anyone would say anything."

Katherine tried to remember how they had waited in the hall, while the guests came streaming out of the woods. It was all so confused, now, that she could not quite be sure exactly who had been the first to arrive. There had been Glen—and Frederica—and Gallia—she frowned to herself—had Henry and Holly come in together? she couldn't place them at all… and then the Inspector had arrived with Benson. Was it her imagination, or was it true that a young man had edged his way into the hall a few minutes before Benson's return. And then, Walters? When did he get back?

Katherine passed her hand across her forehead. "Why didn't you ask someone else?" she said. "Anyone could have told you all I know."

Jeffery looked down. "They couldn't, you know," he said, after a pause. "You found him, Katherine."

Katherine shivered. "Well? I can't go into it all now, Jeffery, you'll have to ask the doctor. He was electrocuted—that's all I know."

"But Kate," Jeffery leaned forward, his face earnest and flushed, "look! Be reasonable! How could he have been? Dash it all! He was only fixing the lights on the Christmas Tree!"

"Hmm…" Suddenly, her brain clearing, Katherine was struck by the full force of what Jeffery had said. If Dimpsie had wished to keep the Christmas Tree a surprise, and no one had been allowed to know what was going on behind the studio doors, how was it that Jeffery knew? "What made you think he was fixing the lights?" she asked as casually as she could.

He looked puzzled. "I don't know. Wasn't he? I must have heard someone say so, I suppose."

Katherine stood up. "Did anyone see you come in here?" she asked.

Jeffery shook his head.

"Well, I can only hope no one will see you leave—I don't really care about entertaining young men in my room in the middle of the night."

"Oh, Kate!" Jeffery looked hurt. "I'm awfully sorry, honestly—I never thought of it in that way. But we're all friends here, after all…"

Katherine made no attempt to hide a yawn. "You're a nice boy, Jeffery," she said sleepily. "Good night."

Jeffery slung the towel on his arm and tiptoed to the door.

"Will you close it after me?" he said. "And if I were you," he added, "I should lock it. Good night, Kate." And he was gone.

Katherine closed the door thoughtfully, and then, smiling to herself, turned the key. She no longer felt so tired. That ghastly, deadeningly sleepy feeling had passed, and now her brain was alert. What was it that had struck her while she was talking to Jeffery? Not only the question of how he knew what Dimpsie was doing in the studio, but something else... something—Yes! she thought triumphantly—how was it that Dimpsie had not locked the studio door, if he did not wish to be disturbed? Surely that would have been the first thing he would have done? She went back to the fire and began to undo her dressing-gown. Surely he would have locked the door; unless—either he thought he *had* locked it—or he was expecting someone; or, more sinister, he *had* locked it—and someone else had a key that fitted. Someone who had a reason for wishing to disturb Dimpsie.

She hung her gown over the chair, and climbed into bed. A hot-water bottle nestled snugly between the linen sheets. Switching the light off by the side of the bed she closed her eyes, trying to think of other things than the ones that were crowding into her consciousness.

2

UNHAPPY CHRISTMAS

I

FREDERICA BROWN WATCHED HER HUSBAND AS HE PACED UP and down the bedroom floor. "If he doesn't stop," she thought, "I shall go mad."

"It's the most incredible luck," Henry was saying. "Just as I'd got him to agree to terms—and now there's nothing signed, and God knows when we'll be able to get our hands on the play!" He threw the stub of his cigarette into the fireplace, stuck his hands in his pockets and mouched over to the window. The snowy landscape was incredibly displeasing to him this morning, and he turned away to resume his walk. "If only I hadn't gone out," he went on, "if only—"

"What the hell's the use of talking like that," his wife broke in. "You know you were only too glad to get a chance of going off into the woods with that little creature... though what you can see in such a vapid young woman passes my comprehension." She lay back on her pillows, her blonde hair curling on her shoulders, her eyes narrowed as she applied a brilliant nail varnish to fingers that bore an unfortunate resemblance to the talons of a bird of prey.

"If you mean Holly," Henry said idly, "she is a delightful young woman, and," he added with marked emphasis, "a thoroughly competent actress."

"If you're trying to be catty, Honey-bee," said Frederica, "you're wasting your time. Everyone knows what it means when Henry Brown says that a common little piece is a competent actress." She dipped the brush in the varnish and painted another nail with the utmost care.

"Now, look here, Frederica," Henry grasped the end of the bed with both hands, "let's get this straight, once and for all. I'm not taking anything from you... and the sooner you understand this the better it will be. It isn't my fault you're no bloody good on the stage... and you can think yourself lucky I picked you out of the chorus—though God knows why I did!" he finished, turning away. He took a cigarette from a box on the mantelpiece.

"May I remind you that you were glad enough to star me before that louse Dimpsie got hold of you," said his wife.

A clock somewhere outside chimed nine times, and a gong resounded from the hall below. Henry threw off his dressing-gown and began to dress without speaking. Frederica ostentatiously paid no attention. Henry wore a Harris tweed suit, a sports shirt open at the neck, with a silk handkerchief decorously twisted into the opening. He brushed his hair carefully, looking into the glass as he did so. His rather vulpine features, the heavy-lidded eyes, aquiline nose and thin lips struck him as being aristocratic and distinguished. He turned to his wife again.

"Allow me to remind *you*," he said, "that Dimpsie is dead—it would be as well to endeavour to curb your tongue for once. And furthermore," he went on, holding up his hand as Frederica was about to speak, "furthermore... there's no need to shoot a line about my not having control of the play. Adams will most probably be able to fix things; and, anyway, I've got the script. Possession, you know..." He smiled, showing excellent teeth.

"That shark!" said his wife contemptuously, "he'll land you in trouble one of these days! I'm surprised you don't go right ahead and put the play on, anyway… you pay little enough attention to live authors so why you should bother about a dead one…"

Henry shivered. "You've got an extraordinary knack of saying things that no one wants to hear. I'm going down to breakfast." He slammed the door behind him.

Frederica sat up in bed. A hundred retorts rose to her lips… she needed all her self-control to prevent herself from throwing the nail varnish across the room; three years ago she would have been out of bed, hurling insults down the corridor. She had learnt a good deal in those years. She had learnt to control her hands; it was too easy to throw crockery about. She had learnt to control her tongue; it was too easy to swear and curse, a few well-chosen vituperative remarks uttered with deadly calm were far more effective. She had learnt to control her face; she had acquired a trick of smiling a slow, lazy smile that maddened Henry far more than a red-faced virago screaming abuse could have done. Sitting up in bed, staring into the space that divided her from the door, Frederica smiled to herself. Yes, she could afford to smile: her marriage to Henry, the marriage from which she had expected so much, and which had come perilously near foundering on the rocks of bad-temper and disillusion, might after all be successful—at least from her point of view.

She had, perhaps, expected too much from her marriage. It was true that at first the mere fact that he had married her was a triumph. But like the fisherman's wife in the fairy tale, that which had seemed unattainable, paled with achievement. It soon became apparent, from sly digs and prying questions, that there were those who supposed Henry had married her so as to have her under permanent contract… that he intended to star her in his plays… that he had married her to be *sure*. They were dismally wrong. Henry had married Frederica because that was the only way. From their first meeting Frederica had known that here was a man she could get—if she played her cards well. But never, in her wildest imagination, had she suspected Henry would propose marriage. She had heard about him, of course, years before she met him. He was a bachelor, subject to the usual theatrical rumours, and Frederica had judged him accordingly. She had yet to discover why he had married her.

The reason was, of course, that Henry was a collector. He had bought Frederica as he had bought his collection of pictures, the beautiful tapestries and carpets that furnished his flat in Berkeley Square, his collection of old china.

Henry Brown's name had originally been spelled Braun; he was a Polish Jew and he had the Jew's real love of beauty. If he had never married before it was because he had never met the woman with whom he felt he could pass the rest of his life; a woman whom he thought was perfectly beautiful. To Henry, Frederica, with her pale gold hair, her brilliant eyes fringed with curling lashes, her narrow, sideways smile, was a unique and rare treasure; her long slim legs and perfect proportions were a constant delight. He felt he would never be tired of looking at her; and that in fact she might be extravagant, pleasure-loving, and stupid did not worry him at all. He had enough money to indulge her whims, and he had no wish for a clever wife. It never struck him that she might have theatrical ambitions; he imagined that she must be only too grateful to be removed from the chorus to ever wish to return to the stage. And in this he was right; until a little bird slyly whispered to Frederica that her husband, after all, was a theatrical magnate and there should be a part for her in one of his plays, should she so desire.

At first she did not consciously think about returning to the theatre; but it occurred to her, after attending dress rehearsals and first nights in which she took no part other than that of her husband's wife, that perhaps she was wasting her time. Henry had so many theatres under his control; surely she might be allowed a try-out, at

the very least. She approached Henry at the first seasonable opportunity. He was slightly surprised.

"My dear, I thought you were content to give up the stage, now
that you are a married woman."

Frederica smiled at him. She went over and perched on the arm
of his chair. "Darling! of course I'm content. I'm divinely happy…
you know that."

"Then—what is it?"

She hesitated. "Sometimes I would so awfully like to go back
to the theatre… only, you see, I've never had a chance. Of course
I realize that I couldn't have a big part—but I'd be content if
I could just get a start. *Do* let me, Henry!" She smiled at him
appealingly.

"You know you'd hate it, really," he said, "and frankly, my dear, I
don't see how you could play a very small part—you have a certain
prestige as my wife, you know."

Frederica knew better than to insist. But in the end she got her
way. After a small beginning, Henry ended by starring his wife in
several comedies. But in spite of her beauty, Frederica was no actress,
and soon Henry began to regret that he had allowed himself to be
persuaded. It became increasingly difficult for Frederica to find a
suitable play and when they decided to accept Dimpsie's invitation
to spend Christmas at Possett Island she had great hopes that he
might have something for her. She felt sure that Dimpson must
have a new play to submit to Henry; she was determined to have
a part in it. But Dimpsie had other ideas, which he communicated
to Henry, and which Henry, as tactfully as possible, retailed to his
wife. There had been little enough time for discussions; and three
days after their arrival Dimpsie had been killed.

Lying in bed, painting her nails, Frederica thought about this.
Thank God she had been out of the house when it happened! She

realized, with a little shock of horror, that probably the police would be arriving—examining everything and everybody. She had better get up and go down to breakfast. Suddenly she remembered that it was Christmas Day.

II

In spite of having gone to bed so late, Katherine woke early. The room was dark, and a shaft of light streaked between the curtains. Outside, on the snow-covered terrace she could hear the murmur of voices and the heavy tread of boots. Reaching for her dressing-gown she pulled it round her, and ran to the window. Below, Doctor Harley stood chatting with a policeman and another man whom Katherine thought must be the Chief Inspector. There were two men with cameras, and sundry cases, and across the lawn walked a dismal little procession, carrying a stretcher covered with a dark cloth. Katherine caught her breath sharply—glancing at her watch she saw it was eight o'clock. Of course, she thought, they wanted to get Dimpsie away before anyone came down. With a rush of gratitude, she realized that Doctor Harley had spared her the pain of going through the whole business again. A quiet tap on the door surprised her.

"Come in."

A pretty girl, her head covered with a mob cap and wearing a pink and white striped gingham dress, came in, carrying a basket of logs.

"Happy Christmas, miss," she said shyly. "May I just kindle the fire for you?"

"Happy Christmas," Katherine replied sadly. "I'm afraid it isn't going to be a very happy one. You're Elspeth, aren't you?"

"Yes, miss." She put a few small pieces of wood on the fire, and blew gently with the bellows. A crackling, followed by a few sparks,

was the result. Deftly she added small logs, and in a few minutes
there was a cheerful blaze.

"Would you care for a cup of tea, miss?" she asked.

"No, thank you. I'll wait for breakfast. But thank you for the fire,
Elspeth, I'm very glad to have it."

The maid withdrew, and Katherine stood in front of the fire,
warming her hands and wondering how she would ever get through
the day ahead of her. She had hardly had a chance to speak to any
of the others last night… there had been so much to see to. She had
had to phone through to London, to get in touch with her paper,
and give them a story that would break after Christmas as one of the
most horrifying yet. She could imagine the headlines only too well…

DEATH ON POSSETT ISLAND

Well-known Playwright Found Dead on Christmas Tree.

And while it horrified her, yet at the same time she knew that
Dimpsie would have relished the notoriety. Poor Dimpsie! She
hurried into the bathroom and turned on the taps; suddenly she
was anxious to know what the Inspector could have said to Doctor
Harley. She dressed quickly, pulling on fur-lined boots over her silk
stockings, and buttoning a heavy wool sweater over her dress. Then
she ran down the stairs and into the living-room. Doctor Harley was
at table, about to begin his breakfast.

The living-room was always used for breakfast, and this meal
was apt to continue well on into the day. Dimpsie had usually made
his appearance about ten o'clock, and from then onward he would
eat and drink interminably, sending again and again for fresh coffee,
and quantities of hot muffins. His guests were expected to stay and
chat with him; although should anyone desire to do their own work,
writing, painting or whatever, the studio was at their disposal, and

they could be sure of remaining undisturbed. But Dimpsie chose his guests carefully, and was always certain to include talkers, who would like nothing better than to sit around a table and smoke and discuss the events of the day, and the scandal of their own particular literary world.

This morning the living-room was warm and cheerful; there was no hint of tragedy in the air. Like the studio, one wall was entirely glazed; electric radiators below the windows prevented the room from being cold, and a log fire burnt briskly in the wide, brick chimney. The walls were built to resemble a log cabin, and there were fur rugs on the floor. A long refectory table was placed near to the window, and on a sideboard stood a variety of cold dishes; a ham, a cold turkey, polished wooden platters on which were piled shapely pears and polished apples, rosy plums and brilliant oranges, bland yellow bananas and dusky grapes. On a trestle-table standing inside the brick chimney were earthenware pots containing coffee and tea. A Cona machine was bubbling, and an electric kettle hissed gently. On the breakfast-table itself little packages were strewn at intervals. They were tied with coloured string and had tiny labels attached. All this Katherine noticed as she walked towards the doctor. He stood up, his hand outstretched.

"How are you this morning, my dear? And may I wish you a happy Christmas, in spite of everything."

"And you," she said, "if you think it's possible." She sat down next to him and turned her chair a little to one side, so that she could face him.

"You were down early," she said.

"Yes," he admitted, "there were certain things to be seen to."

"Tell me, what did the Inspector say?"

Doctor Harley shook his head. "Very little. It seems to be a clear case of accidental death. Poor old Dimpsie—I don't know why it had to happen to him!"

"*How* did it happen?" Katherine asked.

"As far as we can tell," he replied, "he must have been trying to remove one of the little bulbs from the flex. You remember how it was draped over the Christmas Tree? The end of the flex was plugged into the wall—into the power. He must have got impatient, trying to get the bulb off; actually we found it on the floor. Anyway, he had cut the flex and the wire was bare on each side where the bulb had been attached. Why he didn't turn off the current before doing this I simply can't imagine... he only had to pull the plug out of the wall. But there was one other thing... His feet were wet. That's what did it, I'm afraid—he was wearing thin leather moccasins, and they were soaked through. He must have been out in the snow... I don't know why he should have gone out in slippers, but I'm afraid that's what caused his death. You see, he'd got the two ends of the wire together, and that, combined with his wet feet and his metal-rimmed glasses, which acted as a conductor..." He did not elaborate.

"What a waste!" Katherine spoke heavily. "What a cruel waste!"

"I know. It was a chance in a million that anything like that should happen. But it's just when one is careless that accidents occur. The Chief Inspector feels pretty confident that it *was* an accident, but of course the final verdict will rest with the Sheriff."

"Oh, it must have been an accident," Katherine said, "otherwise—it would mean—"

Before the doctor could answer the door opened and Henry Walters came into the room. This morning he was dressed in a dark suit; his white shirt and black satin tie looked sombre against the doctor's tweeds. He greeted Katherine, nodded to the doctor and sat down at the end of the table. Katherine, looking at him, thought his eyes looked red behind his spectacles; she wondered whether he had been very devoted to Dimpsie.

Walters poured himself out a cup of coffee, and drank it without speaking; his entrance had put a stop to the conversation of the other two, and now the room was quiet, the only sounds the clatter of china and the crackling of the burning logs.

Walters put down his coffee cup and looked up wistfully. "I feel *so* dreadfully embarrassed," he began, "I really don't know quite *what* I ought to do... what do you suggest, Doctor Harley?"

"I really can't see why you have any cause to feel embarrassed," the doctor said. "Just what is it that's troubling you?"

"Well—it's this business of Christmas. You see, Dimpsie left everything to me... but everything!" He fluttered his hands expressively. "And now I really don't know quite what one should do about presents, for instance."

"I don't think anyone will be in the mood for presents," the doctor said.

"Oh, I couldn't agree with you more! But then, what *are* we to do with them? They've all been chosen and wrapped and labelled... one might just as well hand them round... though heaven knows one hasn't a vestige of Christmas spirit now." He sighed heavily.

"Quite, quite," the doctor murmured.

"It's all so *complicated*," Walters went on. He seemed to take a delight in his troubles. "What am I to do with all these people? How to amuse them? You understand that Dimpsie had all sorts of plans worked out—but now one just can't have the interest, can one?" he appealed to Katherine.

"I expect most people will be going home," she said quietly.

"But—but the inquest?" Walter said. "Will they be allowed to leave?"

"I think so," said the doctor. "As I told you before, there will be no need for any of them to attend—unless, of course, they know anything about Dimpsie—anything that would explain just why he was all alone in the studio."

A clock in the hall chimed nine times, and they heard Benson strike the gong. Presently the other members of the party joined them.

Gallia Karmanskaya seemed to have benefited by a good night's rest. This morning her eyes were clear and untroubled, she was carefully made-up, and her blonde hair was swept to the top of her head and secured with two tortoiseshell pins. She wore a black sweater with a black tweed skirt and in contrast to this, a china-blue woollen fascinator was draped round her head and secured at the neck with a diamond brooch. Ting-a-Ling was under her arm, his tail drooping sorrowfully. Gallia swept round the table and dropped into a vacant chair next to Katherine, putting Ting-a-Ling on the floor by her side. She was followed by Henry Brown and Glen Hemingway. Glen was a man of forty, tall and rangy, his skin tanned and reddened by exposure to the weather, his bright blue eyes keen and piercing, his hair a greyish brown. His nose was too beaky and his chin too prominent for him to be considered handsome, but he wore his shabby tweeds with distinction, and he had an air of calm assurance and a quiet manner that women found decidedly attractive. Glen, however, was not interested in women; only in woman.

His presence at the breakfast-table seemed to change the atmosphere; the conversation became general, and uncomfortable topics were avoided. Even Walters cheered up a little, and when Jeffery came in, apologizing cheerfully for being late and slipping into a seat next to the secretary, Walters even managed a pale smile.

Jeffery looked tired and there were circles under his eyes. Katherine, watching him from the other end of the table, wondered whether he had slept. Looking round she noticed that there were still two vacant seats... Frederica and—she thought for a moment—of course, Holly. As if in answer to a summons, Holly put her head round the door.

"Hullo everybody!" she called. "Sorry I'm late—I shan't be a minute." There was a clatter as she dropped her skates, took off a sweater and pulled off the little red cap she had been wearing. This morning she wore a red skating dress; really it was little more than a frill, and below it her long slim legs in their white stockings, the white buckskin boots laced to the knee, seemed unusually conspicuous. There was a feeling of tension in the group around the table, but Holly was quite unconcerned. She slipped into a seat next to Henry Brown and smiled up at him disarmingly. Whatever one might think of Holly—although it might seem in exceedingly bad taste to be skating before breakfast on this particular morning, it was impossible to be angry with her. She was as playful and inconsequential as a kitten. Between them, she and Glen brought a breath of fresh air to the breakfast-table. Katherine, although not very much older than Holly, and certainly every bit as attractive, felt herself an onlooker, and was content that this should be so. A scratching at the window made her look round. There, on the sill, his nose pressed to the pane, was a cat.

"Simkin, my darling!" she ran to the window and opened it; the cat sprang lightly into the room. He was a beautiful Persian tabby; the fur on his back black and satiny, a huge beige ruffle around his neck, and his bushy tail long and sweeping. But now his fur was wet and bedraggled, his paws were thick with mud, and he sat down in the hearth, his tail curled round him while he picked delicately at his paws as if he were trying to pull off his long, black-velvet gloves. Katherine poured him a saucer of milk and he lapped it ravenously. He drank three saucersful before he was satisfied. "Where have you been?" she asked him. "You're in an awful state!"

Walters came over to the hearth and inspected the cat. "He went out yesterday morning," he said. "I haven't seen him since. He must have been hunting... he does go off, sometimes." He stroked the cat and it purred loudly. Ting-a-Ling, under the table, made a little dash towards Simkin, but Gallia had tight hold of his lead, and he could only stand still, his head on one side, his tail wagging madly. Simkin, replete at last, and cleaned to his evident satisfaction, lay down at full length in front of the fire; Katherine and Walters returned to the table, and Frederica picked this moment to make her entrance.

There was a lull in the conversation as she crossed the room deliberately and without haste, dropping into the empty chair between Henry and Glen. She looked startlingly beautiful; her golden hair was brushed straight out, and it lay silkily on her shoulders, curling very slightly at the ends. She wore a violet wool housecoat, buttoned from throat to hem, and to the entranced spectators, this matched the colour of her brilliant eyes. She wore no jewellery except a heavy gold bracelet, and a gold signet ring. She was magnificent—and she knew it. As she passed Simkin, asleep on the hearth, the cat jumped up, his back arched, his tail stuck straight up into the air. Twice he spat and then, springing at her, he clawed down the front of her dress with ravening talons. Before anyone present could move, Frederica had taken him by the scruff of his neck and, holding him at arms' length, had dropped him outside the door. Then she walked back to the table with the same deliberate step.

Everyone stood up. "Are you hurt?" "How did it happen?" "I simply *can't* understand Simkin, he's *never* done such a thing!" This was Walters.

Frederica turned to her husband. "Lend me your handkerchief, Henry," she commanded. "He hasn't hurt me at all," she said to the others. "Just a scratch, that's all." She wound the handkerchief round her wrist and turned to Glen, smiling brilliantly. "Darling, what about a cup of coffee for little Frederica? I'm quite famished…" Facing the table again she said: "Please, everybody, go on talking! I know I'm awfully late… so no one must take any notice of me… I'll just have a cup of coffee and pretend I've been here right along."

Everyone sat down again and endeavoured to take up conversational threads, but something in the atmosphere was not conducive to talk, and it was almost with relief that they heard Elspeth's announcement that Inspector Smith had arrived and would like a word with Mr. Walters.

"I've shown him into the parlour, sir," she added.

"All right," said Walters testily. "He might have waited till we'd finished breakfast… but they're all the same, these police, incredibly tiresome." He threw down his napkin and walked elegantly from the room.

"Police?" said Holly, wide-eyed, "what does that mean, Mr. Brown? Shall we all be questioned?" She looked up at him eagerly, confidently.

Katherine giggled. "You'll find out soon enough, Holly," she said.

"Better take care they don't lock you up," Jeffery counselled.

Henry Brown drained his coffee cup and wiped his lips with his napkin before replying.

"Just remember," he told her, "that no matter what they ask, it's always better to tell the truth, Holly. It pays in the long run."

III

Henry Walters hurried into the parlour, pausing just outside the door to light a cigarette. He found Inspector Smith standing in front of the fire, chatting with a short thick-set policeman who he introduced as Sergeant Appy. Inspector Smith was a tall, thin young man, with a pale face and melancholy blue eyes; his dark hair was parted in the centre, and he wore horn-rimmed spectacles.

"I must apologize for bothering you to-day," he began, as Walters entered, "but I understand that Mr. McCabe had several guests staying here for the holiday, and we thought it might be better if I had a word with them at once. It is possible that they might wish to be leaving, and we do not want to cause any inconvenience, you understand."

"Of course, of course," Walters said quickly. "Won't you sit down, Inspector, and you, too, Sergeant?"

The Inspector sat down at the desk, and the Sergeant, taking a small chair by the window, pulled a note-book and pencil from his pocket.

"I shall just want to ask a few questions," said the Inspector. "A matter of routine, you know." He spoke as if it were of little or no importance. "Won't you sit down, Mr.—er—I don't think I know your name, do I?" he looked at Walters expectantly.

Struggling with an insane desire to say he was Clark Gable or Charlie Chaplin, Walters gave his name, adding that he had been with McCabe for ten years.

"Ah, then, Mr. McCabe's guests would all be known to you, of course?"

"More or less. Some of them better than others, naturally."

"Naturally," agreed Mr. Smith. "And is there anything you could tell me about them—any little thing that would be of particular interest...?" He put the question airily, but there was no mistaking his meaning.

Walters flushed. "You'd better ask them anything you want to know," he said. "There's nothing I can tell you."

"Well… there is just one thing," said the Inspector. "What were you doing yesterday afternoon? And where were you when Doctor Harley arrived?"

"Well, actually I had to go to Drumbrunnock," Walters said. "You see, Mr. McCabe thought it would be fun for the doctor and Miss Mickey to arrive and find the house empty. We had organized a treasure hunt in the woods, and everyone except Mr. McCabe was out of the house. He had planned to spend the afternoon in the studio, decorating the tree… he thought that when the doctor arrived he would spring out and surprise them…" He paused a moment. "Well—they were surprised… but in a very cruel and unfortunate way."

"And was everybody else in the woods?"

"As far as I know."

"What about the servants?"

"They were down at the Lodge. They had the afternoon off… and Benson was to be on the look out for Doctor Harley's car. As soon as he saw it he was to let Mr. McCabe know."

"And how would he do that?"

"I suppose he would come over with them and then, going through the kitchen, he could tap on the window of the studio, and Mr. McCabe would know that they had arrived."

"I see. And is that what happened?"

"I couldn't say. You'll have to ask Benson. I was over in Drumbrunnock." Walters' voice was thin and high. His sentences had a staccato quality.

There was a silence for a moment.

"Thank you," said the Inspector. "Perhaps you would ask one of the guests to step in for a moment. I suppose they all knew you had gone to Drumbrunnock?" he smiled unhappily into the fire. "You were getting cigarettes and tobacco, were you not?"

But Walters had hurried out of the room. Back in the living-room he faced a table of incredulous faces.

"He wants to see everyone. I'm sorry," he said, "but there it is. Just a matter of form," he smiled deprecatingly.

Frederica stood up. "Well, let's get it over with," she said briskly. "I'll go first." She swept from the room.

The Inspector eyed her mournfully, but there was a cheerful grin on Sergeant Appy's face. Glamour girls didn't often come his way, and he stared, his eyes popping, at Frederica's shining hair, her trailing dress, and all the accoutrements of beauty.

Frederica gazed at the Inspector. "How can I help you?" she said softly.

"You can tell me your name," he said, "and how long you've known Mr. McCabe, and what you were doing yesterday afternoon…" His voice trailed off into silence.

Frederica sat down in an armchair near the fire, holding one slim hand to the blaze. Slowly and deliberately she gave the Inspector the details he asked for.

"And what were you doing during the afternoon?" he repeated, as she finished.

She shrugged. "We were all in the woods, playing some absurd game. Dimpsie had determined to get us all out of the house… Well, he succeeded."

"And were you alone?"

"Part of the time. But mostly I was with Mr. Hemingway… and one or two of the others."

"Which others?"

"Well"—she hesitated—"my husband… and… and Madame Karmanskaya."

The Inspector rose. "Thank you so much, Mrs. Brown," he said. "And now, would you ask your husband to come in?"

Inspector Smith saw Henry Brown, Hemingway and Madame Karmanskaya in quick succession. Then he saw Jeffery, whose story was much the same as the others, and Katherine. Lastly Holly, who had been rather quiet, sidled into the parlour.

"I expect you'll have heard about me, Inspector," she said, "I'm Holly Temple. Mr. McCabe asked me here for Christmas, and although I didn't know him very well, he was terribly sweet to me." She fluttered her eyelashes appealingly. "This has been a dreadful shock," she confided, before the Inspector had a chance to speak. "Do you know—I've never been in a house with a dead man before." She sank her voice to a whisper. "I felt rather nervous last night, too. There seemed to be so many people walking around…"

"Really?" Inspector Smith was interested. "And who were they?"

Holly shuddered. "Oh—I wouldn't know. But I did see Jeffery Gibson creeping into Katherine Mickey's room… I was on my way to the bathroom, you understand."

"I see. And what time of the night would that have been?"

"Oh, midnight, sure," Holly said, "maybe even later. I'd been in bed some time, and I just got up for a moment…"

Inspector Smith nodded. "Sergeant," he said, "have we seen Miss Mickey to-day?"

"Yes, sir," the sergeant replied.

"Oh well, she's alive then," the Inspector heaved a sigh of relief.

Holly stared at him, her eyes narrowed. Mr. Smith smiled at her, "Have you ever read *Northanger Abbey*?" he asked her.

"No. Would I like it?"

"You might," he said. "I think you ought to read it. Now," his tone became more business-like, "I'd just like you to tell me what you did with yourself yesterday afternoon, if you will?"

"I was in the woods with the others," she said mechanically.

"Which others?"

She giggled. "Well, I started out with Jeffery—but he's only a boy—and then I bumped into Henry, Henry Brown you know, and we found a little hut…" She bit her lip.

"Well?" The Inspector looked down at the desk.

"I suppose this is a confidential report?" Holly asked.

"Definitely."

"Then it's all right for me to say that I stayed in the hut with Henry for quite a little while. Then Frederica and Mr. Hemingway found us, and we all stayed in the hut together for a bit. Then Henry said it was time we all went to look for the treasure, so we got the clues and went out."

"And what did you find?"

"Nothing... well, nothing much."

"What did you mean, exactly?"

"Well... just that I didn't find the treasure... but I found Simkin. He was up a tree, swearing and carrying on like mad. When I called to him he just went higher up the tree and wouldn't come down at all."

"And who is Simkin?"

"The cat. Dimpsie's cat." Holly's cheeks were flushed, her eyes bright with anger. "I believe that Ting had been chasing him. He never goes up trees as a rule."

"No? But you haven't known him very long, have you?" said Mr. Smith persuasively.

"I suppose I haven't," Holly pouted. "Is that all, Inspector?"

Mr. Smith cocked an eye at the fire. "Yes, I think so," he said. "By the way, when are you going back to London?"

"I don't know... it depends on the others. Dimpsie brought me here in his car, you see..." She stopped, a big tear forming in each eye.

"Well, good-bye, Miss Temple," the Inspector stood up, "and when you get back to London, don't forget to read *Northanger Abbey.*"

He waited till she had left the room, and then lit a cigarette. "We'll see the servants in their own quarters, Sergeant," he said.

3

I THOUGHT YOU SAID MURDER

I

SOMEHOW CHRISTMAS DAY DRAGGED TO AN END. FOR HOLLY—
who had constituted herself the life and soul of the party—the
time had not been entirely wasted. Holly had come to Possett Island
determined to make an impression, and she felt she hadn't done too
badly. Dimpsie's death did not worry her at all, except that as his
guest she had felt slightly protected. But she had known all along that
her footing was precarious and that at any moment he was likely to
become extremely bored with her kittenish charms. Once or twice,
in fact, he had been actually rather horrid; had greeted her rudely. As
for instance, the time she had come upon him closeted with Jeffery
in the little room they called the Parlour. "Hullo, Repulsive!" he had
said mockingly, "I'm not at all in the mood for your kitty-ways...
go and find a cat your own size to play with!" She had run away,
laughing vivaciously, but there had been murder in her heart for a
moment. No, Holly wasn't sorry Dimpsie was dead.

She had spent the morning with Jeffery on the lake. She skated
well—and there was no telling who might see her. As it happened,
Henry Brown *had* just chanced to stroll by... there had been time
for her to perform an extremely difficult acrobatic turn before he
walked on... but he had seen her, and his voice had carried on the

still air. She had distinctly heard him say, "… charming—and such ease and grace!" He must, of course, have been talking about her. In any case, she knew he was attracted to her, one could always tell. He was walking with that Russian woman—Gallia something-or-other, but she was old—he couldn't possibly be interested in her—and of course his wife was a stick! Everyone knew that! Holly preened herself in front of the mirror… she *was* attractive, no doubt about it. She tossed her curls airily and fixed a new cupid's bow on her mutinous little mouth… there! Now she would go and find Walters; there were so many questions she had to ask him; and he might be able to tell her something about Henry Brown's plans. After all, as Dimpsie's secretary, he must know what was going on… Henry was going to put on one of Dimpsie's plays, and she, Holly, was to have a part… that was why she was invited for Christmas. So far, she had only once had a chance to talk to Henry Brown, and even then it was only for a few moments in the woods that afternoon. They hadn't been able to talk properly… and then he'd been silly when they were hiding in that little hut. Holly giggled—even if he *was* rather old he was a lot of fun. The only thing was… she faced the horrid fact for a minute… everyone seemed to have fixed up except herself. Frederica had got Glen—well, she was welcome to him, Gallia seemed to have fixed her claws on Henry… Holly bit her lip, she would have to do something about that; and even Katherine had got the little doctor dangling after her. Of course, there were still Walters and Jeffery, but they were buddies in a way, and neither of them really showed any interest in her. Jeffery had been far too taken up with his own skating to spare her so much as a glance, and he had even seemed to think that Henry's words of praise had been meant for him. Stupid little idiot! Just because he was Dimpsie's protégé! Holly's cheeks were hot with annoyance. Still, she thought, if she couldn't get Henry away from that old Russian woman… once again she looked in the glass. What she saw reassured her... the dark curls clustered around her head, her brown eyes sparkled, and her mouth curved sweetly in that delicious cupid's bow. She fastened a little enamelled sprig of holly in the dark curls, and ran downstairs. She knew she would find Walters in the parlour.

The parlour was the small room next door to the dining-room. It had been used by Dimpsie as his study, and one of the main features was the large flat-topped desk at which Inspector Smith had sat and which stretched across the entire wall. The walls were papered in a dark red damask, and on each side of the fireplace bookcases rose to the ceiling. The chairs were Victorian, covered in striped satin and trimmed with a silk fringe. There was an overmantel of green plush, and some waxed fruit under glass. Holly hated this room, and could not understand why Dimpsie did not make it over; her taste ran to modernistic decor, twisted wire chairs and glass tables, terra cotta masks on the wall and lots of coloured satin cushions. She opened the door quietly, and peeped in. Walters was seated at the desk; all the drawers on each side were pulled open, and papers were overflowing on to the floor. Walters was scrabbling about as if his life depended on it.

"Hullo!" Holly said cheerfully.

Walters jumped, and turned round quickly. "Oh—it's you!" he said. "Well, Holly, what do you want?"

Holly came into the room and shut the door behind her. "You don't seem very pleased to see me," she observed. "What are you up to? Going through Dimpsie's private papers?"

Walters flushed. "It isn't any of your business, Holly," he said. "Now, be a good girl and go away—you can see I'm busy."

Holly seated herself on a little chair by the fire. "I haven't any-where to go," she said gaily, "and we haven't had a talk, have we? There's so much I want to ask you, Henry dear." She put her head on one side and fluttered her lashes at him.

Walters pursed his lips with annoyance. "You're being very tire-some, Holly. *Do* go away—I've got such a lot of things to see to. I can't possibly talk to you now... go away, go away!" He waved his hand in the air, as if to brush her out of his sight.

Holly giggled. "Oh, Henry!" she sighed happily, "you *are* funny! You may as well talk to me—because I haven't the slightest inten-tion of moving."

Walters flushed, the dusky red mounting slowly from his neck to his temples. Holly giggled again. "Henry!" she exclaimed, "you're blushing! I believe you've got some guilty secret... Ow!" she broke off indignantly, as Walters suddenly towered over her, picked her up and deposited her outside the door in one continuous movement. Standing in the corridor, her hair rumpled, her dress untidy, she heard the key click in the lock. Resisting an impulse to kick the door she walked slowly away; she'd go and sit in the living-room... perhaps she could find Henry Brown.

II

Glen had not been sorry to find himself alone with Frederica. He had not had an opportunity of talking to her since the afternoon of the day before. Dimpsie's death had been a nasty shock. Glen could not remember the last conversation he had had with the playwright... if only Dimpsie hadn't been so childish! Well, he sighed heavily, it was no use regretting. He'd better make the most of his opportunities now, he might not get another chance. He waited till the last person had left the living-room and then turned to Frederica.

"Darling—you look so beautiful! Do you mind if I just tell you that?"

Frederica stretched out her hand to him. "I love you telling me."

"And am I going to see you to-day? Alone, I mean?"

She tightened her grasp of his hand. "Leave it to me. But we shall have to be careful…"

"I began to wonder whether perhaps Dimpsie didn't suspect?"

"Dimpsie! My dear, that's what he was hoping for. He'd have been tremendously disappointed if there'd been nothing to suspect." She chuckled. "I hope Henry fixed it up about the play."

"Dimpsie wanted me to do the lighting, you know."

"Yes—" She was busy with the handkerchief at her wrist. "Of course, Henry may have other ideas…"

"Darling! has that wretched animal hurt you?" He was all attention.

"No—only the handkerchief working loose. Tighten it for me, please." She held out her hand.

He bent over it, folding the linen carefully round the scratch. "There!" He turned her hand over, kissed the palm, and handed it back to her. "Darling! about the play—couldn't you use your influence with Henry?"

"Me? He wouldn't listen, I'm afraid. You'd better speak to Walters… after all, he was Dimpsie's secretary."

Glen looked dubious. "Hmm—well, I suppose I could… I'll wait and see what turns up. Anyway, I might want to go off—and it wouldn't be at all convenient to be tied up with the theatre."

"Oh?" Frederica looked surprised.

"Darling—I don't really want to, you know that… but it might be easier for both of us."

Frederica stared at him, and her beautiful eyes were full of tears. "Don't," she said, "don't even speak about going away, Glen." She stood up, pushing back her chair, and walked over to the fire. Glen followed her, and for an instant they faced each other. Then, with Frederica in his arms, Glen forgot about his doubts and fears, and was conscious only of her body melting into his. At last she released herself and pushed him away gently. Making the excuse that she must tidy her hair, she ran upstairs to her room. Staring into the glass as she powdered her face, she smiled.

"No need to worry in *that* direction," she told herself.

III

Katherine and Doctor Harley left the Sheriff's Court together, and hurried back to the car. Walters remained behind. There were a great many things to be seen to, and in particular the details of Dimpsie's burial. "The Tatler" had wished to be buried in his own woods on his private Island, but according to the undertaker there might be difficulties and complications in such an unusual case, and so Walters, who was determined to uphold the dead man's wishes, had announced his intention of staying to get things settled.

"And it's absolutely no use for that ridiculous little man to argue with me," he had said to the doctor, "because, after all, it's Dimpsie's own Island… I shall insist on getting my rights!" He took his spectacles off his nose, slipped them into their case and snapped it firmly together. "Whatever next!" he said, angrily.

Katherine sank into the car with a sigh of relief. "Thank God that's over!" she said.

The doctor drove through the red brick archway and out on to the road before replying.

"It was a pretty near thing," he said. "I was very much afraid, at one time—" he stared through the windscreen concentrating on the road ahead of him.

"Quite frankly, when they started to get technical, I couldn't follow what they were saying," Katherine said. "That Sheriff seemed determined to get to the bottom of everything…" She looked at her watch. "We've been in there for hours," she said.

"They're pretty cautious fellows, the Scotch," Doctor Harley said. "Personally, I think it's all to the good. But of course we must remember that there was very little conflicting evidence. I don't really see how they could have brought in any other verdict... Yes, I suppose it might have been worse."

"You mean—it might have been murder?"

"Very easily."

Katherine gasped. "Oh, come now," she said, tell me just one person who might have wanted to murder Dimpsie. Goodness, he wasn't all that bad! I mean—everyone knows he used to tease people... but that wouldn't make anyone want to kill him."

"It's a curious fact," the doctor said quietly, "that, on the whole, most motives for murder are incredibly slight. One might, in fact, say that all motives are inadequate, because, after all, for what reason may one take the life of a fellow being? No, Kate, however teasing or tactless Dimpsie might have been, it certainly would not be a motive for murder."

"That's what I said."

"Ah, but... it might have been the *reason* for the murder... if it was a murder, that is."

"You don't really think—" Katherine said tentatively.

"I don't know what I think, dear child." The doctor drove for some miles in silence, and Katherine, her mind in a turmoil, tried to make some sense out of what he had been saying. Mentally she reviewed her fellow guests... Gallia, Frederica, Henry Brown, Holly, Jeffery, and even Walters. None of them, she thought, could possibly have wanted Dimpsie to die... on the contrary, most of them stood to gain by keeping him alive.

"You've worried me," she said, after they had driven for several miles on the long, snow-covered road over the moors.

The doctor smiled kindly at her. "I'm sorry, I had no intention of worrying you. Oh dear!" he added whimsically, "why can't I keep my big mouth shut?"

She chuckled. "Elaborate, please!"

"We've had the verdict," the doctor said, "perhaps we'd better let it alone."

Katherine stared out of the window. The moors stretched white away into the distance; there was no colour anywhere except for a clump of trees growing in a little hollow near the roadside, and even these were thickly covered with snow. The effect was desolate and lonely. There was no sun, the clouds were leaden against the whiteness of the snow, and overhead rooks and crows wheeled and turned in the empty sky.

"It's a dismal landscape," the doctor said, "no time for talking about depressing things."

"No time like the present," Katherine said. "Come on, Doctor Harley, let's have it!"

"Do you think you could call me William?" the doctor said shyly, "after all, I call you Kate."

She grinned. "Why not? I think, though, I'd rather call you Bill. Would that be in order?"

"Very much so. No one calls me Bill."

"Good. Well, Bill, won't you please say what's on your mind?"

"It's this, then. You know I've looked after Dimpsie for years? He was flabby, and out of condition, and much too fat. He never took a walk, and he hardly ever went out of doors on foot, if he could help it. In London he taxi'd everywhere... and I know he never would have thought of taking a walk in the snow or going into the woods."

"That's true enough," she agreed. "What then?"

"That electric shock might not have harmed an ordinary person... Oh, I'm not saying it wouldn't have made them jump a bit... if you turned on the light, for instance, took out the bulb and stuck your finger in the hole—it probably wouldn't kill you, but you'd feel it all right." He stopped to take out his cigarette-case and pass it to Katherine.

"Light one for me," he said. "Well—what I'm saying is this: agreed that Dimpsie's out of condition—so a shock would have been more liable to hurt him than it would most people—there are two factors that I simply cannot reconcile. One is that the plug was in the socket... I'm sure even Dimpsie would have known enough to pull it out... and the other is that he was wearing thin suede moccasins—and they were wet through."

"I know," Katherine said. "What of it?"

"What of it?" Bill Harley began to get excited. "What of it! Only that his wet feet were a conductor—they made the job certain. Don't you see... that, and the plug, and his spectacles... all those things together made it practically certain that he'd get a lethal shock. I *can't* believe it was all coincidence, Katherine."

"Why didn't you say any of this to the Sheriff?"

"Well... mostly because I've got nothing to go on except my suspicions. I did warn him that Dimpsie's heart was in a very weak state... I explained that he was thoroughly out of condition. But I had thought it all over very carefully—and it seemed to me—" He stopped the car, and turning to Katherine, spoke very slowly and quietly. "Katherine, you do know that everything that I'm saying, that I've said, is in the strictest confidence?"

Katherine smiled. "Of course, Bill. If you're thinking of the paper..."

"Well—I am, in a way. You see, dear child, it's like this: although I have this feeling—I can't call it anything else—that Dimpsie's death was not an accident, at the same time, I cannot imagine any possible reason for a murder—or anyone who could have done it. So there you are—" He shrugged, and started the car again.

"Oh dear!" Katherine said, "I simply hate going back to the castle and meeting them all again... although, as a matter of fact, I've seen very little of them, really. There's been so much phoning to do, and H.B. wanted me to write something about Dimpsie—his life, and that sort of thing—and then all about 'The Tatler' and his broadcasting plans. I haven't had a lot of time for being social."

"I expect most of them will be going back to town to-night or to-morrow."

"Me too," she said. "First opportunity."

"Well—do you want to go to-night?" he asked, "or will the morning suit you better?"

"Oh, Bill, that's terribly kind," she said. "Well—how would it be if we wait and see what the others are doing? It might just be worth our while to wait until they all go—what do you say?"

"An excellent idea, Kate," he said. "We'll wait and see."

They found the rest of the house-party in the living-room. Frederica and Glen were playing backgammon, Henry and Holly were having a cosy chat on the sofa, and Gallia, her chair almost inside the fireplace, a small table in front of her, was playing her interminable Patience. She looked up when Katherine and the doctor entered, and beckoned to them.

"You poor things! You must be so cold! Come at once to the fire, Kate, and warm yourself!" She got up from her chair and began to help them off with their coats, fussing over them and pulling them to the fire. The others went on with what they were doing... as far as they were concerned, no one had entered the room.

"So!" Gallia said at last, "and what did the Coroner say?"

Bill Harley winked at her. "Very surprising!" he said loudly.

"What do you mean?" asked Henry Brown quickly.

The doctor stared at him, his eyebrows raised. "I beg your pardon?"

Henry stared back coldly. "Did I understand you to say that the Coroner's verdict was surprising?"

"That was what I said to Madame Karmanskaya, yes."

"Perhaps you would be good enough to tell us exactly what the verdict was? I think we shall all be interested to know."

Katherine watched, from the fire, how everyone was listening—their anxiety more—or less—veiled. Holly, with elaborate unconcern, was powdering her nose; Frederica's hand was poised—her whole attention on the backgammon board; Glen was staring openly at the doctor, and Katherine could see one hand, under the table, clenched until the knuckles showed white. Gallia was waiting, frank interest on her face, and Henry Brown was, as usual, impassive. Only Jeffery, in a corner of the room, supposedly deep in a book, was watchful—alert.

Doctor Harley looked slowly from one to the other. "You'd rather I told you?" he asked, "you don't wish to wait until Walters returns?"

Henry Brown bit his lip. "There really is no point in waiting, is there?" he asked. "I presume you were there for the verdict?"

"Oh yes, we were there," said the doctor cheerfully.

There was a minute's silence. Then—

"It was Accidental Death," the doctor said.

"I see." Henry Brown turned to Holly. She had replaced her powder puff, and was now concentrating on her lips. She turned to Henry, smiling, and ready to chat.

"Shall we take a walk before lunch?"

He frowned. "Why does the Coroner's verdict surprise you, Doctor Harley?" he asked.

Doctor Harley grinned. "The *Sheriff's* verdict," he corrected. "Well—it surprised me because… oh, I don't know… I thought it might have been… Death by Misadventure, for instance."

Holly laughed shrilly. "Why, that's the same thing, isn't it? I thought at least you were going to say *murder*!"

For an instant there was a stunned silence. Then everyone began to talk very brightly, and Henry Brown led Holly gently from the room.

4

T HE DAY OF THE FUNERAL FOUND THE ISLAND CHANGED TO A
fairytale world of crystal. The trees, which first had been
shrouded with snow, and then bowed down under the torrential rain,
were now stiff and hard, covered completely with ice that sparkled
and glittered in the sunshine like the frosted decorations on a wedding
cake. The funeral party moved solemnly across the lawn. Underfoot
the snow was crisp, and as they approached the woods they were spell-
bound by the beauty of the scene before them. The mass of trees, the
infinite variety of shapes, the pines, firs, spruces, each was as if made
of glass; the icicles drip-dripping with a tinny, tinkling sound. On the
north side of the wood, the side furthest from the sun, the ice was of
a different quality. Here it was frosted, rather than clear, and the low
bushes massed against the edge of the Loch were powdery and dry.

Inside the wood the trees were thicker, but they were still covered
with this heavy layer of ice, and through this it was almost impossible
to see the dark green of the leaves. Occasionally an icicle snapped
off as one of the party brushed against a tree, and as it broke the
branch would swing back against another, and two or three more
of the brittle icicles would break off, tinkling against one another
like fairy music.

The grave had been dug deep in the wood. The Pastor had accompanied the undertaker from Drumbrunnock, and the ceremony was

soon over. One by one, each of his friends dropped a little posy of leaves on to the coffin; it was left to Walters to crumble the first earth into the grave, and then, silently, they returned to the house.

By common consent the rest of the day was spent almost in silence. No one had anything further to say, and the one thought uppermost in their minds was how soon they could get away from Possett Island.

5

"SEEK AND YE SHALL FIND"

I

BOTH KATHERINE AND DOCTOR HARLEY WERE THANKFUL TO be back in London. Holly, to whom they had given a lift, had been somewhat disgruntled at being relegated to the back seat, and although she became slightly better-tempered towards the end of the journey, it was with a sense of relief that they dropped her at her digs in Hammersmith. Standing on the step, her suit-case beside her, she waved good-bye to them.

"Attractive little thing, isn't she?" said Katherine.

"Hmm," the doctor was noncommittal, "not my choice for a desert island. A little too uncertain, I'd say."

"Hardly Dimpsie's type, I should have thought."

"I believe Henry wanted her. Had a part for her in the new play."

"Oh." Katherine was thoughtful. "Well—that accounts for it, then."

"Where shall I drop you?" he asked.

"Could you take me to Baker Street? I shall have to go home first and tidy up."

"Of course." He turned up Campden Hill and they drove for a few minutes in silence. "What are you doing about lunch?" he said at last.

"Is that an invitation?"

"It is. If you'd accept it."

Katherine smiled happily. "I've got to go down to the city... and H.B. may keep me hours... I'd love to lunch, but it's doubtful whether I'll get away in time."

"Dinner, then?"

"I'd adore it."

"I'll pick you up here at seven. All right?" He drew up outside the flats.

Katherine began to collect her things. "That will be grand," she said. "I'll look forward to this evening, Bill."

Doctor Harley saw her into the flat and said good-bye. Driving to his consulting-room he let his mind wander for a few moments... it was delightful to look forward to an evening alone with Katherine. He hoped her Chief was not the kind of man likely to send her off on a wild goose chase back to Possett Island: from his limited experience of newspaper men he had learnt that time and distance were no object where a story was concerned. Remembering his conversation with Katherine after the inquest, he smiled to himself whimsically. "Why can't I keep my big mouth shut?" he thought again.

Having said good-bye to the doctor, Katherine hurriedly parked her cases, snatched up some letters that she found lying on the mat, and took a taxi down to Fleet Street. The offices of the *Sunday News* were housed in a little courtyard off Fetter Lane; the yard was crowded with vans and motors, boys on bicycles, and even one or two horses and carts. Katherine pushed her way into the central hall and inquired for messages. Horace Brain, her Chief, was waiting to see her as soon as she arrived, and she went directly to his sanctum. This meant passing through several rooms occupied by typists, messengers and other journalists, many of whom waved and called ribald greetings. H.B. was at his desk. He was a man of about forty, with a thick mane of straight black hair, deep blue eyes concealed behind horn-rimmed spectacles, and a dry, puckish sense of humour. He, too, had been devoted to Dimpsie, and his greeting to Katherine showed her how much he felt a sense of loss at the death of his old friend.

"So you just arrived," he said, when Katherine was seated in a chair facing him. "I got the story all right…" He paused, and looked straight at her, removing his glasses and laying them on the desk. "What's behind all this?" he asked.

"All what?"

"This being buried in the woods way up in Scotland like that. Was that really what Dimpsie wanted?"

"How should I know, H.B.?" Katherine asked. "I only know that Walters had quite a lot of trouble to get the Sheriff to agree to it… though what it had to do with the Sheriff I can't imagine."

"Scottish law, Scottish law," grumbled Brain. "What about the Will? You've seen that, I suppose?"

Katherine shook her head. "I don't know a thing about it, H.B. Walters was awfully touchy—it was very difficult to ask anything. Altogether, the whole thing was… beastly." She shuddered, remembering.

"I know," H.B. was sympathetic. "But you've got to remember that Dimpsie had hundreds of friends—thousands, one might say. And each one of them wants to know exactly every little detail… there's nothing too insignificant to interest them—and Dimpsie would have been the first to recognize that. Have you seen Archie Tittop?"

"No. I haven't had a chance. He wasn't up there."

H.B. doodled on the blotting-pad in front of him. "Archie and Dimpsie never got on well—not really well. Of course, Dimpsie always thought Archie should have worked for him for nothing," he smiled reminiscently, "you can't blame Archie for not agreeing to that point of view. Tell me, what do you think about this accidental death business?"

Katherine hesitated. "I don't know what I think?"

"Well," H.B. leaned back in his chair and lit a cigar, "I'll give you"— he glanced at his watch—"five minutes to make up your mind." He closed his eyes and puffed dreamily on his cigar. Katherine chuckled.

"If it'll help any," she said, "I'll tell you what I think—but it's strictly what I *think*, H.B. I don't *know* anything."

"Go ahead."

"Well—I can't really believe that Dimpsie wouldn't have checked the plug to make sure it wasn't in the wall. Even the biggest dope in the world knows enough to disconnect the current, surely?"

"What else?"

"No one seemed to know why Dimpsie's slippers were wet. Doctor Harley thought he must have been out in the garden…"

"Of course, Bill Harley was there. What else did he say?"

"He didn't say anything. Look, H.B., I've been over and over in my mind till I'm positively dizzy… there wasn't anyone there who could have wanted Dimpsie out of the way. They all loved him, they were his friends… dash it all, he'd asked them to spend Christmas with him. And besides—practically everyone of them had a reason for wanting him to be alive."

"How so?" H.B. sat forward in his chair, staring at her interestedly.

"Take Walters—he was Dimpsie's secretary, wasn't he? He didn't want to be out of a job, he'd been with Dimpsie for nearly ten years. They were real friends—they understood each other." She looked at H.B. expectantly. He nodded.

"Go on."

"Jeffery Gibson was there. He was Dimpsie's protégé. Dimpsie had been terribly kind to him—I can't imagine what he'll do now unless, Dimpsie's provided for him in some way. Then there was Madame Karmanskaya. She said she and Dimpsie were going to announce their engagement... and even if she was exaggerating, she still must have been very fond of him. Then the Browns... Henry was up there to discuss theatre, I think he has an option on a new play. And Frederica wouldn't have any reason to dislike Dimpsie."

"Wait a minute. You don't *know* what reason she might have had."

"That's true," admitted Katherine, "but as far as I do know, they were good friends... good enough for him to have asked her and Henry for Christmas."

"What about that Temple girl?" H.B. said. "What was she doing there?"

"Holly? I think Henry was rather interested in her. There was some talk of her having a part in the play. Dimpsie must have thought her amusing... I don't know," she shrugged helplessly.

"Did you like her?"

"Well—I think she'd be all right in different circumstances. I didn't care for her, myself... but that doesn't mean she wasn't a perfectly nice girl."

"Who else was there?"

"Glen Hemingway... the big game hunter. I think he and Frederica are having some sort of an affair. Henry didn't seem to mind, I must admit."

"And you and Bill Harley made up the party?"

"Yes. Now, do you see what I mean, H.B.—how could any one of those people have killed Dimpsie? How could they?"

H.B. was silent. He sat back in his chair, chewing on the end of his cigar, lost in thought.

"If you'd been there," Katherine said, "if you'd been there with them... I feel sure that not one of them could have done anything so utterly heartless and callous."

"My dear child," said her Chief quietly, "the fact remains that Dimpsie is dead. You have a hunch that it was not Accidental Death, haven't you?" he asked suddenly.

Katherine stared. "What if I have?"

H.B.'s eyebrows shot up into his hair. "What if you have?" he roared, "what if you have? My God! you, a newspaper woman, sit there and tell me that! Get out of here, Katherine Mickey—get out! And don't come back till you can tell me who killed him… and give me proof, too!" He stood up, his hands gripping the desk, his eyes blazing.

Katherine retreated to the door. "Expenses?" she said meekly.

"All right," he said. He scribbled something on a piece of paper and brought it over to her. "Go out and get him," he said kindly, putting his arm round her shoulders and piloting her out of the room. "You can give this to Marble. He'll look after you. But don't come back until—" He opened the door and pushed her outside gently. "Good hunting," he said.

II

"But, darling," Henry Brown spoke soothingly, "you must try and realize that it doesn't rest entirely with me. If it did—" he made a gesture, signifying that for his part he would gladly give her the world, moon, sun and stars.

Holly drooped her eyelids and smiled at him through her lashes. "I know you'll do what you can," she said. "You know what it would mean to me… Dimpsie's play, produced by you—why, that would absolutely make me! I'd be set up!" She looked up at him appealingly. "You're so sweet to me, Henry, taking me to lunch, and being nice… I can't help being fond of you, you don't mind, do you?"

Henry smiled in spite of himself. He never could make up his mind whether Holly was very naïve, or very, very clever. She was a dear, pretty little girl, and, as he had told Frederica, a competent actress; he didn't really think she knew very much about men.

"In any case," he promised, "you can read the part."

"May I?" Holly snuggled a little closer to him, "that's sweet of you, Henry. I do *hope*—" she did not finish the sentence.

"What do you hope, Puss?" he asked.

"It's only—I know it sounds silly—but sometimes, people get jealous—but if *you* think I'm right in the part, you will say so, I know that."

"Of course I will. Now don't worry your little head any more about it." Henry signed to the waiter for the bill. "Now, what about a little chat—we've several things to talk about that can't very well be discussed here. Shall we go over to your flat?"

Holly sighed. "Yes—do let's! Darling Henry!" she snuggled still closer. "You've never seen my flat, have you? It's small... but it's awfully cosy..."

Henry laughed. "Now, puss!..." he said. "Now, puss!"

As they left the restaurant she tucked her arm through his and glanced up at him demurely.

"You know," she said, "when we were up at that horrid old castle, I began to think you didn't like me after all..."

Henry patted the little hand resting on his sleeve. "Tut-tut!" he said, "little girls shouldn't think—they just want to go on being pretty and cute. Now—what about a taxi?"

III

Katherine left the offices of the *Sunday News*, and walked slowly down Fleet Street. Although she had been unable to refrain from voicing her suspicions to the Chief, she felt she really had very little to go on, and, as she wandered thoughtfully away from the office she could not help feeling somewhat dubious about her chances as a private detective. It occurred to her that she had not had time for any lunch, and she turned into a milk bar that was conveniently situated on the corner of the first crossing.

At this time of day the bar was almost empty, and she perched herself on one of the high stools ranged alongside the counter. A slovenly blonde in a dirty jacket that had once, no doubt, been white, a limp frill on her peroxide frizz, leant across the bar to take the order. With a grimy rag she wiped a few crumbs off the scarred linoleum and smiled as she pushed the dirty card that served for a menu in front of her customer. Katherine, knowledgeable in the ways of milk bars, ordered a cup of tea and a tomato sandwich. The crockery, though cracked, was clean and polished, and the sandwich was good. The blonde retired to the far end of the bar, and Katherine thought about Dimpsie, and tried to make up her mind what to do next. There were several calls she would make, she decided, but perhaps there was one that was more important than the others. It might, she reflected, be an idea to visit Dimpsie's flat. Smithers, the butler, knew her, and no doubt could be persuaded to let her in. She finished her meal, and walked out into Fleet Street again. Now that she had decided on the beginning of a campaign she felt a little better; she jumped on a bus that would take her to the embankment.

Dimpsie had occupied the basement and ground floor of a small house in Cheyne Walk. The house was one of four that stood in a small terrace near the Albert Bridge, and was owned by a retired butler and his wife. Mr. and Mrs. Smithers lived in the basement of the adjoining house, and ran the two houses as service flats. This arrangement had suited Dimpsie very well, and had enabled him to leave the Bensons permanently in Scotland where they could keep the castle in good order, so that should he choose to go there at a moment's notice, everything would be ready for him. Dimpsie's flat consisted of his own suite; bedroom, bathroom and study which were slightly above ground level; also on this floor was a drawing-room and cloak-room. Downstairs, on a level with the garden, were the kitchen, dining-room and two bedrooms, one for Walters and the other for an occasional guest. The Smithers ran the flat efficiently; Dimpsie was seldom in to meals and if he suddenly decided to stay home it was always possible to make a little impromptu meal in the tiny kitchen. Katherine, on her way to Cheyne Walk, remembered sadly how often she and Dimpsie had spent an evening there, discussing literature, plays, radio and the hundred and one things which interested them both so vitally. She did not relish the idea of going through her old friend's personal belongings, but unless she did so, she felt sure that whatever mystery was concealed by his sudden death would never be brought to the daylight.

As she had been a frequent visitor at the flat, there was no reason for her to feel nervous or uneasy, but despite this, as she stood on the step, her hand on the bell, she could not help shivering at the thought of the task in front of her.

After what seemed a long wait she heard footsteps, and the door was opened by Mrs. Smithers. She was a tiny shrew of a woman, with bright red hair and eyes that were sharp as a vixen's. On seeing Katherine her smile revealed two long, yellow eye-teeth, the intervening space being filled by some blue-white specimens that clicked up and down as she talked.

"Come in, miss," she said at once. "Mr. Walters sent us a telegram to tell us about poor Mr. McCabe. We've been ever so upset—and Smithers... he's in bed with lumbago, poor man... he says he can't understand it. Mr. McCabe was ever so handy with things like that—he fixed up all sorts of lamps and gadgets when he first moved in here." She led the way into the first of Dimpsie's rooms, talking all the time. "You know, I can't seem to realize it, somehow," she went on, "one of the last things the poor gentleman said to me was that he'd be back right after Christmas. I can just see him, standing there, so kind as he always was, and telling me about how he was going to decorate up a great Christmas Tree and all. 'And just because you won't be there,' he said to me, miss, 'here's a little something for you to buy comfits with,' and he handed me three pounds, miss, as true as I'm standing there. Ever so kind, he was, and all them old-fashioned ways of his! I said to Smithers, 'Comfits!' I said, 'there's a word you don't often hear nowadays,' and Smithers agreed with me. But I mustn't keep you, Miss Mickey, with all my talk. What was it you wanted, miss—perhaps I could help you?" Her little vixen eyes searched Katherine's face.

"Oh—Mrs. Smithers, it's awfully kind of you… I think I know where to find it. It's just some work of mine that Mr. McCabe had… stories and so on, you know. I expect I'll find it in his desk."

"Oh—that'll be locked, I shouldn't wonder," Mrs. Smithers said quickly. "Mr. McCabe always locked everything before he went away."

"Did he?" said Katherine thoughtfully. "Well—I'd better just have a look round, now I'm here." She could feel the woman's indecision. Another minute, she thought, and she'll refuse to allow me to touch anything. "You see," she went on, forcing herself to speak brightly, "there are several addresses I ought to find—people that I must write to on Mr. McCabe's behalf. I expect I shall have to go back to Possett Island, and in that case there are things Mr. Walters will be wanting, too." She ran her tongue over parched lips.

Mrs. Smithers jumped to her cue. "I'm ever so sorry, miss," she said, "if it were for me to say, I'd be only too pleased for you to go all over, you being an old friend of Mr. McCabe's an' all, but a gentleman come down—from the solicitors, he said he was—and I've got strict orders that nothing's to be touched. I suppose, by rights, you didn't ought to be in here at all..."

"Oh dear," Katherine said, doubtfully, "of course I quite understand..." Her brain was working furiously, trying to find some way out of the difficulty. "I really ought to have told the solicitor I was coming along... I suppose you couldn't possibly allow me—" But before she could finish the sentence, the door bell rang. Sharply. Imperiously.

"Drat it!" Mrs. Smithers flushed with annoyance. "That bell does nothing but ring! I suppose I'll have to answer it." She opened a door and motioned Katherine inside. "It can't hurt for you to wait in here, miss," she said, and padded away, leaving the door ajar.

Katherine stood in Dimpsie's study. She waited, stock still, in the middle of the floor, until she heard the front door open and then, swiftly, she ran to the big roll-top desk that stood against the wall near the window. As Mrs. Smithers had said, it was locked, and there was no time to try the keys she had brought with her. As she hesitated, wondering what was her next move, she heard the sound of voices, and quick footsteps. They were coming into the study. Katherine looked round her in horror. The last thing she wanted was to be caught snooping in Dimpsie's study. Fool! fool! Mrs. Smithers must have been mad to let the woman in, whoever she was. Quickly Katherine opened the door that led into Dimpsie's bedroom, and stepped inside, closing it softly after her. There, by the side of the bed, stood an old walnut secretary, it looked as if it might have belonged to its late owner from childhood days, and no doubt, in there, safe from Walter's prying eyes, Dimpsie might have hidden his more personal letters.

The secretary was very small. Down each side were tiny drawers, their bun handles shining with the patina that comes from loving care and attention. In the centre was a desk with a slanting lid, and below this a deep cupboard. Her heart beating rapidly, lest Mrs. Smithers should come in, Katherine opened drawer after drawer, only to find them filled with bottles of pills, tubes of various kinds of pastes and unguents, bundles of cotton wool and gauze, packets of powders, and altogether a variety of stuff from the chemist's that Dimpsie must have bought from time to time, and been unable to bring himself to throw away. As she pulled open the cupboard and searched through the desk she began to despair of finding anything that would help her, and all the time she could hear Mrs. Smithers talking to the visitor.

"I'm afraid I can't let no one into Mr. McCabe's rooms, ma'am," she was saying. "You'll have to go, ma'am, and I must ask you to leave at once."

"Really!" said the voice, high-pitched with indignation, "I'm afraid you're exceeding your duties, Mr. McCabe was a very dear friend of mine. I have a letter from him…"

"I couldn't help it, ma'am," Mrs. Smithers said, "not if you was to have a letter from the Pope himself. No one's got to come into these rooms. So if you'll just come along…"

"Certainly not!" the voice said. "I shall report you to the land-lord." Katherine could hear steps hurrying over to the communicating door. Hastily, she closed the door of the cupboard.

Mrs. Smithers' voice, hard and definite, reached her.

"I *am* the landlord, ma'am," she said. "And now, if you please…"

"Oh!" the voice sank to a seductive whisper. "Then, in that case, perhaps we could arrange…"

Katherine, straining to hear what was happening, thought she could detect the rustle of notes. But Mrs. Smithers was not to be bribed.

"I'm sorry. I must ask you to leave at once." Her voice held a menacing note, and the caller must have been alarmed.

In the silence that followed Katherine pulled down the lid of the desk—and in that moment she remembered the sliding panel that

Dimpsie had shown her. Tremblingly she put her two thumbs in the very centre of the panel—and pushed. The panel slid away, and below, in the concealed space, lay a thin, white envelope.

Katherine caught her breath. It was fantastic. And yet it was so exactly right. She had been so certain that somewhere—somehow—she would discover hidden treasure, and in the flashing moment that followed her discovery it seemed as if she had known, all along, that she would find what she sought in that very place. She closed the desk and slipped the envelope into her pocket. And at that moment Mrs. Smithers spoke again.

"Come along, please. There's no use in your waiting…"

"But there's someone in there," the voice said angrily. "I can hear…"

"It's the girl doing the room," Mrs. Smithers answered, "not that it's any business of yours. Now come along, please."

The footsteps that had sounded so close, began to retreat. Katherine heard them cross the hall, and in that moment she tiptoed into the study, and ran to the window. She could see an indeterminate figure in a black coat, a scarf tied peasant-wise on its head, hurrying down the steps. The black coat was loose and shapeless; it was impossible to tell whether the person was tall or short, fat or thin. It struck Katherine that the coat was a little long… but she was unable to recognize a single feature of the anonymous visitor. She watched the figure jump into a waiting taxi, and be driven away.

The front door slammed, and Mrs. Smithers padded quickly into the room.

"I'm ever so sorry, miss," she began, but Katherine broke in. There was something she must make quite clear.

"I hope you didn't mind my going into the other room," she said quickly. "You see, I thought it might be a little awkward for you if I were found in here…"

"You did quite right, miss, I'm sure," Mrs. Smithers said. "The cheek of it, miss. Said she was a friend of Mr. McCabe's. She wanted a book she had lent him. She was sure she'd be able to find it! Lent it to him just before Christmas, she had!" She sniffed indignantly. "A pretty poor excuse, if you ask me."

"You didn't recognize her?" asked Katherine idly.

"No. Never seen her before. Not that I *could* see her, now you come to mention it. I don't believe I should know her again if she came in right this minute." Shaking her head at the craftiness of people, she locked the bedroom door, and put the key in her pocket. "I shall keep the rooms locked," she said, "and take away the keys. You can't be too careful, can you, miss?"

"You're quite right," Katherine said, feeling slightly uncomfortable.

"Can I offer you a nice cup of tea, miss? Smithers be ever so pleased to see you, I'm sure."

"It's very kind of you," Katherine said, holding out her hand, "but I'm afraid I shall have to hurry away. I do hope I haven't put you to too much trouble."

"Not at all, miss." Mrs. Smithers shook hands... hers was surprisingly flabby. "As a matter of fact, we was expecting you."

6

OF LOVE AND MURDER

I

SOMEWHAT TO HIS SURPRISE GLEN HEMINGWAY FOUND THAT he enjoyed the long drive with Gallia Karmanskaya. The journey did not seem as interminable as he had feared, and at the end of it he was glad to accept Gallia's invitation to stay and have a meal with her.

Gallia had taken a small house in Chelsea, in one of the little streets leading from the river. There was no garden in front, and a small square pavement was protected from the street by chains. Behind a scarlet front door the tiny hall was gay with flowers. Ringing the bell for her maid, Gallia led the way into the sitting-room.

"This is a tiny room, Glen," she explained, "but I think it is so cosy. Tania has made a good fire for us, and we will have our coffee in here I think." She motioned him to an armchair on one side of the fire, and flung herself down on the couch facing him. Glen looked round the room appreciatively. He liked the plain white walls and the furniture covered in beige tweed; on each side of the fire bookcases had been built in, and were filled with brightly coloured books and china. The windows were draped in fine muslin, and long brocaded curtains hung down to the ground. In front of the fire was a white bearskin rug, and Gallia, her shoes kicked off, sank her feet into its depths. Tania waddled into the room. She was a typical Latvian peasant; enormously fat, with black eyes and black silky hair twisted into a knob on top of her head. She wore a navy blue jersey and skirt, and reminded Glen of an old salt chewing tobacco on an upturned boat. He felt a pipe would have completed the picture.

"First you fetch the rest of my baggage, yes?" Gallia told her, "and then Monsieur Hemingway and I will have a little supper, I think. Coffee, and eggs, and ham—whatever you have got, Tania."

Tania nodded. "There is a cold chicken… some sausage… a salad," she said. "I bring it to the fire, yes?"

"Yes, yes!" Gallia said. "Hurry! We are terribly hungry!"

"Look here," Glen said, "I'll fetch the rest of the things out of the car, shall I?" He stood up as he spoke and went to the door.

"Oh—if you do not mind to do so?" Gallia smiled at him, "then—while Tania prepares the supper, I will change out of this uncomfortable skirt…" she was undoing it as she spoke, and before she could take it right off, Glen hurried out of the room and into the street. It was the work of a minute or two to fetch in all Gallia's baggage, but by the time he had got it all stacked in the hall and had kindly walked Ting-a-Ling as far as the corner, Gallia had changed into a velvet tea-gown and was stretched out on the couch by the fire.

"It's very cosy in here," he remarked, when Tania had wheeled in the trolley containing their supper, and had arranged it on a convenient table. "I must say I wish my flat were as snug."

"Poor Glen," Gallia said, "you are not comfortable where you are, no?"

He shrugged. "It's all right, I suppose, but no one could say it was luxurious. I've got a bedroom and a bathroom, a sitting-room and a kind of cubby hole where I can cook a meal if I want to."

"But where do you do all your marvellous electrical effects?" she asked. "I so hope that you are going to show me these wonderful lightings that you have arranged."

Glen smiled. "They are nothing very extraordinary," he said. "I do most of my work in the garage. I live in a mews flat, you see, and I have the car right underneath me. It's a double garage, so I have the extra space for my work."

"And have you always been interested in the stage?" she asked.

"In a way," he said, "although, of course, I'm really a hunter. That's what I like best. I think it was in the jungle that I first got some of my ideas for lighting… the curious greens and reds…" He stopped apologetically. "I'm sorry, this must be awfully boring…"

"But it is not," she said quickly, "I am very interested indeed. My poor Dimpsie told me that you were to do the lighting of his new play…" She dabbed at her eyes with a ridiculous handkerchief. "I do not think you knew that we were engaged?"

"No…" Glen tried not to show any surprise he may have felt. "No, I didn't know. I'm dreadfully sorry."

She nodded. "Yes, of course. My poor Dimpsie… you understand I shall never get over it! But tell me, you who understand all about electricity, how is it possible that such a thing can have happened to him? That he could be killed while he fixed up the tree!"

"I'm afraid I don't know anything about it," Glen explained. "I can only suppose that there was a short circuit…"

"Short circuit?" she repeated slowly. "No—I do not understand it at all. But you say that it is possible, yes?"

"Well—" Glen hesitated, "it must have been—because it happened. It was the one chance in a million, I suppose." He shook his head sadly. "Heaven only knows how it could have happened—but it did."

"But if someone understood about electricity," Gallia persisted, "and that person wanted to do such a wicked thing…" She stared at Glen.

He smiled at her, gently. "I didn't kill Dimpsie," he said, as if he were talking to a child, "and I think that anyone who really understood electricity would have chosen to commit a murder in a less amateurish way."

Gallia frowned. "Then it was an accident," she said sharply, "you are sure?"

"As sure as anyone can be," he said.

She relaxed again. "Well, all right. You say so—and I am only too ready to believe what you say. Come"—she began to arrange the supper dishes—"you must eat! you are hungry!" She piled a plate lavishly. "It is lucky for me that Tania is so good a cook. She has been with me so many years... when I was in the theatre she was always with me... and now that I have retired she looks after the cuisine. Yes... there is no doubt I am lucky to have her."

"You must have missed having her up at the castle?" he said.

"Yes. But the little Elspeth is so good... she has looked after me very well. I expect that Dimpsie has said to her that she must be attentive... I do not know."

"He was a wonderful host, wasn't he?"

"Ah yes! Indeed he was! And he loved to entertain his friends. I wonder so much what will happen to the new play?"

"Won't Henry put it on?" asked Glen idly.

"Henry Brown? I cannot say. I know that Frederica was anxious to play the lead..."

"Well, if her husband is putting it on that should be easy."

Gallia shrugged. "Who knows? Dimpsie was against it."

"Now why?" asked Glen quickly. "I shouldn't have thought he could have got a more beautiful woman, anywhere!" He flushed a little and pushed his plate away from him.

"You are in love with her," Gallia said, nodding wisely. "Oh yes! you cannot hide it from me! You are right, she is very beautiful... but take care, Glen, she can be dangerous, too."

"What do you mean?"

"She is a beautiful woman—she has a rich husband—so it is dangerous for you to play with fire. Better for you to return to the jungle, I think... the lions are not so dangerous. You are well prepared for their claws."

"Well," Glen stood up, "I must be getting along. Thanks for the supper." He strode to the door. "See you sometime, Madame Karmanskaya."

"Oh!" Gallia smiled at him bewitchingly, "but I have offended you! I am so sorry! You must forgive me—I think only for you!"

"That's very nice of you," his tone was icy. "Good evening!"

Before she could cross the room, he had hurried through the hall, slammed the front door and was starting up the car. Shrugging, Gallia returned to the fire, kicking off her shoes and stretching out her feet to the blaze. The maid, Tania, stood inside the door, her dark eyes narrowed.

"Well?" she said.

Gallia shook her head. "Not well at all," she replied, "very, very bad, Tania. Now Mr. Dimpsie is dead—and so I do not know what we shall do at all..." She stared mournfully into the fire.

"And what about that Mr. Henry Brown that you was talking about? Won't he come up to scratchings?" asked the maid.

"How do I know? Some stupid little girl that was at Possett Castle has been running after him... I do not know what will happen. I must think." She lay back on the couch and closed her eyes. "Leave me!" she commanded, "I shall lie here and make a plan."

Silently Tania closed the door. For a few moments Gallia lay completely still. Then, she jumped to her feet, took a pack of cards from a drawer in the writing-table under the window, and began to deal them out on the rug. She did this with the utmost concentration.

II

Katherine enjoyed her evening with Bill Harley. Now that Possett Island was far away, the misgivings that she had had about Dimpsie's death seemed like some frightful nightmare, and the fact that she had discovered nothing of importance in the flat added weight to this. She said as much to the little doctor, when they were having a cigarette with their coffee.

Bill Harley examined his cigarette. "You're probably right," he said, "if there had been anything wrong, the police would have been on to it, I'm sure of that."

"The only thing that does worry me a little," she said, "is this person who came to the flat while I was there. I can't think what on earth she wanted!"

He grinned. "Same as you, I expect," he said, "wanted to have a look round."

"I suppose so. But why, Bill? Why should anyone want to go searching about in Dimpsie's flat?"

"Dimpsie was a funny old cove, you know. There's no telling what secrets might be hidden away there… he knew a lot of things about a lot of people, Dimpsie did. Not that he ever dreamt of using the knowledge—I think it gave him a sense of power…"

"What sort of things do you mean?" she asked curiously.

"Oh, I don't know. He told me once that Henry Brown used to spell his name Braun, and that he came from Latvia or somewhere… I wasn't very interested, naturally. But," he looked up at her and grinned, "you said you found an envelope, what was in it?"

"Of all things, a marriage certificate."

"Good lord! Not Dimpsie's? Don't tell me *he* was ever married!"

She laughed. "No! Some weird names… Faustine someone and a man called Benenberg… I've never heard of them."

"Probably some of his circus friends. Where did the marriage take place?"

She frowned. "I believe it was New York. Anyway, I can't think why Dimpsie wanted to keep it so carefully. I'll put it back if I get a chance. Otherwise I'll just stick it away in case it's ever needed."

"Dimpsie had masses of queer friends, you know," Bill Harley said. "He wanted me to go with him to Paris last year, he had some crazy plan of going with the Cirque d'Hiver on their spring trip through Provence. But not me... I'm not mad on circuses."

"But he did go, didn't he?" Katherine said. "I remember he sent me some postcards from Avignon. Lovely, they were," she smiled reminiscently.

"Yes... he was a good sort," Bill Harley sighed, "one couldn't help being fond of him."

"Do you know Archie Tittop?" she asked. "Dimpsie's Agent, you know."

"Do I? I've met him... I doubt whether even his own wife really knows Archie," Bill said grimly.

Katherine giggled. She remembered Archie Tittop, with his pale blue eyes cowering under tremendously fierce black eyebrows, and the enormous guard's moustache. "Well, he's coming over here now," she said quietly.

Bill Harley looked up. Archie Tittop was willowing his way across the room towards their table.

"My dears!" he said as he reached them, "I had no idea you knew each other... this is too pleasant! May I sit down?"

Katherine smiled and put a hand on the chair at her side, and Bill, welcoming Archie, made a sign to the waiter. "What will you drink?" he asked.

"A glass of water, if I may?" Archie sighed. "I'm not allowed to touch a drop of anything stronger. Too, too tedious, my dear fellow, but there it is!" He looked up at the waiter winsomely. "Just a glass of cold water," he murmured, and then turned to Katherine. "My dear! I have to drink ten or twelve glasses of water every day. It's tedious, my dear, tedious, but what can one do?"

"Well, I suppose it might be worse," Bill said unfeelingly, but Katherine smiled at Archie sympathetically. "Nothing serious, I hope?"

He frowned, his shaggy eyebrows meeting in a black, furry line.

"I've taken it in time, I trust. Well," he turned his chair so that it was squarely between them, "this is a sad business about our poor old friend," he said.

"Dreadful!" said Doctor Harley.

"I had a line from Walters to-day," Archie said, "I'd written to him about Dimpsie's new play... the one Henry is hoping to do. Henry Brown, you know."

"Yes, he was up at Possett Castle," Katherine said, "with Frederica."

This time Archie's eyebrows went up. "Was she there too? You surprise me."

"Why shouldn't she be?" Bill asked.

Archie smiled. His teeth were rather long and yellow, giving him a slightly wolfish air. "Dimpsie loathed her guts," he said, "and she loathed his."

"But I thought she was to be in this new play?" Katherine said.

"Hmm... she wanted to be, there's no doubt about that. But Dimpsie had made up his mind that nothing she could do would induce him to let her have a part. He'd told Henry that he wouldn't give him the play unless he swore to keep Frederica out of it. He said to me, only the day before he went back to the Island, 'Over my dead body,' he said, 'that woman gets into my play!'"

"My God!" Katherine stared at him, transfixed. "Did he really say that?"

Bill Harley chuckled. "Now, now, Kate," he said gently, "pull yourself together. Even if he did…"

Katherine took a deep breath. "Of course," she said, "I must be going dotty!"

Archie was staring at them both as if he were in a dream. "I've no idea what this is all about," he began, "but what I'm trying to tell you is that when I wrote to Walters to ask for a script of the play, he wrote and said he hadn't got one. Now, what do you make of that?"

"I don't make anything of it," Bill answered, "probably he hasn't got a copy. I expect Henry Brown has it, if he's doing the play."

Archie shook his head. "There must be more than one copy," he said. "Dimpsie always had at least half-a-dozen from the first draft alone. I should have thought Walters could have laid his hands on several… I can't make it out!" He took the glass of water, and sipped it slowly. "Delicious! Quite different from the water at home—and the office is different again. Strange!" He sipped reflectively.

"I expect Walters is going through all Dimpsie's papers," Katherine said, "and perhaps the play has got mislaid. Anyway, Mr. Brown's sure to have a copy."

"I've no doubt he has," agreed Archie sourly. "Well—we shall see. But he needn't think he can get Frederica into the show—because I definitely won't stand for it."

"He probably doesn't want her in it," said Bill mildly.

"It doesn't much matter what *he* wants… it's what *she* wants that counts," Archie said.

Katherine giggled. "But Henry may have other ideas," she said slyly, "don't be too sure of anything."

"Really? You don't say? No, dear," he shook his head decisively, "I'm afraid I don't agree at all. And even if he had, our little Freddie would know just how to dispose of them."

"You sound quite sinister, Archie," said Bill.

Archie grinned. "I'm not, though... Look here, I mustn't waste any more of your evening." He stood up, leaning both hands on the table. "Come and see me, sometime, both of you." He drifted gracefully away, and they saw him eeling through the crowded room to his table.

What a queer creature Archie was, Katherine thought. She could not help feeling slightly relieved when he left them.

III

Glen Hemingway's flat was tucked away in a mews leading from Beecham Square. That it was small was no real hardship to him, since he spent the greater part of his time in the garage. He was there the day after his return to London, and Frederica's arrival was not as unexpected as she might have hoped. She came in her own car, a beautifully built Dusenberg coupé, its shining black body enhanced by the chromium fittings, and its interior of palest biscuit leather a fitting background to her severe black suit and sable coat. She drove silently into the mews and drew up outside the garage. Glen, intent on his work, did not hear her, nor did he look up as her shadow fell across the doorway.

"Darling!" she said softly. "Glen darling!"

Glen raised his head. His face lit up, and he hurried to meet her, his hands outstretched.

"Didn't you expect me?" she asked, as he led her up the little narrow staircase to the flat.

"Well"—he hesitated—"I was hoping you'd come... I didn't know whether you'd be able to manage it. I thought perhaps you'd phone me..."

"I haven't interrupted anything, have I?" She let him take her coat from her and then turned to face him, her hands on his shoulders. "Would you rather I went away again?"

His answer was to draw her to him, to crush his mouth down on hers. Frederica returned his kiss passionately and for a few moments they remained without speaking.

"And what sort of a journey did you have?" she asked, when they were sitting on a low couch drawn up to the fire.

He grinned. "Fair enough. She isn't too bad, you know, the old witch!"

Her eyebrows made two delicate arches. "I can't imagine what you could have found to talk about?"

"Oh, I don't know,"—he was elaborately nonchalant. "She talked about Dimpsie most of the time."

Frederica giggled. "She hoped he was going to marry her. Imagine it, that pansy!"

"I don't think he was, you know," Glen said, "I wonder if he would have married her... of course, we shall never know."

"You can be quite sure he wouldn't have," she said, a touch of acid in her voice. "Dimpsie didn't like women—he had no use for them at all."

Glen was silent. There was no doubt that Dimpsie had not had a great deal of use for Frederica, but he could not help feeling surprised that she should feel so bitterly about it. After all, she was an extremely beautiful woman... she had never lacked admiration. As if she could read his thoughts, she said:

"You mustn't take any notice of me—it's just pique because Dimpsie and I never hit it off. Of course, he had masses of girl friends. Katherine and Holly, to mention only two..." She looked up at him, her eyes candid. "He thought I was no good on the stage," she said frankly, "and you couldn't expect me to take that *and* like it!"

"Surely—" he began uncertainly, "it can't have mattered what Dimpsie thought."

"Of course not!" She laughed and stretched out her hand to cover his. "It's just my own vanity. There! now I've purged my sin by admitting it to you! Tell me what you did yesterday when you got back."

"It was pretty late," he said, "by the time I'd put the car away and had a meal. I went round to the local... it seemed the easiest thing to do."

"Didn't she even offer you anything?"

"As a matter of fact I had a cup of tea with her," he admitted, "but after twenty-four hours of undiluted Gallia I was quite glad to get away."

"My sweet," her hand caressed his lovingly, "don't tell me she had designs on you?"

"Of course not! Whatever next! No... but it was a bit tiring, you know. Funnily enough, she talked about the old boy almost all the time." He fumbled in his pocket. "Mind if I smoke a pipe?"

"I love it. What old boy?"

"McCabe. He was mad on the circus, did you know?"

"I?" Her voice sounded preoccupied. "No... I had no idea... tell me more."

"It seems he'd made a terrific study of clowns. He was going to write a book about them—about the circus, and clowns and the whole shoot. Gallia was telling me how he went to Paris and teamed up with the Winter Circus there... followed them down to Provence or somewhere. He'd told her all about it, she said."

"Really?" Frederica almost stifled a yawn, "and are *you* interested in the circus, darling?"

He laughed. "Never been to one in my life, darling," he said, "that is, not since I was quite a kid, and then, I must admit, it was the lion-tamer and the acrobats that I liked. I never was so keen on the clowns."

"And Gallia—I suppose she, too, is a circus enthusiast?"

"She didn't say so, I gathered she was rather bored by Dimpsie's crazy ways. Apparently she was in Paris at the time, and he insisted on dragging her to every circus in town, and always made her go round to the back and chat with the performers in their cabins."

"She needn't have gone," she said sleepily.

"Oh, I suppose she wanted to please the old boy. She said some of the people were quite amusing. There were some Italian acrobats that Dimpsie was awfully taken with... they spent an evening together and it was they who made Dimpsie promise to go down to Provence with them."

Frederica did not answer, and Glen, smoking his pipe, was content to remain silent. It was not often that they had the chance to be alone; and it was already evident that their future meetings might be numbered. Much as he would have liked to remain in England, there was the question of money to be considered. Glen was not a rich man, but he had managed to turn his passion for big game hunting into a profitable sport. There were always people who wanted a guide; someone who knew the country and who would be able to arrange for native bearers, tents, food, transport and who would cope with the hundred and one unexpected difficulties that always seemed to crop up on safari. He had already been approached by two agencies who had parties of Americans who wished to go to Africa and who had asked for him to escort them. It was a tempting proposal... the people in question were known to him personally, and, although he could not go with both parties, since they both wished to travel immediately, either one would be acceptable to him. But as long as there was a chance of his doing the lighting for Dimpson McCabe's play he hated the thought of leaving London. And then, too, he thought, there was Frederica. His teeth gripped the stem of his pipe, and he felt his muscles tense. What was he to do about Frederica? There was no question of begging her to leave her husband and come away with him. That was obviously impossible. He stirred uneasily, and Frederica sat up.

"What's the matter, darling?" she asked him quickly.

"I was thinking," he answered truthfully.

"Thinking of going away, I suppose," she said, with swift intuition.

"No… I was just wondering how long you'll be content to come here… to this dingy flat in this dreary little mews."

She kissed him lightly, and left the sofa to go and look in the glass. "How silly you are," she said quietly, "as if I care where you live! It's you I come to see, not the flat!"

He watched her while she ran the comb through her shining hair and pulled the plain little black felt hat down over one eye.

"Why are you going?" he asked idly.

"I can't stay here all day, my love; beside…" she hesitated, "I've got to go to my dressmaker… he gets so angry if I break an appointment."

Glen walked over to her and took her in his arms. He turned her face up to his, marvelling, as always, at the perfect texture of her skin, and delighting in the curve of her lips and the long black lashes that fringed her eyes.

"Shall I drive you over, my beautiful?" he asked her, murmuring the words into her hair.

She disengaged herself gently. "Better not," she said, "I've got the car, anyway, and it's easier to say good-bye here, isn't it?"

"I suppose so." He kissed her once again and helped her into the sable coat. "Sables become you, my dear," he said ironically. "If you were my wife you'd have to be content with a tiger skin!"

She chuckled. "As long as you'd shot it," she said, "I should be proud to be seen in it. Anyway, I could hardly expect Henry to go about trapping sables, now could I?" She put her head on one side and looked at him comically.

"I've no doubt Henry has his uses," he agreed, "and it's as well to know which side one's bread is buttered, isn't it?"

"Butter? Caviare, you mean!" She turned and ran down the narrow staircase and into the mews. Glen helped her into the car; he watched amusedly while she manœuvred the over-long body of the Dusenberg in the narrow cobbled channel. Frederica drove well, though with elaborate nonchalance, one languid hand on the wheel while the other slid the gears easily into place; she leaned far back in the driving-seat, a cigarette between her lips, the faster she drove, the more unconcerned her manner. Glen wished he might take her on safari; she would be a good companion, he thought.

He watched the big car glide rapidly through the arch which led to Beecham Square, and then, feeling a little flat and depressed, returned to his lighting plant. Frederica's visit had been a pleasant interlude, but the question of what he was to do in the near future still remained to be solved, and the Agency was pressing for an answer. Glen sighed and relit his pipe. If only Dimpsie hadn't died... there would have been no need for him to make the decision.

IV

Gallia was depressed. The little house in Chelsea no longer resounded with humming and singing; she had spent the morning in her room, only coming downstairs at lunch-time, her head wrapped in a woollen comforter, her hair skewered into a limp bun at the nape of her neck. In the kitchen Tania no longer sang at her work; quick to sense the atmosphere and to understand her mistress's feelings, she responded in her own way by cooking little Russian delicacies in the hope of cheering the heart by tempting the palate. But Gallia had no appetite; she toyed with the food on her plate, pushing it about listlessly. The little dining-room seemed lonely and dull, and there was no one she cared to invite to share a meal with her. Dimpsie's death had affected her more than she cared to admit even to herself. Apart from the fact that she had indeed hoped that she would induce him to marry her, he had helped her a great deal financially. Without Dimpsie to push things her way life might be grim indeed. Gallia sat over her fire; she wore a loose housecoat made of purple velvet, her feet were thrust into scarlet flannel slippers, and the comforter she had drawn round her neck was a dull, gold woollen material. As a rule, she found bright colours cheerful, they made her feel gay; but to-day nothing could lift the gloom that had settled on her spirits.

On a little table by her side were her cards, a crystal, and a bottle of Courvoisier. So far, she had not touched the brandy; she had cut the cards, only to find that once again the Ace of Spades, the Death Card, was uppermost. She had looked into the crystal, but she could see nothing but a grey mist, swirling and blending into a smoky mass. From the doorway Tania watched her compassionately.

"Pauvre Madame! You do not care to go out for a little, no?" Her face was screwed into a mask of anxiety for her mistress.

Gallia smiled wanly, "Ah, Tania," she shook her head, "how can I go out? I have not the heart. But you—there is no need for you to stay at home…" She fumbled in a large black velvet bag and brought out a small red leather purse with her initials in gold. "Ah! my little purse that Dimpson has given me! Here!" she held out some coins. "You, Tania, you go to the cinema. Then, when you come back, you shall make me some Boublitsky, na?" she smiled again at the maid. But Tania shook her head obstinately.

"Na. I cannot leave Madame."

"Ah! I want you to go. I *want* it!" Gallia spoke imperiously and held out the coins with a gesture that would not be denied. "Go to the cinema in the Western Road, and you are back by six o'clock.

Na, Tania, I shall sleep here on the sofa." She drew her feet up as she spoke, and arranged the comforter about her head.

Tania looked troubled. "But… if someone should call…?" she said.

"I shall not answer the bell. It is quite as simple as that," her mistress told her.

Tania smiled. "Then… then if Madame is sure?"

Gallia's only answer was a grunt. Tania withdrew and closed the door noiselessly behind her. She hurried down to the basement, where she stoked up the boiler, left a tray prepared for her mistress's tea, and closed the windows carefully. Then she took her coat and hat from behind the kitchen door and hurried out. In a land where she found little to compensate her for her native Latvia, Tania was completely fascinated by the cinema. Although she was not always able to understand everything that was said, she managed to follow the story well enough, and when she was not actually in the cinema, her spare time was spent in reading the lives of her favourite stars in the Movie Magazines. She was thoroughly conversant with the mode of life in Hollywood, and she could have told you just how many times Clark Gable had been married, and which of his wives had been married before and to whom. Her favourites were Spencer Tracy and Edward G. Robinson, whose features had a Slavonic cast that appealed to her tremendously. Gallia saw no reason why she should not indulge herself in her main amusement, and saw to it that Tania had the chance to go to the cinema at least twice a week. She did not care for the movies herself, but she believed in live and let live, and, when she was in an indulgent mood, she would allow Tania to expound by the hour on her favourite film stars.

It was not more than ten minutes' walk to the Forum in Western Road, and Tania hurried, so as to be in time for the big picture. As she paid for her seat she felt a sudden misgiving—had she remembered to lock the back door? This troubled her for a moment, until she remembered that it was unlikely there would be any callers. She was not expecting any deliveries and there was no reason why Madame should be disturbed. Tania presented her ticket to the commission-aire, who tore it in half, returned her a small portion and threw open the doors to the darkened auditorium. Tania, taking her seat between an elderly gentleman and a small boy sucking peppermints, relaxed thankfully. For the next two hours she would lose herself in the adventures of Edward G. Robinson and a gorgeous blonde.

Gallia lay on the sofa, her eyes closed, listening to Tania as she closed the back door and hurried up the area steps, humming to herself. The firm tread grew fainter as she hurried down the street, and presently the only sounds in the little room were the brisk ticking of the clock, and an occasional snore from the woman on the sofa. Suddenly, as swiftly as she had dropped off to sleep, Gallia awoke. She called sharply for Tania before she remembered that the maid had gone to the cinema, and that she was alone in the house. All at once she had a presentiment of evil, and the worries and money-troubles that had been oppressing her became giants, looming over her in the tiny room. She got off the couch and padded softly to the window. It was becoming dark outside although the street lamps were not alight yet. Switching on the light, she drew the brocaded curtains across the windows, and searched in the writing-desk for a little bottle. Once again she settled herself on the sofa; she took two pills from the little bottle and then uncorked the Courvoisier and took a long pull. The spirit tasted like liquid gold, and the warmth comforted and soothed her. For good measure she took another swig—and then another. Her eyes began to feel heavy, and she switched off the lamp. Her breathing became slower and slower... her troubles seemed to lighten and to be wafted away... everything would be arranged... it would be all right... a rosy glow enveloped her and she drifted into a deep sleep.

It was quiet in the room, now. The brisk ticking of a tiny clock, and the flicker of flames in the grate were the only sounds to break the stillness. When at last the front door bell rang, its shrill insistency seemed to shock the room into an even greater silence; but the woman on the sofa did not stir. The visitor, having rung three times, decided that the house must be empty. It was easy to walk quietly down the area steps, where Tania had so conveniently neglected to lock the kitchen door. The visitor walked into the house and up the stairs, peeping into each room in turn. The drawing-room was quite dark now; the fire had burnt low and only a few glowing coals remained to cast a feeble glimmer. The directed beam from a torch picked out the sleeping form on the sofa, and the light in her eyes caused Gallia to stir and wake. For a moment she was too dazzled by the light to do more than blink uncertainly, but even as she swung her legs over the side of the couch the visitor advanced.

When Tania returned from the cinema a short time later she was surprised to find the house in darkness. She hurried through the basement passage and up the stairs, switching on the lights everywhere. Very quietly, lest her mistress should still be asleep, she turned the handle of the drawing-room door. From where she stood she could see the sleeping form, and she drew the door to; then, pausing with her hand still on the knob, the vision of what she had seen still before her eyes, she thrust open the door again, this time switching on the lights.

"Madame," she called softly. "I am back home, Madame!"

But there was no answer, and although she listened intently, no sound of the heavy breathing which she associated with her mistress. Tania approached the sofa cautiously. Gallia lay on her back, one leg dangling uncomfortably and somehow she had managed to pull the sofa cushions right over her face.

"Ach!" Tania exclaimed. "How can she sleep so?" She bent down and twitched away the cushions.

For one dreadful moment she stared, appalled, at what she saw. It was hard to recognize her beautiful mistress in this horror of purple-mottled flesh; the bulging eyes and the blackened lips curling back from teeth which seemed blue-white in awful contrast. Tania, beside herself with terror and still clutching the cushion, ran to the street door and threw it open. Then she screamed.

7

THE POSTMAN CALLS THREE TIMES

I

HENRY BROWN'S OFFICES WERE ON THE FIFTH FLOOR OVER-looking Piccadilly. They were decorated and run on American lines; that is to say, there was a small outer office hung with posters advertising past successes, two or three uncomfortable chairs, and a desk. There was usually a small boy in attendance, who seemed to have nothing to do except read the evening papers. If, however, one succeeded in getting through the small door which was at the other end of the room, one found the next room large and airy. Here, behind a larger and more comfortable desk, sat a young lady whose appearance was apt to vary with the seasons. At this time of year she was a startling blonde. "It brightens me up a bit," she said, in the slow drawl copied faithfully from Lana Turner. During the spring, a surprised but constant caller would be likely to find her with her golden locks changed to auburn, and in the summer she would doubtless deride to be a languorous brunette. Miss Tonkins was her name, and she had resisted countless efforts on the part of enamoured young gentlemen to change it. "And what makes you think it would be for the better?" she was capable of asking pertly the young man of the moment. "It may not be very fancy, but it's my own... and I like it!" Miss Tonkins was twenty years old.

Several of Frederica's best friends had suggested that she might find a more sober secretary for Henry, but Frederica only laughed. She knew her Henry. It was dewy innocence that intrigued him, not dyed hair. "My dear," she would say, "Little Tonkins can dye her hair green for all of me, but she's a darn good secretary, and that's all that matters to Henry."

"But she's so exciting," the friend would murmur deprecatingly.

"To look at? I quite agree." Frederica's smile was dangerously sweet. "I always allow Henry to choose his own staff… I am sure he knows better than I do what capabilities he requires."

"Of course, dear, just as you say."

It was understandable that rumours of these quite frequent conversations should reach Miss Tonkins, and it is equally understandable that she should have become devoted to Frederica. She felt her position secure, and she became even more teasing and impertinent to the young men who surrounded her. Strangely enough, this did not have the effect of chasing them away; on the contrary, they became even keener, and Miss Tonkins could have made two dates for every night of the week, had she so wished.

Henry Brown's office lay beyond his secretary's, and it was here that one felt the full force of the American influence. The room, which had been enlarged four times its original size by taking down the party walls, was painted a soft, dove grey. The walls, the ceiling and the floor, on which was a thick, thick carpet were all a uniform tint. There was very little furniture; just an enormous mahogany kneel-hole desk for Henry, and four enormous armchairs upholstered in the same shade and piped with lemon-yellow. There were yellow cushions, and the grey curtains were splashed with yellow flowers. The fireplace was made of cut steel, and the electric fire was an ultra-modern affair of glass bars and chromium plating. Over the fireplace was a large Matisse, its brilliant blues and greens striking

a sharp note in the misty room. At the other end of the room was
a large portrait of Frederica wearing a violet dress. This had been
painted by a young Polish artist that Henry had come across at a
party. The wall facing the window had been taken back about six
inches to form an alcove and this had been filled with books. These
were mostly plays and books on the theatre, reference books and so
on. Below the books was a cupboard where Henry kept his drinks.
A large radiogram stood in a corner. There was no other furniture.

Henry sat at his desk, the script of Dimpsie's play before him.
He wished, not for the first time, that he had had a couch put in
the office when it was being decorated; it did not occur to him that
it was still possible for him to buy one. He had had the office furnished in this way because he thought it was the right thing to do,
and although at first the austere and modern lines had tormented
him, he had at last become used to it, and even found the effeminate
dove grey rather soothing. Also, it made such a complete contrast to
his home, that he felt he was stepping from one world to another,
which pleased him inordinately. He looked at his desk; at the two
telephones, the two reading-lamps of cut steel with chromium
shades, at the inkstand, pen-tray and clock, all made of modern
cut glass, and he contrasted them mentally with his empire desk
at home. The realization came to him that he was wasting time…
he must come to some decision on the play before getting in touch
with Archie Tittop. For the third time he picked up the letter he had
received that morning from Henry Walters.

"…you know how much Mr. McCabe relied on me" (it ran)
"and how much I was able to help him on his work. This I have
always deemed the greatest of my privileges, and I am sure you
will understand how I felt about being able to help him. It had
been long understood by both of us that this play was to be a

collaboration, and I know he would have wanted me to make this clear to you. There was no question of a contract between us… it was a purely friendly arrangement, and, of course, my name was to be in very much smaller letters. That had been decided and agreed. There was also the question of Mr. Tittop. Normally, he would have handled the play in the usual way; but in these unfortunate circumstances surely there is no need for him to have anything to do with it. As you are aware, the copies were only finished three days before Christmas, and as Mr. McCabe did not suggest sending a copy to Mr. Tittop I see no reason why he should have one now. I shall be glad to hear from you, and perhaps you will be good enough to let me know what you think of the play.

"YOURS SINCERELY,

"HENRY WALTERS."

Henry Brown folded the letter carefully and put it in his wallet. For once he felt thoroughly perturbed and ill at ease. No doubt there was some truth in what Walters had written; it was more than likely that he had helped Dimpsie on many occasions, but as far as he knew, Dimpsie had never collaborated with anybody. Most probably it was a try on—Walters might imagine that he had some kind of a case, but if this was so, how was it that Dimpsie had never mentioned the matter to anyone? And then there was the question of Archie Tittop. Surely Walters could not be serious when he suggested that it was not necessary for the Agent to be shown Dimpsie's new play. In any case, Henry decided, it would be entirely unethical not to allow Archie to handle the play as he had done all the others. He picked up the script and flipped the pages… it was a good play, a money-maker, and there was nothing in it to suggest that Dimpsie hadn't written every word himself. Henry could imagine him indignantly refuting the charges brought by his confidential secretary. His round eyes would become even rounder and more owlish behind the thick lenses, and he would have sat back in one of Henry's grey armchairs, his feet on another, his hands folded comfortably on his capacious stomach, and from his mouth would have issued the quietest, most vituperative stream of language that anyone could imagine. Henry Brown smiled inwardly as he pictured Dimpsie and what he would have said.

"That contumacious, cross-eyed rat-faced son of a she-wolf," he might have begun, rolling the words round his tongue. For a moment a sense of his complete loss swept over Henry, and perhaps for the first time he felt a twinge of personal bereavement. Dimpsie might have raved and stormed and been impossible to deal with; he might have twisted and been a tight-wad; but there was no doubt he had been a law unto himself, and Henry knew that he was going to miss his old friend.

If only, he thought, he could make up his mind once and for all what he was going to do about Walters. Obviously, nothing could be decided until they talked things over. Taking it all round, it made very little difference to Henry; there would be author's fees in any case. But, he thought whimsically, a play by Dimpsie and Walters would not be worth as much as a play by Dimpsie alone... there was a point he could make. He pressed a button on his desk, and Miss Tonkins put her head round the door.

"Take a letter," he directed. He would tell Walters to come to London and they would discuss the matter. In the meantime, he thought to himself, he would have time to think things over.

II

Henry Brown was not the only one who had had a letter from Walters. Katherine had received one, inside a large wooden box, bound at the corners with iron. It had been delivered as she was leaving for the office, and noticing that it came from Scotland, she stopped to try to undo it. It proved to be a collection of handbills and posters, accompanied by a letter from Walters.

"Dimpsie always wanted you to have these," (Walters wrote) "and so I am sending them now. As you know, his collection of circus handbills and posters was quite famous, and if you look through them you may find much to interest you. Jeffery and I are returning to London in a few days' time, and I shall look forward to seeing you. It has been a very sad time for us up here, yet somehow I shall be sorry to leave."

The letter meandered on for a few lines, and then he was hers sincerely.

Katherine looked at the box. It was cumbersome and exceedingly heavy; her heart sank as she wondered where she would find the space to store such a collection. Why on earth should Dimpsie have wanted her to have it? As far as she could remember, they had never even been to a circus together. She tugged at the box and managed to pull it into a corner of the tiny hall. Well, it would have to stay there for the time being—there was absolutely nowhere else to put it.

The letter had been tucked into the outer wrapping, and now she pried open the lid of the box and peered curiously at the contents. But all she could see was rolls of paper, and there was no use in pulling them out until she had time to examine them. On an impulse she rang Doctor Harley's number. After speaking to a secretary and a nurse, and explaining that the matter was not at all urgent if the doctor was busy, she heard his voice over the wire.

"I hope I wasn't interrupting something," she said hurriedly. "I told your secretary it was nothing important."

"Now, Kate," the voice came back softly, "what's on your mind? Come on, now, you didn't ring me up for nothing."

Katherine explained about the box. "Can you imagine why Walters sent it to me?" she finished.

"Surely. Dimpsie wanted you to have it, my dear. You know how mad he was about the circus and circus people… Well, he thought he'd like you to have the collection."

"But, Bill… where am I going to house it?"

A chuckle came over the phone. "Where indeed?"

"I won't keep you," Katherine said indignantly, "I'm sure you're busy… and—and I've got to go to the office."

"Katherine—just a minute," Bill's voice was hurried. "I shouldn't say anything about this, if I were you. It's rather early days… I mean to say, no one knows about the will or anything—it might be as well to keep it under your hat."

"All right. I suppose you know best"—she hesitated—"you mean you don't even want me to tell H.B.?"

"I shouldn't. After all, it isn't of any interest to anyone except yourself, is it? I think it might be as well to wait…"

"Just as you say."

"Shall I be seeing you to-night?"

"Do you want to?" she asked coyly.

Bill laughed. "I'll fetch you at eight," he announced.

"Till then." Katherine replaced the receiver. Picking up her handbag and gloves, and tucking her brief-case firmly under one arm, she ran out of the flat.

By the time she got to Fleet Street it was midday. As usual, the yard leading to the office buildings was in a state of utter chaos. Katherine, pushing her way through, caught sight of a news placard being pasted on to a board. DEATH OF A DANCER she read, and on her way upstairs, speculated as to whom it might mean.

"The Boss wants you, miss," an office boy told her, his eyes alight with impishness. "He's been asking for you all morning."

"Goodness!" Katherine walked quickly through the swing doors and tapped on the Editor's door.

H.B. was sitting at his desk, a cigar stuck in his mouth, his face was red, and the atmosphere in the room was heavy with smoke.

"Oh, so you decided to come to work to-day, after all?" he said sarcastically.

Katherine raised her eyebrows. "I always work," she said coolly.

"Really? Very interesting—very interesting," he said, and thrust a newspaper at her. "What do you know about this, then?" he snapped.

She took the paper and sat down on a chair the other side of the desk. It was a shock to read about Gallia's death in black and white. For a moment the room spun round and she leaned forward in the chair. H.B. hurried round from the other side of the desk.

"Here! drink this," and he held out a glass of water. "I'm sorry, Katherine, my dear, I thought you must have known." His red face was concerned and grave, and he patted her hand gently.

"I'm all right," she said, "but of course, I didn't know. I had no idea…"

"She was up at Dimpsie's place, wasn't she?" H.B. asked.

Katherine nodded. She was reading an account of how Tania returned from the cinema to find her mistress lying dead where she had left her asleep.

"Oh, poor Tania!" exclaimed Katherine. "How simply ghastly for her! No," she returned to H.B., "I haven't seen Gallia… as a matter of fact—I had rather hoped to go and see her. Well," she shrugged, "that's off, poor soul!"

"And how do you suppose it happened?" H.B. asked.

"I've no idea. Heart failure? She looked so well over Christmas. Even after all that crying the next day her skin was clear and her eyes were as bright as a child's."

H.B. hesitated. He walked over to the window and opened it. A blast of cold air streamed in, cutting across the smoke and lifting the papers on his desk. He slammed it to again viciously.

"Wait a minute," he said. "Suppose you tell me about Dimpsie, first."

Katherine looked at him helplessly. "But there isn't anything to tell—so far," she said. "That's one of the reasons I wanted to see Gallia. I thought perhaps if I had a chat with her... and perhaps with that Holly child, although I doubt if she'd be any help, I might see a little clearer."

"You haven't anything to tell me, then?" he asked slowly.

"Not yet."

"Very well," he said, "but you may as well know that Gallia Karmanskaya was murdered."

"No!" Katherine stared at him, horrified.

He nodded. "I'm afraid so. The police have asked us not to rush the story... but of course it's almost bound to leak out. The *Sun* ran a full page in the lunch edition... Her maid found her with a cushion over her head. She'd been smothered."

"But—but who would want to—" she left the sentence unfinished.

"Ah, who... that's the question; and why?"

"It doesn't make sense," Katherine exclaimed. "Hang it all, Gallia can't have had any enemies... not any in that sense, can she?"

H.B. shrugged his immense shoulders. "You'll have to answer your own questions, I'm afraid, my dear," he said.

"What do you mean?" she asked incredulously.

"I can't give you an assignment on this," he explained, "but I want you to go out and find out what's happening... what it all means.

You know all these people, Katherine, and they'll talk to you where they wouldn't allow a reporter in the house. Of course there'll be reporters on this case—bound to be—I shall have to send out Jake and Hamish. But you needn't let them get in your hair... I shall tell them to keep away from you. You're on your own, Katherine my dear, and it's up to you."

Katherine smiled at him. "I'm afraid you're going to be awfully disappointed, H.B.," she said quietly, "but I'll do my best."

For the first time he smiled back at her. "Good kid," he said, "I knew you would."

III

It was dark and quiet in Holly's little apartment. She closed the door on Henry Brown and turned back to the fire, picking up the paper that Henry had left, and switching on the lights in the sitting-room. The paper had been underneath the flowers that Henry had brought her, and she had put it down, thinking he might want it later. But Henry, his mind full of a thousand things, had found Holly sufficiently beguiling to have put all thoughts of the news out of his head. They said a lingering good-bye in the hall, and then, noticing the paper on a side table, Holly picked it up. It was the *Gazette*, she saw with approval, and that meant lots of pictures and headlines. Holly was not in the least interested in world affairs and although a daily paper was delivered at the flat she rarely, if ever, so much as glanced at it. The films and the stage took all her attention, and magazines dealing with these she read religiously. But now, with two or three hours between her and a dinner appointment, she had time to kill. She wandered back to the sitting-room and stretched out full length on the couch. A copy of *Vogue* and some picture papers lay on the floor near the fire and she would look at those if the *Gazette* should prove too boring. But she found the *Gazette* anything but dull. In the outsize headlines for which it was noted, it proclaimed the death by murder of Gallia Karmanskaya; there were pictures of the outside of the house, of the maid, Tania, of the front door and the steps descending to the area, and even a horrible little picture of the sitting-room with a shapeless something on the fatal couch. Holly crumpled the paper and threw it from her in horror. Stretching out her hand, she took a cigarette from her bag; her hands trembled as she lit it and she inhaled deeply. Her whole being was filled with terror and repulsion, there was not the slightest feeling of pity for the dead woman; at this moment all her thoughts were for herself. She tried to remember all that had happened during the few days she had spent in Gallia's company, was there anything the dead woman had done or said that could have incriminated her in any way? Supposing she had left a letter behind? At this thought Holly sat bolt upright. If Gallia had noticed anything—had intercepted glances from Henry Brown—it was quite possible that she might have spoken to anyone about the interest the producer was show-ing in his little protégée. Holly frowned and bit her lip as she raged helplessly up and down the tiny room. If there were only something she could do! But every instinct told her that her wisest course was to do nothing—to carry on as usual. But how could you, she asked herself despairingly, carry on as usual when at any moment the bell might ring and she would open the door to find the police waiting there... the telephone broke in on her thoughts and she started nervously. For a few moments she stood irresolutely in the middle of the floor, the bell shrilling insistently; but at last she picked up the receiver, handling it gingerly as if she were terrified of touching it. It was with a sigh of relief that she heard Henry's voice.

"I've just seen the paper," he said. "I left a copy of the *Gazette* in the flat. You'd better read it."

"I have," she whimpered. "Henry darling... I'm frightened..." She listened anxiously for his reply.

"Nonsense!" he said robustly, "there's nothing to be frightened of. I expect the police will find this was a clear case of robbery... however," he paused for a moment, and Holly had the impression that he was not quite sure what to say next, "...however," he went on, "if you remember what I told you up on Possett Island, you'll be quite all right."

"What do you mean?" she asked faintly.

"Speak the truth," he counselled, "if anybody asks you questions, don't try to hide anything; speak the truth, Holly."

"But surely"—she said miserably—"they won't want to ask *me* anything, will they? I don't know a single thing about Gallia... I can't see why they should imagine I could be of any help..." Her voice trailed off.

"I dare say," Henry's voice was soothing, "there's no need to worry, my dear child, as long as you tell the truth. But there is a possibility that the police may wish to question everyone who was at Possett Island with Madame Karmanskaya, and should this be the case, then I am afraid that they will want to see you."

"But, Henry," she broke in anxiously, "I don't know anything..."

"Of course not," he said, reassuringly. "Just speak the truth, Holly, and you've got nothing to worry about. And now, darling, I must be getting along." His voice softened, and they exchanged a few amiable sentiments. At last he rang off, and Holly replaced the receiver savagely, and slammed the telephone back on to the table. For a few moments she stood still, her eyes searching the room for something—anything, that would serve her purpose. A doll, lying on a pouffe in the corner, caught her restless gaze. It lay on one side, its foolish head dangling over the edge of the pouffe, its legs, in black satin trousers, hanging limp from a sawdust body. Holly took it and jammed it on to the fire, stuffing it into the little grate and poking it into the flames relentlessly.

"There!" she said, between clenched teeth, "burn! Go on, burn!"

She waited till it was fully alight, when the vapid expression seemed to be twisted into something tormented, and the creature's arms and legs were tortured into fantastic and evil shapes; and then, horror-struck, she rushed from the room.

In her bedroom she stared into the looking-glass; the face that looked back at her was flushed, the eyes bright and scared, the nose pinched. At last, she turned away; she fetched a pen and paper from the table by her bed, cleared a space on the dressing-table, and began to write.

IV

Henry Walters searched impatiently through the post-bag. Surely that man Brown, or whatever he called himself, wasn't going to ignore his letter? The long bony fingers turned over the letters to make quite sure that they had not missed the precious envelope, but there was nothing from Henry Brown. Walters bit his lip, and tried to remember exactly what he had written to the producer, while he opened his mail with mechanical precision. There were the usual assortment of bills, fan letters and calls for help with which he had become only too familiar during the past years with Dimpsie, and he sat at the breakfast table, littering his end of it with envelopes and paper. Jeffery, facing him, glanced up now and again from the paper, but Walters was immersed in his correspondence.

"Good lord!" he exclaimed at last, "here's a letter from Holly! What in the world can she be writing to me about?" He turned the envelope about and examined it curiously.

"Open it," suggested Jeffery, "then you'll know, won't you?"

"It's so thick," objected Walters. "I don't know what it can be."

"You'll have to open it, if you want to find out."

Walters inserted the paper-knife slowly, his mouth twisted in a bitter smile. That Holly wanted something from him, he was quite decided, so that he was entirely unprepared for a wadge of papers covered with fine, spiky writing in a language that he could not recognize at all. There were four sheets, in all. The paper was thin and of very poor quality, and was so closely covered that the words almost ran into each other. Walters put the letter on the table and shook the envelope; a card dropped on to his plate.

"Dear Henry," (he read, in Holly's sprawling hand),

"I expect you will have heard about Gallia. I am sending you this letter because I think it must have belonged to her. I found it in the parlour and meant to ask whose it was but I quite forgot all about it, and I've just discovered it in my pocket. I am sending it to you, Henry, because I know you are used to dealing with other people's correspondence, aren't you?

"LOVINGLY,

"HOLLY."

Walters crumpled the card and threw it into the fire without speaking.

"What's up?" Jeffery's eyebrows were raised.

"Only Holly trying to be clever," Walter's voice was cold, his tone acid. "I never could make out what Dimpsie saw in her. Nothing but a common little piece, I always thought."

"A menace," Jeffery agreed.

"I can't make out a word of this," he picked up the letter and looked at it despairingly. "Might as well be written in Chinese," he grumbled.

"Let's see…" Jeffery stretched out his hand. "It's Russian, I should think… or Polish… But of course it might be any one of the Balkan languages. Why did Holly send it to you?"

"I haven't the slightest idea. I shall have to have a few words with that young woman when we return to London." He smiled, showing those long, wolfish teeth. "I rather think she'll have a little explaining to do. And I shall be interested to know exactly what she was doing all alone in the parlour."

"When are you thinking of leaving?" Jeffery asked the question awkwardly.

Walters turned a worried face to him. "You're not getting bored, are you? It's been such fun—just the two of us—you've no idea how much it's meant to me. There's no hurry to get back to town, is there?"

"No—I suppose not," Jeffery said dubiously. "Only—what about Dimpsie's things? And—he must have left a will or something, Henry? Won't you have to get in touch with his solicitors?"

"My dear, I phoned them straight away. I haven't any knowledge of Dimpsie's will—for all I know he may never have made one— but the solicitor bloke will know all about that. There are all sort of papers and things that I must go through, though, and besides, there's a little play of mine." Walters smiled thinly. "Oh yes, I used to scribble a bit before I came to Dimpsie—one of my things turned up the other day and I gave it to him to read. Now, of course, I can't find it anywhere. I must see if I can locate it… otherwise that beast Archie Tittop will get his claws on it."

"It'll be all right if it's got your name on," said Jeffery. "Do you really think that Archie will come up here?"

Walters frowned. "He'd better not," he said darkly. "I wouldn't like to insult Archie, but if he starts any of his nonsense…" He left the threat unfulfilled.

Jeffery stared moodily into the fire. Perhaps it was selfish of him not to be more sympathetic, but he had his own worries. Walters didn't seem to realize that he didn't know where his next quarter's allowance was to come from—or whether it would come at all. Surely Dimpsie must have made some arrangements on his behalf? Jeffery remembered that Dimpsie hadn't known he was going to die. It was funny, he thought, that Henry had never mentioned that he had been going to leave him. Jeffery wondered whether he should say anything about it, and decided against it. He remembered how shocked he had been to hear Dimpsie screaming at Henry, and how the secretary had attempted to calm him down without any success.

"I know perfectly well what you're after," Dimpsie had yelled. "You want to run with the hare and hunt with the hounds. Well, it can't be done, Walters, and the sooner you realize it the better. And as for trying to take my friends away from me—seducing them, that's what it is!"

"But, honestly, there's a mistake," Walters had said, white and shaking. "You know how devoted I am to you, Dimpsie, I always have been."

"Don't stand there lying," Dimpsie had said, his voice icy with contempt. "I suppose you'll have to stay until after Christmas, but then, you can get out, do you hear me?"

Jeffery had not meant to eavesdrop, he had been about to open the studio door—had had his hand on it—and at the sound of his own name he had paused, gripping the door knob.

"Even Jeffery—" Dimpsie had said, "—even Jeffery you've tried to take away from me. Oh, I know he's loyal, he'd never let me down, but that wouldn't prevent you spreading your poison, Walters." Jeffery had stood still, sick and faint at the implication. He knew he ought to run away, to shut his ears, to retreat from the sound of that screaming voice; but he was unable to move; he was at once fascinated and horrified, and he had remained listening until the sound of high heels pattering down the staircase had recalled him to the present.

"Hullo, there, Jeffery!" Holly had called. "Listening to the row?"

"What row?"

"Oh, don't pretend you don't know," Holly said scornfully. "I could hear it in my bedroom. Henry's been getting it hot and strong. And *you're* one of the reasons, my pretty boy."

Jeffery flushed. "Don't talk like that, Holly, please," he said.

"Please, Holly," she mimicked. "Anyway, what were you doing outside the door?"

"It's locked," he said, lying quickly. "I was just going in—but it's locked."

"Oh well—" Holly giggled, her eyes dancing, "let's go and find the others. Leave Dimpsie to his stuffy old quarrel—he'll get over it!" She caught hold of Jeffery's hand and pulled him away.

And now, thinking of all that, it struck him as odd, to say the least, that Henry had never mentioned the quarrel. But perhaps, he reflected, it was out of delicacy... and, anyway, it was all over now. There was no point in bringing up past troubles. And Henry must have been terribly upset, Jeffery thought, remembering the insults Dimpsie had hurled at the secretary.

"I never knew you wrote, too," he said.

"Me?" Walters smiled. "Oh, yes. Of course, during the past ten years I've been lazy... well, perhaps not lazy," he corrected himself, "I never had very much time for writing any of my own stuff—but I did all Dimpsie's corrections, you know, and actually, this is between ourselves, Jeffery, I wrote some of the stuff for him—when he was busy, you know, and couldn't get down to it."

"Really?" Jeffery tried to conceal his astonishment.

"Yes. But, of course, this is strictly off the record, part of a secretary's duties, you know. 'The Tatler', for instance, I often had to get it ready. Dimpsie was awfully bad about being on time. He'd wait till the last moment and then have the most ghastly rush. Sometimes there wouldn't be time to submit the copy—and then I'd have to run up a little something…" He smiled deprecatingly. "It was never mentioned, of course. He wouldn't have liked it to be known. And, I never expected—" He paused.

"But how wonderful of you," Jeffery said. "Honestly, Henry, you *are* marvellous! There's nothing you can't do!"

Walters coughed modestly. "It's nothing," he said. "I just tried to help… and I know Dimpsie appreciated it."

Jeffery stared for a moment, but he said nothing. It seemed to him the height of magnanimity that Henry could be so nice about his employer after all the vile things Dimpsie had said. He hoped Henry would get another job with someone decent—someone who would be fair and just, not accepting all kinds of help, and then— Impulsively he turned to Walters. "I think you're wonderful," he said, "being so nice about Dimpsie, considering everything he said—"

Walters' face was a study. "Everything he said?" he echoed. "What do you mean, Jeffery? Dimpsie never said anything to me. Why should he?"

8

MR. HEMINGWAY SINGS

I

FREDERICA DRAGGED AT THE LITTLE BLACK FELT HAT SHE WORE pulled over her eyes, and dropped it on the floor; she shook out her hair as if the weight of the hat had been too much for her. "You see," she said earnestly, "I get so dreadfully tired... and then I can't sleep. I lie awake night after night... while Henry snores," she smiled gently as she said the last words.

Doctor Harley leant back in his chair and watched her thoughtfully.

"I wonder why you thought of coming to me?" he said. "Could you tell me who your regular doctor is? And have you been troubled like this before?"

"I haven't a doctor," she shook her head, and her eyes looked appealingly into his. "You see, Doctor—or may I call you Bill?"

Bill Harley grinned. "Sure, call me what you like, but go on, please."

"I haven't a doctor," she said again, "I'm never ill. I have what one might call 'rude health'. When Henry found out that I was sleeping so badly he suggested that I see you about it. He likes you, Bill, he's got a lot of confidence in you."

"Has he? Well..." he hesitated, "well... thank you," he said. "Now tell me, how long has this been going on?"

She made a grimace. "Not so very long... but it seems for ever. I suppose it began after Christmas."

"I see. And you haven't done anything about it till now?" He put a professional finger on her wrist and became absorbed in his watch, counting her heartbeats. Abruptly he returned to his chair.

"Not a thing." She remained silent, her hands folded meekly in her lap. Faint blue shadows under her eyes accentuated the normal pallor of her cheeks and her skin, in contrast to the dead black crepe of her dress, appeared even more delicate and fragile than usual. The heady fragrance of the white gardenias she wore pinned at her throat reached Bill across the desk.

He pulled a tablet of paper towards him and made a note on it.

"I'll send you something," he promised. "It'll make you sleep, you know, but I'd like to see you again. You ought to sleep naturally... you don't want to get in the habit of taking drugs."

"Will they be pills?" she asked anxiously.

He stared. "Yes. Why do you ask?"

"I never could swallow a pill," she smiled brilliantly at him, "I suppose..." she hesitated.

"Would you rather take it in liquid form?" he asked. "It won't taste good, you know."

"Oh... couldn't you make it nice? I'm sure you could." She spoke slowly, as if the matter were of no importance, but Doctor Harley, trained to observe every action of the patient during a consultation, noticed that her hands, that had been lying limp, were now clenched, the knuckles white and strained.

"Can you take a powder?" he asked jokingly, and was surprised at her look of relief. "Very well, then. I'll make it a powder... and you can take it with a teaspoonful of jam. That all right for you?"

A little colour came into her cheeks as she nodded. "It won't taste, then?"

He shook his head. "Hardly at all. Just a little bitter, but the jam will disguise it."

Frederica stood up and held out her hand. "Thank you," she said gratefully. "You are a dear."

Bill took her hand, and was surprised to find it was icy cold. "You'll get those powders this afternoon," he told her. "If I were you, I should go home and lie down. You're tired."

"I am," she agreed. "And, Bill—don't tell Henry you've seen me."

"But—but I thought he told you to come and see me?"

"Yes. But I said I wouldn't. Silly, aren't I?" she flashed. "But you see, if he knows I have to take a sleeping powder it will worry him so much. It's far easier just to say I'm sleeping better, and then everything will be all right. See?"

Opening the door Bill smiled down at her. "Anything you say," he agreed. "But I'd like you to come and see me again in a week's time." He watched her walk into the hall before returning to his desk. The scent of the gardenias remained in the air; tantalizing, reminiscent, elusive.

II

The news of Gallia's death had come as a shock to all the members of the Possett Island house-party. They had reacted in different ways, but it was Glen Hemingway who was the most upset by what he read in the papers. Alone in his flat, his first impulse had been to telephone or wire to Frederica, but second thoughts had suggested that this might be extremely unwise and second thoughts had prevailed. He would have liked to have seen Doctor Harley, to find out a little more of the affair; he imagined that Harley would certainly have been called in... but going over the matter again and again in his head it seemed that his wisest course was to continue as usual, and not to try to make any unusual contacts. He tried to put the whole affair out of his mind, but he found himself unable to concentrate on his work and he spent his time in going from the workroom to the flat and back again, in an effort to get something done, or to try to interest himself in a new lighting effect he was working on. Several times he was tempted to ring Henry Brown, and to ask whether anything had been decided with regard to Dimpsie's play, but each time he picked up the receiver to dial the number, an inexplicable feeling, some kind of sixth sense, made him replace it again.

But the end of the day following Gallia's murder, he was in a state bordering on collapse. He had heard nothing from Frederica, and he had come to the conclusion that it would be unwise to try and see her. The only thing left for him, it seemed, was to close with the offer to go back to Africa. His Agent had assured him that both parties were still most anxious for him to take them and, although he would now have preferred to remain in England, as things were turning out, he might be wiser to take this chance of getting away. Sitting hunched over the fire he had smoked pipe after pipe, deliberating on his course of action, and now the relief of coming to a decision was exhausting. He felt tired to death, but he decided to phone his Agent and clinch the affair, so that he could not change his mind again.

Once he had settled with his Agent, a strange urgency oppressed him, and although he was to leave England within ten days, he wished that he might be going immediately. It occurred to him that he could await the Americans in Paris, just as well as in London, and there seemed no reason why he should not do this. He hurried down to his workshop; he would have to pack up his electrical gear and stow it away. Feverishly he began to tear down installations and coil wire; to separate fuses and plugs; and as he worked, a strange sound emanated from the workroom. Mr. Hemingway was singing.

III

To Henry Brown, hurrying away from Holly's flat, the news of
Gallia's death had been more painful than he would have cared to
admit, even to himself. Although Henry was in love with his wife,
and was somewhat captivated, in spite of himself, by Holly's kittenish
charms, he had had a great admiration for Madame Karmanskaya
and had been secretly flattered by the interest she had shown in
him. And although he was fully aware that Gallia was financially
troubled and that she had hoped that he would help her, he could
not help feeling that her interest was not entirely self-seeking. He
had not been deceived by her White Russian pretensions—he had
felt certain that she was either Latvian or Polish, probably the latter,
and he thought none the less of her for wishing to change her status:
after all, he himself had become a naturalized Englishman. And
the very fact that she was not in her first youth, that she must be
the same age as himself, had been an added attraction. For Henry,
Gallia had combined the sophistication of an older woman with the
complete *naïveté* of the Russian. The combination was irresistible.
For although she might not have been born in Russia, she had so
absorbed herself in the part she had to play that it had become a
second nature, and she was unaware that she had ever been otherwise. They had always spoken English together, but between them,
the unspoken knowledge of another tongue lay like a safe-deposit
of which they both possessed a key. It might never be necessary to
use it… but it was there. Safe and hidden from the public gaze. And
perhaps it was this, more than any physical allure, that had drawn
Henry to Gallia with such subtle strength. For no matter how successful he might be, there was always the fact that he was an alien;
and it was something he was unable to forget. Perhaps, had he been
of different parentage he might not have been so conscious of his

birth, but as it was, in spite of his wealth, his *objets d'art*, his pictures and the hundred and one things he had collected and accumulated, he was never quite able to step out from the shadow of the ghetto.

And on top of the shock of Gallia's death, came the swift realization that they would all be questioned. There was no doubt at all in Henry's mind that the police would connect this affair with Possett Island, and that everyone who had been there over Christmas would be sure to receive a visit from Scotland Yard. If only he could be sure of Holly! But, attractive though she might be, she was so impetuous—so reckless—and her tongue was liable to run away with her! She had no love for the dead woman… Henry doubted whether she loved anybody very much… and, when roused, she might be able to make several indiscreet and unnecessary remarks. That they might be untruthful was beside the point. He had practically decided to let her read the part of the ingénue in the new play… although this might mean trouble with Frederica. But there was something about Holly that he found indubitably fascinating. That baby, pouting mouth, the dewy look about the eyes with their fringed lids, and that engaging way she had of nestling up to him. Henry sighed! He'd been a fool and he'd have to pay for it, he supposed, and consoled himself with the thought that better men than he had fallen for little girls.

He had arrived at his apartment before he realized that he dreaded a discussion with Frederica. She had never spoken about Gallia, and the thought that she might do so now filled him with revulsion. But Frederica had no time to waste on dead women; her thoughts were for the living, and almost entirely for herself. She could not but be glad that Gallia was no longer alive, a permanent source of distraction for Henry, even if not a very serious one.

She lay in her bedroom on the chaise longue; in a white chiffon and lace garment that was almost transparent she was at her most attractive. Henry felt his heartbeats quicken as he looked at her, and as he stooped to kiss her the blood pounded in his temples. What a fool he was, he thought again, and cursed himself for his stupidity.

IV

The sky was a pewter bowl, and in the west a livid streak suggested the approach of rain. Katherine hurried down Fleet Street and jumped on a number 19 bus. It was crowded with messengers, clerks, shoppers, two school children and a woman with a dog. In spite of the cold, the smell of humanity was revolting, the atmosphere was raw and damp, and the woman next to her had a head cold and coughed incessantly. Katherine averted her head and tried to concentrate on the traffic outside, but her mind was full of the dreadful news she had just heard, and she felt sick at heart. All the doubts and fears she had experienced over Dimpsie's death were multiplied a hundred fold, and inevitably she coupled the two together: Dimpsie and Gallia. Why was it that the deaths of these two should be connected—and how could they be? These questions went round and round in her head until she felt dizzy, until suddenly the unknown passengers to right and left of her became sinister and dreadful, the bus itself an evil influence, and the conductor, meekly awaiting her fare, a malignant being seeking to destroy her peace of mind. Pulling herself together, Katherine paid the few coppers and left the bus. She found herself at Sloane Square, and determined to walk the rest of the way. The rain, that had been threatening all morning, now began to pour out of the sky in a drenching spray of icy needles, but Katherine walked through it, oblivious to everything save her thoughts.

From the outside, Gallia's little house looked neglected and untidy. The blinds were drawn and the windows tightly shut against the rain; a small collection of milk bottles at the top of the area steps, and a bundle of newspapers stuffed into the letterbox gave mute evidence of the disintegration of the household within. Inside the hall it was dark and quiet; the body had been removed to the mortuary, the photographers and journalists had all gone; except for a couple of policemen the house was empty. Katherine looked curiously round the tiny sitting-room; everything had been left as it was, and she noted the bottle of Courvoisier, the pills and Gallia's capacious handbag on the table by the sofa. A photograph had fallen into the grate and she picked it up and replaced it on the shelf over the fireplace. It was a study of a young man with fair hair cut in a bang across his forehead, his wide blue eyes gazing calmly out of the picture into some cloud-cuckoo land of his imagination. Katherine thought he was sufficiently like Gallia to be a brother, and she turned the picture over in the vain hope of finding an inscription on the back. The policeman, watching from the doorway, spoke up.

"I shouldn't wonder if that's not the man wot's been 'ere this morning. Asking for the Madam, he was, and ever so put out when I told him wot'd happened."

Katherine's eyebrows went up. "Who was he?" she asked quickly.

The policeman grinned. "Couldn't understand the lingo, miss, and that's a fack. I told him to wait; I said the Inspector would see 'im, but I couldn't get 'im to understand wot I meant, and 'e went off in ever such a stew!" He looked ruefully at Katherine. "I felt ever so sorry for 'im, miss... seemed as if 'e couldn't get it into 'is 'ead. And that maid person, they 'ad to take 'er off to 'ospital, she was that upset, finding the body and all."

"So you don't know who he was—or where he's gone to?"

The policeman fished in a pocket and brought out a card. "'E left me this card, miss... I've got to hand it over to the Inspector, but you can 'ave a look at it. As a matter of fact, the Inspector hasn't been down since early this morning, so I'm not doing any harm by letting you have a dekko at it. Acrobat or something, he was, wasn't he?"

The card was a thin piece of pasteboard with an ornamental border, in the centre the names "Faustine & Krasnya" were printed in capitals, and below this was written "Acrobatic Adagio Dancers". In one corner was Cirque Merano, Paris. Katherine glanced at it and handed it back.

"Perhaps he'll be back?" she hazarded.

The constable shook his head. "I'm sure *I* don't know," he said dubiously. "Wotever that lingo was, I couldn't make any sense out of it." He replaced the card carefully and returned to his post at the door. "I just thought it might interest you, miss... I didn't mention it to the gentlemen from the press."

"Thanks very much, Officer." Katherine smiled gratefully up at him. "There *is* just a chance that this might be important..." The words trailed off as the thought occurred to her that the little pasteboard really *might* be important, if only she had the wit to realize in what way the young man was connected with the dead woman. Automatically she went from room to room, her eyes searching for some clue that would throw a light on the murder, but even as she looked, her mind was busy with the pasteboard card that she had just seen. *Faustine & Krasnya*. Somewhere, in the back of her mind, she knew she had seen those names before... but where?

9

COCKTAILS FOR HOLLY

I

THREE HOURS LATER KATHERINE ROSE FROM HER KNEES TO answer the door bell. It was with relief that she saw her visitor was Bill Harley, and she took his hat and coat from him and dumped them on the settee, while she threw open the door of the sitting-room. Inside was confusion. The floor was knee-deep in posters and papers of all kinds. Dimpsie's box that Walters had sent to her stood open in the middle of the room, vomiting papers that threatened to fill every corner of the tiny flat.

Bill Harley stood and gazed at the mess. "What on earth are you up to?" he demanded.

Katherine shrugged. "A hunch." She described her visit to Gallia's house, and the picture of the young man. She told about the card the constable had shown her and repeated the names engraved on it. "Somewhere I've heard these names before," she said, "but where, Bill, where?"

He took out his cigarette-case and offered it. "Dare we light a match?" he asked, waving the case at the papers littering the floor.

Katherine giggled. "I shan't be able to keep all these. I can't imagine what poor old Dimpsie was thinking of. Let's have a cigarette and perhaps you'll be able to help me. I know I've heard those names before... somewhere."

"Have you looked through all the posters?" he asked.

"Impossible! The box is still half full... there's nothing on any of these..." she turned over a handful carelessly.

Bill dipped into the box and brought out a bundle tied up with string. He knelt down and began to untie it carefully, keeping the papers together in a heap.

"It isn't any good, Bill," Katherine said, "even if we do find the names on one of these bills it isn't going to mean anything." She plumped down on the floor at his side, smiling up at him.

"Well?" he said whimsically.

She shook her head ruefully. "Not so well," she said. "I feel dreadfully depressed, Bill. I can't understand any of this, can you?"

"Not a thing, darling," his tone was thoughtful. "Hey! wait a minute!" He stared at her, a faraway look in his eyes. "Do you remember telling me you found a marriage certificate in Dimpsie's desk? What were the names on that?"

Katherine jumped to her feet. "My God!" she said, "it could be." Rummaging in her desk she brought out the envelope she had found in the little bedside desk in Dimpsie's bedroom. Together they opened it carefully.

"It's a marriage certificate all right," she said. "And look... Faustine Pravcek to Krasnya Benenberg. Faustine and Krasnya... what do you know?"

"Must be the same ones, I should think," he said doubtfully. "Of course, Dimpsie knew all sorts of queers... and then Gallia had been on the stage for years. There's no reason why they shouldn't have had mutual friends."

"None whatsoever..." She sat back on her heels, the certificate dangling from her fingers. "I wonder why Krasnya was calling on Gallia to-day?"

"Perhaps he'd heard about Dimpsie, and he wanted to see her... to ask about something or other."

"Bill"—Katherine spoke softly, as if she were afraid to voice her thoughts—"do you think there's any connection between Gallia's death—and Dimpsie's?" She looked at him fearfully.

"I shouldn't think so." Comfortable words were belied by the uncertainty of his tone.

"I wish I'd seen Krasnya," she said again.

"Perhaps he called to get the certificate," Bill suggested.

"Do you think so?"

"No. He'd have gone to Dimpson's flat."

"All right. And then, finding no one there, he went to see Gallia..."

"I wonder whether Walters has ever heard of him," Katherine said thoughtfully. "He's leaving Possett Island in a day or two and coming back to London. I could ask him..."

Doctor Harley pulled some more of the papers out of the box and spread them out on the floor. They were all shapes and sizes, mostly folded into half or quarter their normal size and advertising circuses all over the world.

"There must be several hundred posters here," Bill said. "Are you going to look at all of them?"

"How can I?" she glanced up at him. "You're not really serious, are you? Do you think I ought to go through them?"

"It's up to you, darling," he said, "you're the one that's out for murder—not me."

"I don't think I like the sound of that," she said quickly, "and, by the way, that's the second time you've called me darling."

"Only the second time," he chuckled, "how very remiss of me!"

But something in his tone of voice caused Katherine to take a quick look at him. Strangely enough, Doctor Harley was not smiling.

II

Both Walters and Jeffery were thankful to be back in London. The last few days on Possett Island had seemed interminable, and several times Jeffery had had an uneasy feeling that Walters would have been glad to have the place to himself. To add to their troubles Inspector Smith had paid an unexpected call and had asked a number of questions that Walters had found exceedingly unnecessary. Now that Dimpsie was dead and buried there seemed absolutely no point in going over and over the same old ground. "Let the past bury its dead," Walters said, when the Inspector had observed his intention of taking a stroll through the grounds, or walking on the terrace outside the studio. He seemed to have taken quite a fancy to the studio, Jeffery thought, and he wondered what was going on behind the horn-rimmed spectacles the Inspector habitually wore. It was quite a relief when Walters announced that all the papers were cleared up and there was no need for them to remain on the Island any longer.

Back in town Walters established himself in Dimpsie's apartment. He would have to clear everything up, he said, and he might as well take advantage of the empty flat. He had determined not to let the grass grow under his feet, and he lost no time in getting in touch with Henry Brown. The producer, however, had little to say to Dimpsie's late secretary.

"I'm afraid you'll have to establish your claim to part-authorship of the play," he said tersely. "McCabe never mentioned your name to me in this connection, and therefore you will have to give me some reasonable proof that you did actually collaborate with him... if you will forward this to my secretary, she will deal with the matter."

Walters did not wait to hear any more. Choking with rage he slammed down the receiver and, pushing back his chair, began to pace up and down the room. For the hundredth time he wished that he had been able to retrieve the script from Brown before the producer left the Island. He wondered what Archie Tittop was doing, and whether he knew anything about Brown's plans. No doubt they had even started casting... he flopped into a chair and passed his handkerchief over his forehead. The worry of it all, he thought bitterly, when it might have been so simple! Suddenly, as if a wave of relief had poured over him, he remembered Holly. Taking up the receiver again he dialled her number.

"Hullo, sweetie," he said falsely, and waited anxiously for the reply.

"Henry darling," Holly's voice was sugary, "when did you get back? I'm crazy to see you!"

Walters relaxed. "Me too," he said. "When may I come round?"

There was a slight pause. "Whenever you like," the sweet voice said, "or shall I come round to you... where are you staying, by the way?"

"I'm in Chelsea," he explained briefly, "at the flat. Do come round if you'd like to. I'll make a cocktail..."

"I'd love it," Holly said quickly. "As a matter of fact, I've got to go out. Frederica's giving a party—and she asked me to go along. I could drop in on my way."

"That's fine, Holly dear," Walters enthused. "I'm longing to see you. I won't keep you now—you come around just as soon as you can."

He replaced the receiver and hurried over to the sideboard. Thank heavens there was plenty of drink—Dimpsie had always kept a good supply of gin and whisky, and there had been no one to drink the last order. He fussed round, getting out glasses and arranging the bottles on a silver tray. The fire was burning up well and the room was warm and cosy. If everything went as it should, Walters thought, there was no real reason why he should not keep on the apartment. Mrs. Smithers was obliging enough and Smithers, when he wasn't complaining about his rheumatism, the pain in his joints and his lumbago, was a good cook. Yes, he thought complacently, he might do a lot worse. He trotted into the bedroom and passed the brushes over his hair; replacing them on the dressing-table he took care to see that everything was spick and span—Holly might wish to powder her nose. When he was satisfied that everything was in perfect order, he returned to the fire to await his visitor. But he was unable to relax; the sound of a taxi sent him running to the window to peer out and every footstep he made sure was Holly's. But more than an hour dragged by before she arrived, and when at last he saw the familiar little figure alighting from a taxi it was all he could do to conceal his annoyance at having been kept waiting.

"I'm afraid I'm terribly late," she apologized prettily, "but it wasn't altogether my fault." She took off a little fur tie and dropped it on a chair, together with her handbag and gloves. Then, turning to Walters, she held out both her hands. "Oh, it *is* nice to see you again!"

Walters took both her hands in his and led her over to the fire. "It's lovely to see *you*," he said, smiling down at her. Holly settled herself in an armchair, she leant her head against the velvet cushions and smiled up at him.

"Well, dear," Walters said, "tell me all the dirt." He wafted gently to the sideboard and began to pour out the drinks. "Gin, dearie?"

"Just lemonade, please," Holly said. "I don't really drink, you know, and I may have to have a cocktail at Frederica's. I'd rather just have a soft drink now."

Walters handed her a tall glass, filled to the brim. He poured himself a cocktail and sat down opposite her. Holly sipped her drink and looked at him roguishly.

"You wicked thing! You've put gin in it!"

"Just a drop, dearie, just a drop!" he said calmly. "Now, drink it up and tell Uncle Walters just what's been cooking while he's been away in the frozen north."

Holly shook her head. "Nothing, I'm afraid, that would interest you. You know about poor old Gallia, of course?"

"Umm…" He pursed his lips and looked reflectively at the tiny glass. "Holly—what made you send me that letter?"

"Letter? Oh—you mean that foreign thing—" She was all innocence, eyes wide, mouth dewy and surprised into a tiny O. "Well… I didn't know what I ought to do with it, and I thought that as I'd found it up at the castle I ought to send it back there. You're not cross with Holly, are you?" she put her head slightly on one side and pouted appealingly.

"Well—you were not exactly polite, were you?" he drawled. "Still—Uncle Walters never bears malice… specially when little girls are so sweet and pretty. Besides, that letter may come in very handy, one of these days."

She nodded. "That's just what I thought. You see, it would have been so easy just to tear it up and throw it away… but then I thought, well—if one can't read it, there's no way of knowing whether it's important or not—and so I sent it on to you, darling."

"And what else have you been doing?" he asked politely.

She gave an infinitesimal shrug. "Nothing much…"

"Resting, I suppose." His tone was slightly acid.

For a moment she hesitated. "No," she said, "as a matter of fact, I'm booked to open in the new show Henry Brown is putting on."

Walters got up and went over to the window to conceal a smile of satisfaction. They were all the same, these actors. Only hint that they might be out of work and all the cherished secret plans will come tumbling out. He stood there, looking out on to the street, his mind a turmoil, his brain seething with questions that he was longing to ask. But he wasn't going to spoil the whole thing by rushing it—he would have to pretend to be disinterested; if Holly once thought he had any special reason for wishing to know about the play, she would shut up like a clam. He pretended to be busy lighting a cigarette, and came slowly back to the fire.

"Another drinkie?"

"No thanks," she sounded disappointed. Wasn't he interested, after all? Men were extraordinary. You'd think Walters would want to know every detail about Dimpsie's play. It just showed, she decided, how stupid he was.

Walters poured himself another cocktail and took a sip before speaking again. "Well, dearie, I'm very glad to hear that. Very glad indeed. The First Miss Smith, of course?"

Holly giggled. "The one and only. Henry thinks he'll have to eliminate the two others... he says they only clutter up the play. Still—he may not be able to do that... What do you think?"

Walters shrugged. "They're all alike, these producers," he said viperishly. "No offence, Holly; I know Henry's a friend of yours, but really! Once they get their scissors on a play it's just snip, snip, snip, till they've slashed the thing to ribbons."

"I suppose I oughtn't to have told you—" she said doubtfully.

Walters put a bony forefinger to his lips. "I'll be as silent as the grave, dearie! Not one peep out of me! And tell me, what does Archie say to all this?"

"I haven't seen him," Holly said, "but I don't expect he can say much. After all, it's really none of his business, is it?"

"Well—he was Dimpsie's Agent, you know." Walters spoke lightly, but he watched Holly from narrowed lids to see how she would take this.

"*Was* is the operative word," she said lightly, "I don't suppose he'll have much chance to say anything now."

"Oh," said Walters blankly. "And tell me, dearie, who's doing the lighting? I suppose Henry will be having Glen, won't he?"

"Oh, I suppose so," she agreed. "But it's early days to talk about that… the play isn't cast yet." Suddenly she giggled. "And we open next month, I believe!"

Walters raised his eyebrows. "Do you, now," he said quietly.

Holly finished her drink and put the empty glass on a small table.

"I shall have to go," she said, standing up. "Frederica will be furious if I'm late." She picked up her fur and gloves, and held out her hand to Walters. "It was sweet of you to give me a drink, Henry," she said. "You will drop round to the flat some time, won't you?"

"Of course I will—I should love to," he assured her. "And perhaps I'll be coming to some of the rehearsals, Holly. Anyway, we'll meet soon." He ushered her to the door and into the hall. As he opened the front door a cruising taxi came slowly down the road. In less than a minute Holly was safely on her way to Frederica's. Walters returned to the sitting-room and poured himself another drink. Sitting by the fire, he sipped it reflectively, wondering how much truth there was in Holly's statements, and how much was said with the object of impressing him. He was not surprised that Henry Brown and Frederica had not invited him to their party; in the circumstances he could hardly have expected an invitation.

III

Holly had felt diffident about accepting Frederica's invitation. There was no doubt that Mrs. Brown must have at least a slight inkling of how things lay between Holly and her husband. Although they had been as discreet as a mother bunny preparing for her firstborn, still Holly could not help remembering certain episodes at Possett Island, and how several times Henry had paid her a good deal of attention. He had paid attention to Gallia, too, she reflected with a slight shudder... but it was to be hoped that his affection for the Russian woman had nothing to do with the murder. There was a moment when Holly had seriously considered refusing the invitation on the plea of a previous date; but second thoughts had pointed the foolishness of this course. The only way, as she saw it, was to face up to things and deny everything that might do her harm. Of course, she was obliged to flirt with Henry. As the wife of a producer Frederica must realize that it was difficult enough for a girl to get a job without definitely antagonizing people who would be inclined to hold out a helping hand. It was all very well, Holly thought, for people to say that if you had talent you would get on—would be bound to make a success. But what about if one hadn't a lot of talent? What about a girl like Holly, who had only her looks and a certain pleasant little way with her? Holly knew that she wasn't the stuff that stars are made of. It was up to her to get along the best way she could—and, she giggled to herself, a girl couldn't afford to be choosy. Henry might be a bit old, but he was attractive all right, and knew how to make love convincingly. He was slick, that's what he was.

"You goin' ter sit there all night, miss?" The taxi-driver opened the door and poked his ugly face round at her. "This is w'ere you said, i'n it?"

Holly started guiltily. She hopped out of the cab and fumbled in her bag. Shamed into giving the driver a larger tip than she would have done normally, she hurried into the block of flats. Inside the hall everything was very cool and quiet. A thick fawn carpet almost covered a marble floor, and heavy velvet hangings gave an imposing air of richness. The lift was sufficiently old-fashioned to have the right air of solidity and yet was not slow or draughty. The Browns' flat was on the top floor, and Holly, accustomed to a gimcrack, modern apartment, was surprised to find that even when the door was open and she was admitted to the hall by a demure parlourmaid, there was still that air of hushed silence, and only a murmur of voices gave any indication that a party was in progress.

Following the maid, Holly could not help a slight feeling of uncertainty which grew to a moment of positive nervousness when she entered a room in which she could not see a familiar face. But she had not taken more than a few steps forward when her hostess detached herself from a group of people and came to greet her. Frederica was dressed to-day in a coffee-coloured satin dress that was quite unlike anything Holly had seen before. Very plain and fitting tightly to the figure, it was difficult to see how there was room to walk, and yet, as Frederica moved across the room towards her, Holly observed that the skirt was cut in such a flowing line that it was the personification of ease and grace. With this dress Frederica wore an enormous topaz brooch at the neck, and on her wrists two large bracelets studded with the same stones.

"Darling!" she said, taking Holly's hand in hers, "how sweet of you to come! Henry isn't here yet—but I want you to meet some friends." She brought Holly up to a group of people and made quick introductions. "Meet Henry's new discovery," she said. "Holly's going to be a terrific success in the new play! We're all madly excited about it!"

A young man whose name Holly didn't catch murmured something and fetched a drink from a nearby table. Bowing from the waist he handed it to Holly, his eyes twinkling.

"We must all drink to this," he said, raising his own glass.

Frederica patted Holly's shoulder. "I have to run away for a moment," she said, "you'll be all right, won't you?"

"Why, yes," said Holly. She twinkled back at the young man and, easing his way over to her, he indicated a sofa in the next room.

"Shall we?" he said, "you'll find it tiring, standing about."

"I am a little weary," Holly admitted. He was a rather gay young man, she thought, and definitely attractive.

"I don't think I've seen you here before," he said, as they settled themselves on the sofa.

Holly shook her head. "And I almost didn't come to-day."

"Really? Me too…" The conversation became the usual exchange of banalities, and Holly, while enjoying her chat, did not forget to keep an eye on the door, so that she might check on Henry's arrival.

Henry Brown had remembered that his wife was giving a cocktail party, and the thought of it bored him. It had not occurred to him to suggest that Holly should be asked, he was only too well aware of Frederica's feelings in that direction, and so it was with considerable surprise that he found her there on his arrival. Holly was chatting away with a group of young people, and for once had neglected to keep an eye on the doorway, so that Henry's voice in her ear came as a surprise. He had taken care not to arrive too early, and by now many of the guests had drifted away; Holly, however, in spite of several attempts to leave, had been restrained by Frederica.

"Henry will be dreadfully upset if you go before he arrives," she said. "Do stay for a bit longer, Holly." She smiled down at her, charmingly. "Make it a special favour to me."

It was difficult for Holly to respond to these overtures of friendship. For one thing, she had for so long been under the impression that Frederica disliked her that she found it hard to readjust her impressions so quickly, and for another, although she prided herself on her *savoir-faire*, and was able to cope easily with neglect or rudeness, she found it much harder to deal with kindness, particularly when it came with such spontaneity from such an unexpected quarter. And there was no doubt that Frederica had treated her with the greatest kindness and friendship.

"I believe she doesn't dislike me as much as I imagined," Holly said when she had a few moments alone with Henry.

"Of course she doesn't dislike you, child—why should she?" he said, his eyes on the beautiful figure of his wife.

"Well—" Holly mused. "I could think of a reason…"

Henry patted her hand. "Well, don't, dear," he said decisively. "It isn't wise to dwell on such things."

Holly pouted, but in a flash changed the pout to a smile. Her good sense told her that to show her feelings at this stage would be the height of stupidity. Instead, she smiled winningly at Henry and said, "She's beautiful, isn't she?" indicating Frederica.

Henry laughed. "Yes, my dear, she is," he agreed.

For a moment they sat in silence, and then Henry stood up. "I've got to run along," he said. "Will you be at home this evening?" This was more a statement than a question.

"I—I guess so," she said quickly.

"All right." He patted her cheek with a lean, brown hand. "I may be seeing you," he said, and left her.

For a moment or two Holly continued to sit where she was. She felt rather flat and disappointed. If Henry had not turned up just at that moment, no doubt one of the young men would have suggested dining with her—as it was, she would have to go home to an empty flat, and cook herself an egg. A wave of resentment swept over her. Men were impossible! She was tempted to rejoin one of the groups, to wangle an invitation somehow… it still wasn't too late. But before she could rise to her feet, Frederica was in front of her, a mink coat draped carelessly over one arm, a good-looking young man in tow.

"Holly darling!" her voice was hurried, breathless, "could you be an angel and have dinner with Henry? I've got to rush out—I forgot I had a date, and Peter's taking me." She flashed a quick smile at the young man standing at her side. "Henry didn't dare ask you himself—but could you? Would you?" she pleaded.

In spite of herself Holly couldn't help smiling back at her. "I'd love to," she said, "of course I would."

Frederica squeezed her hand gratefully. "Angel! You've saved my life!" she whispered. Aloud she said, "I'll tell Henry—he'll be thrilled."

But Henry received this piece of news with mixed feelings. Frederica had explained to him with the utmost sweetness that her date with the young man in question was of several days' standing, and she had offered Holly, on a plate, as it were, with such guilelessness and an obvious desire to please that for once Henry was inclined to take the whole thing at its face value. After all, what more natural than she should try to arrange an evening's amusement for him? Henry, returning from the front door where he had just said good-bye to the last stragglers, was not too displeased to find a personable young woman waiting for him. He came up behind her, as she was powdering her nose in a looking-glass over the fire, and put his hands on her shoulders, turning her round so that she was in his arms. Masterfully he brought his mouth down on hers, and Holly surrendered gladly to his kisses.

IV

Jeffery Gibson could not help feeling quite glad to be alone at last. Although he had been flattered by Walters' suggestion that he stay on at Possett Island, he had never been able to rid himself of a slight uneasiness over the whole affair, and it was with real satisfaction that he unpacked his bags in the little room he rented in Gordon Square. Now he could look forward to several days of uninterrupted work, for although he had had plenty of time on his hands during the last few days at the castle, he had never been able to settle down to study. Always some unpleasant thoughts would obtrude upon his consciousness, and more than once he had pushed away his books in despair and, laying his head upon his arms, had given way to a fit of crying. This was altogether unlike himself, and he knew that in some subtle way the castle and Possett Island must have been undermining his nerves. He was not at all a neurotic type of young man, nor was he given to worrying himself unnecessarily; the fact that he still needed another year's work at the university before he could hope to get his degree was not weighing on his mind. Somehow, he knew he would manage to get sufficient money for his fees, and until such time he put the matter resolutely out of his head and refused to waste time dwelling on his difficulties.

But in spite of himself, he was very lost and sad whenever he thought of the death of his old friend. He had known Dimpsie for many years, and the playwright had always been unfailingly kind to him. Several times during the Christmas holiday Jeffery had found himself wondering just how much any of the guests had missed their genial host. The tears came to his eyes as he remembered the last luncheon they had had together. Dimpsie had been at his gayest, though most vitriolic, and he had caused more than one member of the party to wince; but it had all been fun and games, where Dimpsie was concerned and the friends that he invited to the Island knew better than to take him seriously. Jeffery remembered how Henry Brown had been advising Dimpsie over the new play; Henry had spoken of the structure and coherence of the plot, had enlarged upon the need for conflict in the second act curtain, and had suggested cutting out one or two minor characters. Having listened to all this in silence, Dimpsie had pushed his glasses firmly on to his nose and leaning both elbows on the table squinted across the table at Henry. There had been a moment's silence—a silence tense with undercurrents of meaning—and then, quietly, mildly, Dimpsie had summed up the situation as he saw it.

"The trouble with you producers," he had said, "is that you refuse to admit that you suffer from constipation. And I don't mean constipation of the bowel, Henry, I mean constipation of the brain! If you had two ideas worth rubbing together you'd have been screaming them from the top of the Albert Hall! But no"—his voice rose higher and higher until the calm manner in which he had begun the speech expanded into a furious tirade. "You producers," he screeched the words, "you producers are nothing more than frustrated writers. You're incapable of doing more than tear other people's work to pieces. Oh, I know you, Henry, you obnoxious, illiterate Polish scum, you'd cut your own mother's throat if she'd written a play and wouldn't allow you to slash it to ribbons!" Suddenly his temper dropped away from him as suddenly as it had arisen, and he smiled gently at the glowering producer. "Dear me! What am I saying? Henry, you mustn't take any notice of me, you know I can't bear criticism!" Pushing back his chair he had turned to Jeffery. "Let us go into the parlour," he suggested. "We'll have a quiet game of backgammon." He turned benignly to Henry. "I've arranged a charming afternoon for you all," he said. "Walters will explain everything to you. I shall be busy in the studio—I do *not* wish to be disturbed." He had flashed a wicked look at his guests as they sat round the luncheon table and, taking Jeffery by the arm, had led him from the room. Outside the parlour door Dimpsie had said, "I don't really want to play backgammon. I've got some work to see to… Keep everyone away from the studio, dear boy, and I'll be seeing you this evening." Jeffery had watched him amble down the hall and enter the studio. That had been the last time he saw Dimpsie alive, and more than once he had attempted to reconstruct the entire scene to see if there were not some hidden clue to the mystery of his unexpected death. Once again, in his solitary room high above Gordon Square, Jeffery remembered that day, and it was with an ever-increasing sense of loss that he thought of his old friend. He was a trifle uneasy about his new friendship with Walters. During Dimpsie's lifetime the secretary, while on friendly terms with all the guests at the Island, had never attempted intimacy with any of them; now Jeffery found himself drawn into something he neither wished for nor encouraged. And Walters demanded so much from him! There had seemed no end to the confidences he was prepared to make, and there was so little that Jeffery could offer in return. He resolved firmly that once back at the university, he would endeavour to throw off Walters, it shouldn't be difficult, since he would have a great deal of studying to do. Downstairs, in the draughty hall, the telephone began to ring, its insistent call reaching Jeffery in his attic. He opened the door and hung over the bannisters. Presently the heavy footsteps of his landlady ascended the basement stairs; he heard her answer the phone and presently her voice floated up to him.

"Mr. Gibson! Fourth floor! It's for you, sir. Can you hear me?"

He hurried down, his heart pounding. If it should be Walters, what excuse could he give? The old one about working was wearing a bit thin, truthful though it was. What could he say that would sound convincing? He picked up the receiver, while his mind was anxiously occupied in finding some reason to prevent a meeting. But the voice that answered his hullo was not Walters'.

"Tittop here," said the Agent. "Is that Gibson? Fine. I should like to see you. Can you come down to the office?"

"Rather." In his relief Jeffery was almost too eager.

"Make it to-morrow morning, then," Tittop said, "about eleven. You know the way, don't you?"

Jeffery assured him he did, and replaced the receiver. He had been so thankful not to have to speak to Walters that it had never occurred to him to ask why Archie Tittop wanted to see him. Now, as he went upstairs, he could not imagine why the Agent should have phoned him. Most probably it was to ask some questions about Dimpsie. Thoughtfully, Jeffery opened the door of his room, and went in. How peaceful it was, he thought. He went over to the window and looked out on to the tree-tops in the Square. The branches stretched black withered fingers into the cold, grey sky; below, the lamps were springing alight, little drops of flame in the winter's afternoon. Pulling the curtains, Jeffery went back to the table. Soon he was deep in his books.

I O

THE INSPECTOR BACKS A HUNCH

I

KRASNYA BENENBERG WALKED GLOOMILY THROUGH LEICESTER Square and turned into Charing Cross Road. All round him the traffic surged in an ever-flowing stream; the girls, boys, pimps, touts, prostitutes, pederasts and the whole of the humanity which is the mainspring of tin-pan alley rubbed shoulders with him as he shambled past. But Krasnya, deep in thought, never noticed anyone. Only by keeping exactly to the routes marked on his map was he able to find the way back to the dingy little hotel where he was staying. He had studied this map industriously on the journey from Paris to London, and so well had he learnt the specific path, that now he walked almost without looking at those undecipherable hieroglyphics which were the names of the streets. He stopped at the paper shop to buy a copy of *Le Matin*, and with this shoved into his pocket he walked into the nearest milk bar. Seating himself on a high stool at the counter he opened the paper and began to read.

"Wot d'jer want, dear?" The flossy brunette behind the bar wore pearl earrings clipped into unbelievably tiny ears.

"*Pardon?*" For a moment he stared. "Tea," he said firmly. "No milk." He twisted his tongue round the unfamiliar word.

She poured out a cup of steaming liquid and put it in front of him. "Sugar, ducks?" The tiny lumps were on a dirty plate. He took one, dropping it into the cup and not attempting to stir it.

"Go on," she said brightly, "take another. They're all yours." She pushed the plate towards him.

He dropped another lump into the cup, and fumbled in his pocket, bringing out a handful of money. He held it out to her, smiling.

"You take what you need," he said. "Me, no understand."

She selected a sixpence, rang up fourpence on the till and presented him with two coppers. While he sipped his tea she watched him from the other side of the bar.

"Mademoiselle," he said presently, "you go to theatre, yes?"

"Wot, me?" She laughed, showing bright, new teeth. "No, can't say I do. Pictures for yours truly—more in my line, you know."

"Pictures?" He looked surprised. "You—artiste? *Artiste-peintre?*"

"Naow. Pictures, you know. Spencer Tracy. Clark Gable. That's the style."

He shook his head. "No. Explain, please."

She looked at him, curling her lips into a smile of utter disbelief.

"Go on!" she said, "want to tell me you never heard of Greta Garbo? Where you bin all this time?"

"Ah! Greta Garbo! The cinema—I understand." He turned on his stool and pointed in the direction of Shaftesbury Avenue. "No… the theatre—the stage. La Danse, you understand. You have never see La Karmanskaya?" He gesticulated with his hand, making the impression of a ballet dancer.

"Karmanskaya?" She frowned at him. "Wait a minute." Diving down under the counter she brought up a paper. "Look!" With a dirty finger she pointed at the headlines. DEATH OF A DANCER, he read. GALLIA KARMANSKAYA FOUND ALONE IN CHELSEA HOUSE.

Krasnya Benenberg pushed the paper to one side. His eyes filled with tears. Gulping down the rest of the tea he crossed the floor of the café. At the door he turned to smile at the waitress, but she was busy filling one of the urns.

Drearily he stumped out on to the street and into the narrow turning which led to the hotel. The street was deserted at this time of day, and the hotel lobby was quite empty. He took his key from the hook and walked up the stairs to his bedroom. Opening the door, the unfamiliar room filled him with nostalgic desire for Paris and, flinging himself on the meagre counterpane, he wallowed in the misery and depression that was becoming more and more unbearable.

At last he pulled himself together and went over to the basin to wash. He swilled the water over his face, and then emptied a bottle of Eau de Cologne on his hair. The pungent scent delighted him and he began to feel a little better. Sitting on his bed he turned out his pockets. A last letter from Gallia was among sundry papers. Reading it through carefully he decided that, perhaps, after all, it would be as well to call on Mr. McCabe. He remembered McCabe very well… a monstrous fat little man with owl eyes behind inordinately thick glasses. He remembered McCabe's interest in the circus, and how he had insisted on being shown every little detail of the circus life. Krasnya had thought the little man would be bored at the idea of going behind the scenes, but that had been just what McCabe had enjoyed. And it had ended by his joining the circus for a whole month. There hadn't been anything for the playwright to do, but he had attached himself to Krasnya, and was never tired of hearing stories of circus life, and the various personalities. And yet, somehow, Krasnya had not been sorry when the month had come to an end. In some mysterious way, Dimpsie had managed to worm all sorts of stories out of him, stories that he had really never intended to repeat. On the whole, he was thankful to say good-bye to McCabe. It was only then that he had mentioned his sister, Gallia, and it had astonished him to find that McCabe and she were old friends. And now, reading Gallia's letter for the third or fourth time, and noting the kindly way she spoke of the playwright, it seemed a wise idea to go and see the little man. If he had been fond of Gallia, he too would be suffering, and perhaps they might console each other.

Krasnya passed a hand over his chin—no, he would not shave. That could wait. Now he would go and pay a call on Dimpson McCabe. That, he thought, was what Gallia would have liked.

II

Superintendent Buller leant back in his chair and looked thought-fully at the Inspector. He was a short, plump individual with a fair, scrubby moustache and cold grey eyes. He tapped an empty pipe on the desk and there was a faraway look in his eyes.

"There's no evidence," he said at last.

Inspector Smith evaded the issue. "I was due for leave," he said casually, "and I'd promised myself a holiday in London. It's six years since I went up North, you see."

"I know, I know," said the Superintendent. "So you said, Inspector, but what I want to know is—what makes you think there's anything in what you say?"

Inspector Smith's melancholy blue eyes were fixed on the empty pipe.

"It's a hunch," he said after a long pause. "Just a hunch. I have an idea, Mr. Buller, but it's *only* an idea… it wouldn't be fair for me to mention it—to put it into words, if you get my meaning. But when I heard that Madame Whosis, I never could get my tongue around her name, when I heard that she was—well—bumped off, then I felt pretty sure of my ground. I'd been meaning to go and see her, as a matter of fact, there were one or two questions I wanted to ask her... well, I left it too late." He sighed heavily and took off his glasses. Pulling out his handkerchief he began to polish the lenses, while the Superintendent watched him without speaking.

"You see, sir," the Inspector said at last, having replaced his glasses on his nose, "I don't altogether agree with the finding on Mr. McCabe's death. You heard about that, I have no doubt?"

"Yes." Buller's words were terse, his tone crisp. "Electrocuted, wasn't he?"

"Exactly. He was found dead in his studio. He had been decorating the Christmas Tree."

Buller raised his eyebrows. "They're all alike, these amateur electricians, think they know a hell of a lot—and then they get careless. I know the sort of thing."

The Inspector smiled. "Yes, of course. I thought the same thing—it was too easy."

"What do you mean?"

Inspector Smith was only too pleased to enlarge. He told how Dimpsie had been found, and explained exactly what the doctor had said. He gave details of the inquest, and of the guests at the castle.

Superintendent Buller listened in silence to this recital. Then he pulled out his cigarette-case and offered it to the Inspector. They smoked for a few minutes, and then Buller said:

"But what motive was there—what made you suppose it might be murder?"

Inspector Smith frowned. "We couldn't find a motive—there didn't seem to be any reason why anyone should have wanted to do away with him. There was no evidence that anyone had been in the room with him—no finger-prints, nothing. What else could we do?"

"I see. Then whom did you suspect?" Buller put the question half-tentatively.

"No one. How could we? There wasn't a shred of any kind of evidence. But at the time, I thought to myself if this is a murder there'll be another. Why, I said to the chief…"

"Wait a moment!" The Superintendent's eyes were gleaming shrewdly and his mouth was pinched into a thin, pink line beneath the scrubby moustache. "Wait a minute! D'you mean to tell me you actually thought there might be another murder, and yet you took no steps to prevent it?"

"How could I?" Inspector Smith was meekness itself. "What could I do? I tell you, Superintendent, it was a *hunch* that I had. And there's no room for hunches in the police force."

"So you waited till you were due for leave," Buller mused, "and then you tootled down here just too late to save Madame Karmanskaya."

"Oh, I don't know about that," said Smith. "After all, I couldn't have done anything—I couldn't have waited outside the door all day, the good lady would never have allowed it."

"No—but you said you were thinking of calling on her. Well, if you'd done that the day after you arrived, you *might* have been there when the murderer rang the bell… if he *did* ring the bell."

"Surely he wouldn't have?" queried Inspector Smith.

"Might have done. There's an electrical arrangement for bells in the basement passage… when a bell rings a tab showing which bell it is shoots up from a little box. It stays put until another bell rings—works on the cash register system. The last bell that rang that day was the front door."

"Then—you think, maybe, the murderer was someone she knew?"

"Possibly." The Superintendent examined his nails. "Of course, it's just a theory of mine, there's probably nothing in it, but it occurred to me that whoever rang the bell intended making a formal call. When there was no answer, they tried the back door, found it open, and trotted in. There's a possibility that they never meant to murder the woman at all—or rather, that they hadn't intended it when they rang the front door bell."

"If the murderer really rang the bell," said Inspector Smith very slowly, "that bears out my theory."

"And what might that be?" asked Buller.

"Well—just that Madame Whosis was not surprised to see this person, whoever it was… because if she had been attacked by a stranger, surely she would have at least jumped off the couch. She had been a dancer you know, and she was quite an athletic woman."

"You were talking about a hunch," said Buller. "Just how would it fit in with this?"

"Well"—said Inspector Smith, leaning forward, his elbows on the table—"has it ever occurred to you…" his voice dropped, and Buller leant forward to listen to him. It was with a shock of annoyance that he realized that the phone was ringing at his elbow. He picked up the receiver and barked into it. Then he listened. A look of surprise dawned on his face, and he brightened visibly. "Show him in," he said quickly. "I'll see him at once." He turned to Smith. "This'll interest you," he said. "It's Madame Karmanskaya's brother."

III

Glen Hemingway looked round the empty garage with satisfaction. It had taken him longer than he had expected to dismantle his electrical apparatus and pack it ready for storage, but now that it was done, and the last of the packing-cases had been taken off to the Repository, he felt a great sense of freedom and relief. Now, at last, he could get back to the life he loved. He thought of the veldt,

with its mile after mile of enchanting emptiness; where there would
be nothing between him and the cloudless sky; of the jungle, and
the weird birds and enormous butterflies, of the trailing creepers
and the gigantic bamboos; of the kraals; of the plantations; of
the sun; and most of all he thought about lions. Now that he was
at last able to return to that life, he realized just how long he had
been away, and how much he had missed it. That there would be
a party with him did not disturb him in the least. That was part of
his life, and he enjoyed the company of his fellow men. The jungle
was large—a mother whose capacious bosom could encompass a
family far larger than any he was likely to bring to it. And now he
longed to be off. The ten days or so that he would have to wait until
his party assembled stretched before him, an interminable desert of
boredom. For a moment he wished he had not arranged to spend
the time in Paris, he could have amused himself in London. There
was Frederica, too, who might be sorry to say good-bye to him. His
mouth twisted in a wry smile as he recalled their last meeting. Her
love certainly would not stretch as far as Africa.

He folded back the garage doors and went upstairs to his flat
There were just the last few remnants of his packing to be attended
to, and then, his wry smile changed to one of pure pleasure, then it
was good-bye. He went into the tiny bedroom where his suit-cases
were strapped and ready, he tied labels, and checked his keys, doing
everything slowly and methodically, unhurriedly. Then, taking a case
under each arm, he ran down the stairs and put them in the back
of the car. When he had packed five cases into the car he returned
to the flat for the last time. Almost regretfully he looked round the
sitting-room, making certain that he had left none of his few pos-
sessions, then he went back into the bedroom to gather up the last
few objects. All at once he was in a fever to be gone; he stuffed the
last few garments into a hold-all, hastily shoving in the sponges,

toothbrush and soap that are always left until last, and ramming
his pyjamas and dressing-gown in on top of them. Triumphantly
he zipped up the gaping maw and turned to run down the stairs.
Almost he was panting, so eager was he to be away, so fearful lest
anything delay him. A last quick look round kitchen and bathroom,
a last peep into the sitting-room and, with his foot upon the stair,
he was jolted back from flight. The telephone was ringing. Shrilly,
insistently, the bell called him back from the staircase. And as he
put down the hold-all and turned to answer it, he knew that it was
the one thing he had hoped to avoid. It was the telephone he fled…
the telephone he dreaded… and now, his hand poised, he stopped
to wonder whether he need answer, whether, perhaps, if he waited,
the hateful little bell would stop.

But even as he listened, he could hear, through the paper-thin
walls, the voice of his neighbour, Mrs. Dewlap, calling angrily out
of the window.

"J'ear that bell? W'y doesn't 'e take and answer it? Waikin' up
my Edie, 'e is, wiv that orful row."

And the answering call. "Dunno w'y 'e wants a phone, I don't.
Never troubles to answer it… can' be bovered, I should fink."

And then, "Mr. 'Emingwaiy! MR. 'EMINGWAIY! YER PHONE'S
RINGING!"

Wearily, despondently, he picked up the receiver.

IV

Reading an account of Frederica's cocktail party in her paper the
following morning, it occurred to Katherine that it was rather odd
that Doctor Harley had not been invited. Both Henry and Frederica
had shown themselves to be friendlily disposed to Bill, and it was
strange that neither one of them had asked him to the flat. It did

just strike her that perhaps he had been asked, and decided not to accept, but then surely he would have mentioned the fact to her. It was odd, she reflected, that none of Dimpsie's guests had been really friendly. It was he who had loved them, and it was the thread of his personality that drew them all together. Without him, they drifted apart without seeming even to be aware of the fact.

She noticed that neither Walters nor Glen Hemingway were among the listed guests and it was with a faint shock of surprise that she read Holly's name. Out of all the people at Possett Island, Holly was the last one she would have expected to find at the Browns. Evidently Frederica had changed her ideas—or Henry had insisted on the girl's presence. Katherine wished she might have been there—a fly on the wall—to be able to watch them all and yet be unnotice-able. The more she thought about it, the stranger it seemed. Holly, the only one of the Possett Island group to be invited! Frederica must have known that her husband was having a slight affair with Holly—everyone at the castle must have known—so why invite her to the house, and leave out Hemingway?

Katherine gave it up, it was too difficult. Theatricals were noto-riously insincere, and there was no way of telling who were their real friends. She fluttered the pages of the newspaper in search of the Theatre Column. "WHISPERS" overheard by Becky Sharp, generally managed to find interesting snippets of news, although most people thought the column should have been titled Shouts. To-day the column was headed—"New Play by an old favourite. An alluring starlet tells me she is to make her London début in a new play by Dimpson McCabe. Theatre-goers will recall Mr. McCabe's tragic death a few weeks ago at his Scottish home. The play will be produced by Henry Brown." Katherine chuckled. So that was why Holly was at the cocktail party. No doubt that also accounted for the inexplicable absence of Archie Tittop, and Walters. Henry evidently intended to carry things off in a high-handed manner. For a moment she was tempted to phone Holly, to inquire how she enjoyed herself and whether she had signed the contract, but second thoughts prevailed. It would be much wiser to go and see her... the phone was always so unsatisfactory. She resolved to call on Miss Temple at the first opportunity. All at once she remembered Frederica's offer of friendship on the morning she had left the castle; well, that hadn't meant very much. Katherine folded the paper and began to clear away the breakfast things. She carried the dishes into the tiny kitchenette and dumped them in the sink, turning on the hot water so that it flowed in a steaming jet. While they were soaking she dusted the sitting-room, and tidied up the rest of the flat. Then she took the dishes out of the water and wiped them, replacing them on the dresser. She took a pride in her little flat, and everything was kept in perfect order; it was rather like living in a doll's house, she felt, everything was so trim and neat. That it was small was an advantage—she had little time for playing at keeping house. When everything was tidied, she sat down at her desk. There was a good deal of work that she could get through at home, and there was no reason for spending more time in Fleet Street than was absolutely necessary. Looking through her notes she realized that she still had not been able to check up on Gallia's visitor, the elusive Mr. Benenberg. Immersed in her writing, the front door bell rang several times before she heard it. She hurried to open it, but at the sight of the man on the threshold, she stepped backwards in surprise.

"Kate, my dear," he said, "I had to come."

11

SURPRISE MEETING

I

MISS TONKINS ALWAYS DREADED THE FEW WEEKS BEFORE A new production. The office was besieged morning, noon and night by out-of-work actors and actresses, and she had the unpleasant task of telling them that there was nothing doing. She had developed this to a fine art—a supercilious lift of an eyebrow, the curve of a lip—it was hardly necessary for her to open her mouth, but in spite of this there was a constant crowd in the outer office, and it became increasingly difficult to get rid of the stayers, the people who would be willing to sit in the office all night if it meant an interview with H. Brown the following morning. Miss Tonkins could feel her patience ebbing away.

"It's no use your waiting, Mr. X," she would say, "Mr. Brown won't be in to-day. Why not try next week?"

"It doesn't matter," the victim would reply. "I've no one else to see this morning—I'll just wait on the chance."

"If you like to leave me your name and address," firmly, "Mr. Brown will get in touch with you."

"Thank you. I think I prefer to wait." And he would settle himself in his seat, his hat on his knees, and cigarette tucked into the corner of his mouth, prepared to wait and wait interminably.

It was a relief when the play was cast and in rehearsal. Then Miss Tonkins could relax a little—although there would always be the unsuccessful playwrights, musicians and designers who continued to batter at the door of the office, in the hope that one day Henry would realize that they had just the item he was looking for. Still, she was thankful for small mercies. Now that Dimpsie's play was well under way, the outer office had been empty for the last few days. She had had the happy thought of putting up a notice saying that Mr. Brown would be back at such and such a time, and then changing the card at the critical moment. This way she kept the road clear for Henry, and was able to get on with her own work.

Henry, too, was relieved that rehearsals had started. He had been a little worried over Archie Tittop's continued silence, but he at last came to the conclusion that the Agent had decided to retire from an unequal contest. Nor had he seen Walters. The secretary had not replied to Henry's letter, and there did not appear to be any reason why he should do so. A try-on, Henry thought contemptuously, and said as much to Frederica. He was surprised to see the light of malice in her eyes.

"I wouldn't trust him," she said. "I think he's a despicable character, mean and sly. Why, I should think you could prosecute him, Henry, saying he'd written Dimpsie's play!"

Henry shook his head. "No. I couldn't," he said. "And I wouldn't. He isn't doing me any harm."

"Isn't he? Just you wait and see," she said, her mouth a thin pale line, and her eyes hard with anger. "He's probably going round London saying you've stolen the play from him."

Henry raised his eyebrows and did not reply.

"Just because you're a Jew," his wife said, "you think no one can get the better of you."

Henry stared at her. "My dear girl! What's come over you? What's the matter, what have I done?"

"It's what you haven't done," she said bitterly. "Do you think it's pleasant for me to know everyone in London is saying you're a crook? That you've stolen Walters' play and won't do anything about it?"

"Now, my dear, you must really try to be sensible," Henry said calmly. "There is no reason at all for this hysteria, and I don't understand it. You need not pay any attention to Walters—if he is not satisfied with things as they are, he has the remedy in his own hands. And I can take care of my own reputation, thank you very much." He patted her cheek tenderly. "You must not allow yourself to be so angry, Freddie, my darling, it is not at all becoming to you. I suggest that you rest a little—and then come down to the theatre."

Frederica bit her lip; for a moment she stared at her husband, then she laughed. "I'm such a fool," she said. "You ought to know me better by now. Of course, Walters is just a little piece of dirt— you are quite right not to consider him at all." She kissed Henry on the cheek. "Now—go to the theatre and this afternoon I will come down and see you. How's that?"

She watched him check his brief-case, take his hat and overcoat and leave the flat. Running to the window she opened it and looked down into the street. She saw Henry get into the car and drive away. Nor, until he was out of sight, did she go to the telephone. The number she dialled would have surprised her husband, and he would have been still more surprised could he have heard the ensuing conversation.

II

Archie Tittop's private office was an oasis of comfort in a dusty, overcrowded desert. A severe brass plate enlivened the uninteresting doorway and, inside, the hall was dark and narrow. The rooms on each side were given over to the packing and filing departments, and at the end of the dingy corridor was the waiting-room with its rogues' gallery of celebrities ornamenting the walls. Twentieth century literature was well represented here and most of the portraits were inscribed to "My dear old friend Archie Tittop" or "My dear Archie". The portraits of women and men were equally divided and there was even a photograph of two dear little girls in Victorian dress with large hats and flounced dresses, and long tresses of hair. Dimpsie's picture was in a place of honour facing the door. It was an unusual photograph, showing the playwright sitting in front of the mike with a script in his hand. The pose was easy and familiar, but the photo was one that Dimpsie had never allowed to be published. It did not please him that the general public should see him at work in an informal way. He had liked to be wrapped in mystery, which accounted for his buying Possett Island and living in such an inconvenient spot. Archie never ceased to regret that he had not been invited to the fateful Christmas party. He could not help a sneaking feeling that had he been there things might have turned out very differently. Never for one instant could he believe in the Sheriff's verdict of Accidental Death; and he felt convinced that somehow, in some way, the truth would be brought to light.

However lazy, flippant, lackadaisical and irritating his clients might find him, Archie was no fool. He looked after his authors in the best possible way, saved them endless time and trouble, and saw to it that they made money. Most of them, having begun by threatening to leave him almost every week of the year, had settled down to an amicable relationship of quarterly rows. But it was very occasionally that a Dimpson McCabe would turn up. Dimpsie, who made a great deal more money than he knew what to do with, scrutinized his accounts with miserly precision and haggled over every halfpenny. But in spite of this, and in spite of the fact that Archie knew that Dimpsie despised all agents, calling them "Rats" and other choice epithets and saying that they lived off the brains of their clients, he had been fond of the irascible playwright. However aggravating Dimpson had been he had at least never been dull, and he had always been content to leave Archie to fight his battles. He had enough to do, he said, getting his stuff out, without trolloping about with the people who bought it. And although he grumbled unceasingly about the stinginess of the contracts, about how shockingly he was losing money, about everything that he could think of, Archie knew that at heart he was satisfied.

Archie had been in business for thirty-odd years. He had run his agency carefully, choosing only those authors in whom he had faith, and going for quality rather than quantity. Dimpson McCabe had been one of his first clients, and they had built up their reputations together. Archie knew just exactly what a play by Dimpson was worth—he knew why Henry Brown had been asked to Possett Island—he knew, of course, that the play was finished, and there were many little birds only too anxious to whisper about it as soon as it went into rehearsal. However, he did not approach Henry. There was plenty of time for that. He did not know whether Dimpson had made any private arrangements with the producer, but it was extremely unlikely that he should have done so. Archie sat in his office; he felt absolutely secure—he could afford to wait.

He was not altogether surprised to receive a visit from Henry Walters. He had expected the secretary to phone him, and for several days he had felt that a visit was quite on the cards. He saw at once that Walters was extremely nervous, and he was surprised. He rang for Dimpsie's file, and passed a box of cigarettes across the desk. Walters lit one slowly, and Archie, watching him, saw how he was holding himself back, biting his lips and trying to conceal his nerves.

"You must have had a very trying time," Archie said, while they were waiting for the file.

"Oh—yes; unbearable," Walters said. He spoke in little gasps, and his face was white and shiny. "I don't suppose you know why I have come to see you," he went on. "I guess Dimpsie never told you about the new play."

"Oh, yes," Archie interpolated smoothly. "I know all about it."

Walters was silent for a moment. His mouth was dry, and he passed his tongue over his lips to moisten them. "Yes. But did he tell you"—he swallowed—"did he tell you we wrote it together?"

Archie stared for a moment, and then smiled. "No, he didn't, I'm afraid. I've never known Dimpsie to collaborate before, this is quite surprising, isn't it?"

"Well—not to me," Walters said. "You see—I used to help him a good deal. I wrote most of 'The Tatler' scripts, you know. We'd talked about this play for several years... and we wrote it together... together," he repeated firmly, his voice rising a little.

Archie nodded. "Really? How interesting. No, Dimpsie never mentioned that to me. But he told me all about it, of course, and we had discussed the cast... but only very vaguely, you understand."

"You know the play is in rehearsal?" Walters asked.

"Yes. It will be produced at the end of the month," Archie said. "I think Henry has been very wise in giving that child Holly Temple a chance. I believe she will turn out to be a clever little actress."

Walters wasn't listening. "But the contract—" he said, "what about the contract?"

"Oh—it's the usual one," Archie said, quickly. "Henry Brown has produced so many of the plays that it hardly seemed worth while to draw up a fresh one. So it will be the usual contract, Mr. Walters."

"But what about me?" Walters asked, and his voice was a cracked whisper. "What about me?"

Archie smiled. "I'm afraid I don't quite understand," he said.

"My contract," Walters said. "My permission was not asked—I was not consulted! And I have no contract with Henry Brown, damn him!"

"Do you want me to get the play back?" asked Archie.

"I want you to get me a contract," Walters said. "I should get the same contract as McCabe. Why not? I wrote most of the play, didn't I?"

"Did you?" asked Archie gently. "I'm afraid I shall have to ask you to prove it to me."

Walters stared at him. "What do you mean?" he asked loudly.

"Just what I said. You will have to prove that you collaborated in the play before I can get you a contract."

Walters laughed. "That's easy." He pulled out his brief-case. In it were innumerable drafts of the play in his writing, with corrections put in both by him and by McCabe. "There you are," he said, "if it's proof you want."

Archie shook his head. "I'm afraid I should need something more than this," he said. "Have you a letter from Dimpsie, or an agreement, anything in writing to show that you were collaborating?"

"Of course not," Walters said. "Why on earth would he have written to me—we were both living under the same roof. Be sensible, man, for heaven's sake!"

"I beg your pardon," Archie said with raised brows, "but I must repeat that I shall need to have concrete proof of the collaboration before I can do anything for you." He stood up. "It shouldn't be difficult to find," he said disarmingly. "I'm sure you'll be able to find something from Dimpsie—something that you've forgotten, perhaps."

But Walters did not move from his chair, and Archie spoke again.

"Have you looked through all the papers? I'm sure you must have overlooked something—perhaps just the very thing. I don't need a whole letter, necessarily, so long as it's signed... and acknowledges the collaboration."

"I see." Walters' voice was dull and he spoke slowly. "You realize, of course, that as McCabe's secretary I've had to go through all his papers... if there were anything else that I could have brought—" he spread his hands helplessly.

Archie Tittop sat down again and put both elbows on the desk.

"Why don't you go and see Brown?" he suggested. He poured himself a glass of water from a crystal jug that stood on a small table by his side. "Yes," he said, "I should go and see him—talk it over with him. After all, it's up to him... he's putting up the money."

"Yes." Slowly Walters stood up and held out a fishy hand. "Yes... that's quite an idea. Thanks, Tittop. I'll go and see Henry Brown." He edged over to the door and opened it. "Well... thanks. I expect we shall be meeting again?"

"Sure... sure..." agreed Archie. "Good-bye, Walters."

The door closed behind Walters and Archie heaved a sigh of relief. He poured himself another glass of water and sipped it. Well—there was no telling what people would try on, he thought. Not for a moment did he believe Walters' story. Why, he thought contemptuously, they're nothing but a bunch of crooks, the whole lot of them! Who he included in this statement he did not specify, even to himself.

III

Krasnya Benenberg walked through the cobbled yard and under the ugly red brick arch that was the entrance to Scotland Yard. He found himself in Whitehall, and turning towards Trafalgar Square began to trudge towards Soho. The interview with the Superintendent had been tiring; it was extremely difficult for Krasnya to make himself understood, and even more so to understand what was being said to him. The shock of finding that his friend Dimpson McCabe was dead, had sent him hurrying to the police. All at once he had the feeling that an enemy was at work—and that perhaps no one knew or cared. It was a relief to know that, indeed, the police cared very much, and that his sister's death was a matter for grave concern. The Superintendent had assured him that every possible avenue would be exploited, that no clue would be too small to be followed up. As for Dimpson McCabe—that was another matter. They tried to explain this to Krasnya, but he could not understand what they were trying to tell him—it was too complicated, and at last he agreed to leave everything in their hands. Inspector Smith had been anxious that he should remain in town, but Krasnya had done his best to explain that he must return to Paris almost immediately. The reason for his visit to London had paled into insignificance beside the horrible thing that had greeted him. He trudged solemnly up Whitehall and into Trafalgar Square. He stood a moment watching the pigeons, and it occurred to him that he must have seen pictures of the square on the coloured postcards on sale at every tobacconists. He sauntered across the square and stood, waiting to cross the road, opposite St. Martin-in-the-Fields. He watched the traffic with admiration, it was so well-regulated, and the cars in their steady streams did not attempt to race and shove as they would have done in Paris; here, in sober London, each line of traffic moved quietly along; it was just a question of waiting for the lights, and one could cross the road only too easily. With his gaze held by the great church opposite, he stepped off the kerb. An enormous car bore down on him; for a moment everything went black, while lightning streaked across his eyes, and purple balls exploded heavily in his head. He felt himself being dragged backwards... heard a voice speaking roughly somewhere far away.

"You want to look where you're going," the voice said indignantly, "walking into the road like that! Whatever were you thinking of, I should like to know."

Krasnya sat up and opened his eyes. A small crowd had collected, but the voice urgently shooed them away. "Go on, now, leave the poor man alone! He's had a nasty fright, but no bones broken, thank God!" She turned to Krasnya, and he saw a woman of fifty, plump and rosy, with twinkling eyes, a firm mouth and good teeth. She was dressed in a cheap brown tweed coat and carried a large handbag. She might have been a country woman, up for a day's shopping from a little village.

"You're all right now, aren't you?" she asked him. "But take my advice and look where you're going another time. It's easy to see you're not a Londoner," she spoke with good-natured contempt.

Krasnya stood up. "Madame," he said, "I thank you. You did save my life."

A smile broke on her rosy face. "I expect I did," she agreed gaily. "Well, thank goodness it was no worse." She pulled her coat tightly round her and prepared to cross the road. "You're all right now, aren't you, so I'll be getting along." She stepped off the kerb and was lost in a stream of people hurrying across the road.

Krasnya Benenberg walked up St. Martin's Lane in a dream. For in that instant—that second before he was struck by the car—he thought he recognized someone, someone who might make all the difference to his life, if only he could find her again.

12

WILL YOU WALK INTO MY PARLOUR?

I

HOLLY WAS INTENSELY GLAD THAT REHEARSALS HAD STARTED at last. In spite of the contract Henry had given her, she had not allowed herself to feel sure of the part until the production was actually under way. Henry was an excellent producer—he always knew exactly what he wanted and, with infinite patience and tact, he saw that he got it. The cast was a small one and Holly thought they seemed quite friendly; but she knew enough to wait until she was spoken to, and she made no attempt to push herself forward. She did not see quite so much of Henry now; he was always very discreet, and the little luncheons and the afternoon sessions at her flat were becoming a thing of the past. Soon after they began work in the theatre, Frederica came down to watch the rehearsals. She liked to drop in unexpectedly, at odd moments, and she would stroll casually to a seat in the stalls where she would sit, a mink coat flung over her shoulders, smoking innumerable cigarettes and making occasional remarks in a husky whisper. It was at the second of these appearances that she invited Holly to lunch with her at her club. Holly, her hair tousled and her face shiny with sweat, was flattered. She was still young enough to enjoy driving in a beautiful car, Henry always used taxis, and she was thrilled to be lunching alone with

Frederica. In the dressing-room she made up her face carefully, wiping off superfluous lipstick, and generally toning down her rather highly-coloured appearance. Mary Webb, another member of the cast, with whom she shared the dressing-room, grinned at her and remarked laughingly:

"Going up in the world, aren't you, dearie?"

But Holly did not smile back. "I've met Frederica socially," she said noncommittally.

"Yes, we all know that," Mary flashed, "and you've met Henry too, haven't you?"

"Well, so what?" said Holly, evenly.

"Henry going to lunch with you two girls?" asked Mary.

Holly laughed. "That," she said, "I wouldn't know."

She pulled on a little scarlet beret, adjusting it carefully, and pinning it in place with a tiny diamond arrow. She wore a black tweed coat, buttoning high in the neck, and above the fastening glimpsed a scarlet kerchief. She picked up her handbag, and tucked it under her arm.

"Good-bye, darling," she said, "see you later." And she ran out of the room. Mary Webb listened to the sound of her high heels pattering sharply in the stone corridor; for a moment she almost wished that she, too, had been going out to lunch, but the rumours that she had heard about Frederica were not reassuring. In spite of herself she liked Holly. The child was foolish, of course, and far too cock-sure, but that was her extreme youth, thought Mary whimsically. Mary was thirty and happily married. She could afford to be nice to Holly, and she was, although it was difficult to resist teasing her sometimes. The young take themselves so seriously.

Driving through the crowded streets to her club, Frederica did not trouble to chat. She drove well, if a trifle negligently, and Holly noticed that she never lost an opportunity to get ahead, even when it seemed impossible to advance an inch. The big car edged its way in and out of the traffic, manœuvring so that it was first away at the lights and taking full advantage of the slightest gap to nose a way through. At last they arrived, and Frederica parked the car and strode into the club, Holly trotting along at her side. Holly began to feel just the tiniest bit uncomfortable—her hostess had hardly spoken to her since they left the theatre. Frederica scrawled her name in the visitors' book and together they entered the restaurant. Mrs. Brown was evidently an old and valued customer, for the head waiter, bowing and smiling, showed her to an excellent table in the window, and placed a vase of deep red roses on the table. Glancing around her, Holly noticed that they were the only people to have such a table decoration; she would have liked to remark on the flowers, but somehow she felt shy and ill at ease. Frederica ordered the lunch without consulting her guest, and not until the cocktails were on the table did she smile at Holly, and lift her glass to her.

"Good luck!" she said briefly, but her smile was kind, and Holly, sipping nervously, echoed her words.

Frederica drained her glass and set it on the table. "Shy of me?" she asked Holly.

Holly grinned. "Not really," she said, "but I was beginning to wonder why you asked me?"

"I suppose so," said Frederica slowly. "Well, Holly, it's very simple... I've always wanted to see more of you—that's why I asked you to the cocktail party. But it's difficult for me to pay too much attention when Henry's casting... you see, other people might think there was some favouritism. Of course, that's absurd, Henry wouldn't dream of listening to me, But you know what the theatre can be, my dear. Now that the production is well under way, I can chat to anyone without being afraid that someone is going to gossip about us." She smiled confidentially at Holly. "I can't bear gossip, can you?"

Holly shook her head. "I don't expect anyone would want to gossip about me," she said. "Why... I'm hardly known at all."

"It's surprising how people will talk, though," said Frederica. "You remember Madame Karmanskaya?"

"Yes, of course," Holly murmured.

"The things she used to say!" laughed Frederica, "quite incredible, sometimes. Did she ever tell you anything about herself?"

"I don't believe... yes, wasn't she connected with a circus, or had a brother, or something... I'm not sure. Perhaps Dimpsie told me, I don't remember."

Frederica shook her head. "I never heard that one," she said, "but I know she used to tell a lot of tall stories, poor old thing!"

"Was she Russian—or Polish?" asked Holly. "I know she used to speak some language that sounded rather like German—but I never knew what it was."

"Russian, I should think," said Frederica briefly. "I believe she was in the Imperial Ballet years ago."

"Yes, I remember her telling me about her brother," said Holly. "He was an acrobat or something. He was married to some girl he adored, and she ran off and left him. Gallia was rather fed up about it—said it ruined his career... she got a letter from him while she was up at Possett Castle, and she told me about him then."

"Oh," Frederica was not listening. She was busy with a cigarette and a refractory lighter. "Holly, we'll have our coffee in the lounge, shall we?"

Holly glanced at her watch. "I believe I ought to get back to the theatre," she said.

"There's no rehearsal this afternoon," Frederica told her. "Henry had to call it off—didn't you see the notice?"

"Well—if you're sure," Holly said doubtfully, as she followed Frederica into the lounge.

It was over coffee that Frederica confided how badly she had been sleeping lately. "The doctor has given me some tablets," she said. "But the trouble is that I can't get any rest at home. The phone simply rings and rings, and even if I've told Williams I'm out or that I'm not to be disturbed, it doesn't seem to make any difference. I lie there with every nerve on edge, waiting for the next sound… it's agony, Holly."

"But—but couldn't you have the phone disconnected?" asked Holly. "It's too bad you have to be disturbed in that way."

"Well—I don't want to tell Henry," Frederica explained. "And if I had the phone cut off and he wanted to get on to me, he'd be worried to death, as you can imagine." She laughed helplessly. "Oh well, I shall have to struggle on, I suppose!"

Holly hesitated. An idea had occurred to her, but she felt shy of suggesting it to her hostess.

"Are you supposed to rest in the afternoon?" she asked.

"Well—that is the idea… but, as I say, it's impossible at the flat. I'm going to give up the whole thing"—she made a weary gesture—"I can't cope any longer."

"If you'd care to rest at my flat—" Holly said tentatively, "it's perfectly quiet there…"

"How sweet of you," Frederica said, taking Holly's hand in hers. "But of course I'm not going to give you all that trouble. Why should you have to put up with me in your flat…" She gave a deep sigh. "Oh! it would be wonderful to get away for an hour or two… where no one could badger me!"

"Well… do come back with me," Holly urged. "I can assure you no one will disturb you. I can go out, if you like… and you can have the place to yourself."

Frederica looked deep into her eyes. "Do you really mean that?" she asked.

"Of course I do," said Holly. Frederica's intense look disturbed her and for a moment she wondered if she were being foolish. But it was too late to draw back now. "Of course I do," Holly said, "and you shall have the flat to yourself. I can do a bit of shopping while you are having your sleep."

"My dear," Frederica was apologetic, "I don't want to turn you out…"

"Honestly," Holly said, "honestly, I've got all sorts of things to do… I shouldn't be going home, in any case."

"Really? You really mean that?"

Holly nodded. "Of course I do." She wondered vaguely whether she had tidied up the flat before she left. No doubt Mrs. Gonner would have seen to things; if not, well, it was just too bad. Frederica would have to take her as she found her. The Hollys of this world don't have personal maids, and housemaids, parlourmaids, butlers, footmen, and all the other accoutrements of a large household. It wouldn't do Frederica any harm, thought Holly, to see just how people have to live when they're hard up.

"You know—I remember the time when I lived in an attic on the top floor of a restaurant in Frith Street," Frederica said once they were on their way to Hammersmith. "It was a cheap little room—the house belonged to the proprietor of the restaurant, and when his wife was away he used to give me all sorts of bits and pieces; cold roast chicken and things. God! I used to be hungry." She smiled at Holly. "Well, it gives me a certain satisfaction to remember those days." She smoothed the mink coat lovingly.

"Turn left at the next traffic lights," Holly said, "and then it's the second turning on the right, the fourth house down." Frederica's confidences struck a jarring note.

Frederica turned the car into the side street, took the second turning and drew up in front of a small brick-built villa. The front garden contained a blackened laurestinus and something that might once have been a cotoneaster. The path leading to the front door was made of concrete blocks and the footsteps of the two women rang out sharply. White net curtains filled the windows which were surprisingly clean and in the bay stood a florist's basket of orchids and carnations, which gave an unexpected touch of glamour to the drab little house. The front door was painted the usual dreary chocolate colour, and Holly drew a key from her handbag to open it. Inside was a tiny hall and a staircase which was sealed off with another front door. Holly opened this and they went up the narrow staircase and into the tiny flat. The little sitting-room was cosy enough, with its divan pulled up close to the fire, and one or two tables with cigarettes and magazines. There was a sideboard in the best Tottenham Court Road manner and a gate-legged table against one wall. The carpet was what Holly called modernistic, and a curious unframed mirror hung over the fireplace. Frederica looked about her with interest.

"What a nice home," she said at last. "Is it yours, Holly?"

"No. Belongs to a friend of mine—ever such a nice girl she is. She went to New York with the Mercurio Ballet and they offered her a job there. She said I could have the flat till she came back. She's been away three years," Holly chuckled. "I wonder if she ever will make up her mind to leave New York for dear old London?"

"You were lucky," Frederica said.

"Yes, I *am* lucky," Holly agreed, "born with a silver spoon in my mouth, mother used to say." She pushed open a door. "Look, this is the kitchenette—nice, isn't it?"

It was more like a glorified cupboard, but even though she might be sluttish in some respects, Holly kept this little cooking-place spotlessly clean. A tiny electric stove, some shelves and a sink comprised the furniture. A table let down from the wall on a little hook, and a meat safe hung outside the window. Frederica nodded, and stifled a yawn.

"Ooh... I'm sorry." Holly ran through the sitting-room and opened the bedroom door. "Look! you can lie down in here, if you'd rather."

Frederica looked at the bed, with its tousled satin counterpane and dingy headboard. The room smelt of stale scent and the dressing-table was covered with a fine layer of powder. Satin curtains covered the windows and a greasy rug was at the side of the bed. In comparison, the other room was fresh and shining.

"I think," Frederica said, "I'd rather rest on the divan... if you wouldn't mind. It will save disturbing the bed, won't it?"

Holly shrugged. "Please yourself," she said. "Well... make yourself at home. I think I'll pop down to the High Street and do my little bit of shopping." She took a string bag from a peg in the hall. "I'll come back in about an hour," she suggested. "All right?"

Frederica was already slipping her feet out of her shoes. "Grand," she said. "You're an angel, child."

Holly went slowly down the stairs. "Just tell the operator you won't take any calls for an hour," she called back, "then you won't be disturbed."

"Okay!" Frederica went into the sitting-room and closed the door. From the window she watched Holly hurry down the street and turn the corner. Then she turned back into the room.

II

Inspector Smith put two lumps of sugar in his tea, and stirred it carefully. It was strong tea, with very little milk, and it was exactly as he liked it. He took a long drink and returned the cup to the table. His hostess watched him attentively—it was the first time she had entertained a policeman and she found Mr. Smith very good company.

"Another cup?" she asked.

"No thank you." Mr. Smith took out his horn-rimmed glasses and settled them comfortably on his nose. "Now... if I could just have a look at those posters..."

Katherine stared at him. "All of them?"

He nodded solemnly. "Every single one, I'm afraid. But tell me where they are and I'll get them... I don't want to be a nuisance."

"That's all right, Inspector, you can help me carry the box out, if you will." Together they lugged it from its hiding-place and Mr. Smith began to examine the contents. "This is the one," Katherine said, "the one that has the same name as the marriage certificate."

She held it out, and together they gazed at it. "Mr. Benenberg has gone back to Paris, you say?" said Katherine. "It's a pity we couldn't have asked him about this, really."

"*What* about it?" asked Mr. Smith, a gleam of interest in his sad, blue eyes. He smoothed his hair back and looked smilingly at Katherine.

"Well—about Faustine—who she was... and if he still works with her... Why?" she was struck with a sudden thought, "it might have been Gallia herself, mightn't it?"

"No, I don't think so," said Mr. Smith. "We know who Faustine was, all right... it's who she is now that's puzzling me for the moment."

"Why—what happened?" asked Katherine interestedly.

"The usual trouble... they had a fight and Faustine ran away. He thinks she never really meant to stay with him... she just married him to get to Europe. Once they were there she picked a fight and disappeared."

"Heavens! And is he looking for her?"

"No. He came over here to see his sister and borrow some money. When he found out what had happened to her he was broken-hearted, poor little man. Then he went round to see an old friend, Dimpson McCabe, and found that he, too, had died. Poor Benenberg was in a terrible state; it must have been a terrific shock to him, Miss Mickey, and he seemed almost out of his mind with worry and grief."

"Has he got enough money to get back to Paris?" she asked.

"Oh yes. I don't think it was a question of immediate funds... it's very difficult to understand him, because he has very little English. As far as I could make out, he wanted the money to finance some new big act he wants to put on; I imagine he thought he could get it from his sister, but I understand she was in debt herself... so I guess Mr. Benenberg will return to Paris right away."

"Poor man," Katherine's eyes were soft with pity. "I hope he's got someone over there to go to."

"I shouldn't worry about him, miss," said the Inspector, "these people pull a hard-luck story, you know. We get used to them." He was going through the papers as he spoke, dividing them into three piles, and folding them carefully to avoid creasing. "By the way, have you seen anything of Mr. Hemingway since you returned to London?" His voice was carefully casual.

"Not a thing," said Katherine cheerfully. "But then, he was Frederica's—Mrs. Brown's that is—beau, not mine. I didn't expect him to look me up. There wasn't any reason why he should."

"I understand he's to do the lighting for the play that Mr. Brown is putting on. The play that Mr. McCabe wrote. I suppose he would have to know a good deal about electricity for that?"

"Well, he certainly would... but he isn't doing it that I know of. I heard that Henry has decided to use his pet electrician. But, of course, I might be wrong. You know how rumours float around in the theatre!" She grinned up at him cheerfully. "I don't really think Henry would have liked to have Glen doing the lighting... too difficult altogether. He'd have had Frederica in and out of the theatre every five minutes... not that he won't get that anyway."

"You don't like Mrs. Brown, I take it?" asked Mr. Smith gently.

"I don't know..." said Katherine slowly. "You know—I can't really make up my mind about her. At Christmas she started off by ignoring me completely and then, just as she was going, she asked me to look her up in town. Then, if you please, she gives a cocktail party and doesn't invite anyone who was at Possett Island except Holly... of all people!"

Mr. Smith shook his head. "Queer," he said, "but maybe she will ask you to something more intimate... I've never been to a cocktail party, but I understand that people give them as an excuse for inviting a whole crowd together. Less trouble than a dinner party, and not as expensive as a dance."

"Embarrassing one's friends and frustrating one's enemies," Katherine murmured. "Personally, I never like them. You haven't missed much," she assured him.

"Give me a nice cup of tea," he said, putting the posters together again. "I'd rather that than all the cocktails."

"Oh, do have another cup now," Katherine urged him, "there's plenty in the pot."

"No thank you, Miss Mickey. That was a grand cup and I enjoyed it very much. Now," he rose to his feet, dusting his knees carefully, "I must be getting along. I think I'll just drop in on Mr. Hemingway. You wouldn't happen to know where he lives, by any chance?"

Katherine shook her head. "I'm dreadfully sorry," she said, "I've got absolutely no idea."

"Ah well," the Inspector reached for his hat and held out his hand to Katherine, "I dare say I can locate him. I'll be saying good-bye to you, Miss Mickey, and maybe we shall meet again."

Katherine opened the front door. "I hope so," she said, "I'd like to know what happened to Faustine."

"So would I," said Mr. Smith, as he rang for the lift, "so would I."

III

Jeffery returned to his room in Gordon Square with a light heart. The interview with Archie Tittop had been more than satisfactory; he felt immeasurably relieved and unutterably grateful to his old friend. Far from forgetting him, Dimpsie had made ample provision for his welfare; not only were there sufficient funds for his university career, but there was also a sum of money to be invested in his name which would bring him in a tiny income.

"Dimpson had no one to leave his money to," Archie had said. "No relatives, that is, and he wanted to make sure that you would be well equipped to face the world. He hasn't left any other legacies, except a small one to Katherine Mickey."

Jeffery could not help thinking of Walters, and as if he could read his thoughts, Mr. Tittop said:

"He left one hundred pounds to Henry Walters, provided he was still in his employ. But I understand that he was under notice to quit, so I don't know quite how that will work out. Better not mention anything about it, Jeffery; I ought not to have told you, really."

Jeffery nodded. "Close as the grave, that's me," he said. "Poor Walters, it's hard luck on him… if he really was leaving."

"He didn't say anything to you, then?" Mr. Tittop asked.

"No. Not a word."

"Did he mention anything about collaborating with Dimpsie on a play?"

"Well… I believe he did say something about it. I know he used to write a lot of Dimpsie's stuff for him. When he was busy…" Jeffery's voice trailed away.

"Now look here," Archie said severely, "I know you're only repeating what Walters has told you, Jeffery, but you must understand here and now that Dimpsie always wrote every line himself—and corrected his own proofs. He never let anyone touch his stuff until it was absolutely finished. All that Walters ever did was to take it down in shorthand, and type it out. He never did another thing… as for writing anything—that's sheer nonsense. He couldn't write a line to save his life."

Jeffery shifted uncomfortably in his chair. "I expect I misunderstood him," he said miserably. "I'm awfully sorry, Mr. Tittop, if I said the wrong thing. Of course, I know Dimpsie never had a ghost, or anything like that."

"It wasn't a question of ghosting," Archie said, "Dimpsie just wrote every word himself, and let me tell you—he was a tyrant over proofs. Not one word would he have touched… I can't tell you the trouble I used to have with Editors." He pulled out a cigarette-case and offered it to Jeffery. "No," he went on, "I had an idea that Walters might be trying to cash in on some of Dimpsie's material… and I'm going to put a stop to his little game."

"I don't think—" Jeffery began, but Archie interrupted him.

"You owe a good deal to Dimpsie," he reminded the discomfited young man, "and there's nothing to be gained by trying to uphold Walters. You'd far better leave him to look after himself. And now," he added pulling a mass of papers towards him, "we'd better go into a few accounts."

*

In his room high above Gordon Square Jeffery reflected on this conversation. There seemed to be no doubt in Mr. Tittop's mind that Walters was up to no good, and Jeffery recalled various scenes at Possett Island with a growing sense of dismay. For a moment it almost seemed to him as if Walters had wanted Dimpsie out of the way, but he put the thought from him in horror. Of course Walters had been devoted to Dimpsie, he decided, and Mr. Tittop had absolutely no grounds for the suggestions he was making.

Jeffery sat at his table, his books in front of him, his pen in his hand; but he could not study, he found it almost impossible to concentrate. The secretary's face was imprinted on the page before him, and past conversations rang in his ears. The shrill voice of his landlady calling him to the telephone came as a welcome release. He hurried down the stairs to pick up the receiver and talk glibly into the mouthpiece before he realized that it was actually Walters who was on the phone. It was too late to draw back.

"I'm awfully sorry," he said lamely, "but I've simply *got* to study. I've got such masses of work to get through before Term starts…"

Walters' voice came thinly back across the wire. "… it's frightfully important, my dear chap, otherwise I shouldn't trouble you."

"Can't you explain over the phone," Jeffery urged him, "Perhaps I can help if you tell me what it is?"

"Must see you," the voice squeaked. "Impossible to try and talk over the phone."

"Oh, very well," Jeffery said at last, "I'll come round."

He slammed down the receiver, snatched his mackintosh from the hall-stand, and ran out into the Square. The journey from Tottenham Court Road to South Kensington was long enough to give him time to reflect on his actions and to decide what course to pursue. Evidently Walters was in some kind of a mess, and now was the moment when he, Jeffery, would have to make a firm stand.

Tittop had been perfectly right, he thought, and it certainly looked as if Walters was out to make trouble.

Arriving at Cheyne Walk he rang the bell, and the door was opened by Walters.

"Oh, there you are!" said the secretary fussily. "Well, come along in." He led the way into the sitting-room and Jeffery took a seat near the fire. "Thank goodness you've come! You're really the only one who can help me." He looked appealingly at the young man.

"What can I do?" said Jeffery. "What's the trouble, Henry?"

"It's that devil Archie Tittop," Walters said, his face red and angry. "That man's a fiend, Jeffery, I warn you."

"What's he done?" asked Jeffery mildly.

"What's he done? Oh, only tried to make out that I was under notice to leave Dimpsie when he died... me! I ask you, Jeffery, have you ever heard of such a thing?"

Jeffery shifted uncomfortably on his chair. "Well—" he said at last, "what happened exactly?"

"He wrote to me and asked whether there was any money owing to me—salary and so on, incidental expenses, housekeeping and all that. So I wrote back and sent in my account, and took the opportunity to ask him whether Dimpsie had made any kind of provision for me. He always told me he'd left me something... several times he's mentioned that. And that beast Archie wrote back and said that had I been in Dimpsie's employ at the time of his death there would have been something, but that he understood I had been given notice to quit! Me! Dimpsie's greatest friend!" His voice was high-pitched and his hands shook as he clenched them.

"It's frightfully bad luck," Jeffery sympathized, "but honestly, Henry, I don't see how I can help."

"Oh yes you can," the secretary said, "you can tell Archie that it's completely untrue... after all, you were there. You know that

Dimpsie never even thought of sacking me. Why in the world should he?"

Jeffery flushed. The memory of that overheard conversation between Dimpsie and Walters was too vivid for comfort. "Honestly, I'd do anything I could," he began, "but I don't know a thing about it."

"On the contrary," said Walters grimly, "you know a great deal… perhaps too much. It isn't good for people to know too much, is it? I'm afraid Gallia knew too much… that might be why someone found it necessary to liquidate her, eh, Jeffery?"

Jeffery stood up. "I don't know what you're talking about," he said hotly. "I don't know too much about anything. I think you're talking a lot of nonsense, Henry, and if you're not careful you'll get yourself into trouble."

"Very well," said Walters, his voice trembling, "if that's your attitude, Jeffery, you must do as you wish. But I would just like to suggest that in future, when you are visiting ladies in the middle of the night, you would do well not to take a torch with you. It's surprising how far a small beam can travel." He opened the door with a gesture. "Good-bye," he said, refusing Jeffery's hand. "You may be feeling very pleased with yourself now—but just wait, perhaps later on you'll be sorry you treated me this way." Without waiting for Jeffery to go he returned to his chair by the fire, his whole attitude one of complete dejection. But Jeffery was only too anxious to get away, and without so much as turning his head, he almost ran out of the room and out into the street. The atmosphere of the flat was sinister and horrible, and Walters' veiled threats extremely unpleasant. He was thankful that matters had at last come to a point where he need no longer see the secretary, and he resolved that in future he would be out should Walters phone or call on him.

IV

As he stood on the jetty watching his car being lifted high in the air, Glen Hemingway was conscious of a feeling of intense relief. In front of him the little steamer was getting under way; porters were running up and down the gangways, and last minute passengers were hurriedly counting their suit-cases and bags to reassure themselves that nothing had been left behind. Very gently the giant crane lowered the car on to the deck, and Hemingway decided that it was time that he, too, took his place with those on deck. In four more hours, he reflected, he would be in Paris... away from it all; even in his thoughts he did not specify exactly what it was that he was anxious to leave behind. He handed his ticket to the steward and looked around for his porter. Consulting his watch he saw that he had one minute to spare, and he used this time in going down to get his passport stamped. There was already a queue at the little office, and he returned to the deck, surprised to find that they had not yet cast away. There was a slight disturbance at the gangway, and a slight, pale man in a dark suit was talking earnestly to the steward. In a moment they were joined by another man whom Glen guessed to be the Captain. He watched them disinterestedly, hardly bothering to wonder what was going on, his mind occupied with his own affairs. It was with a start of surprise that he realized that someone at his elbow was speaking to him.

"... we won't keep you a moment, sir."

Hemingway turned and saw that the speaker was another of the stewards. "What do you want?" he asked.

"Would you come this way, please, sir," the steward repeated, leading the way to the little group at the top of the gangway. Hemingway followed him, a sinking feeling at the pit of his stomach; surely there could be nothing wrong with the papers for the car—quickly he checked off the various details. Then he noticed something vaguely familiar about the gentleman in the dark suit; he felt sure he had met him somewhere… it was difficult to place him. He had not long to wait.

"Mr. Hemingway?" the stranger asked. Glen nodded. The stranger smiled. "I am Detective-Inspector Smith. Mr. Hemingway, I'm afraid I shall have to ask you to return to London with me."

Glen stared at the Inspector. "But I can't possibly do that," he objected, "I'm going to Paris. If you want to ask me any questions, you'll just have to come along too."

The Inspector smiled. It was a movement of the mouth only, his eyes were cold, blue and tired-looking. "I'm sorry," he repeated firmly. "It will make things much easier if you will return with me now—much easier. I would prefer not to have to insist, Mr. Hemingway."

Glen stared for a moment, anger giving way to something deeper. "Very well," he shrugged, "I suppose I shall have to come." Turning on his heel, he walked quickly down the gangway and on to the dock.

I 3

DEATH AND DISCOVERY

I

IT SEEMED TO KATHERINE, AS SHE TRIED TO PIECE THE FACTS together, that somehow Holly held the key to the mystery. Walters had explained how he had received the letter from Holly, and he had even gone so far as to show it to her, but although she could neither read nor understand a word of it she realized only too well that it must have been written by Krasnya Benenberg to his sister. Obviously it was the letter announcing his arrival, and it would be extremely interesting, Katherine thought, to know just how Miss Temple had come by it. Accordingly, she went down to the theatre hoping to catch Miss Temple in an off moment. She noticed with interest that the boards advertising Dimpsie's play were already in position, although the date of the opening was not yet announced; Holly's name was prominent among the cast, and a large photo of her was hung in the entrance. Katherine inquired at the stage door, showed her card and went down the narrow corridor that led to the wings. It was ten-thirty. The stage was bare, except for a table and two armchairs and the rehearsal was already in progress. Holly was nowhere to be seen and, replying to her whispered question, the stage manager told her that she had not arrived this morning.

"She isn't on in this scene," he said, "so it doesn't really matter. I've phoned her flat, though, and there was no answer—she's probably on her way here."

Katherine crept down to the stalls and took a seat at the end of a row; but her attention was not on the stage, and she found herself wondering why Holly had not turned up to the rehearsal at the proper time. It was hardly likely that she would be late without some very good reason; she would be only too anxious not to put a foot wrong where Henry was concerned. The minutes dragged slowly by and Katherine waited impatiently. She tried to fix her attention on the stage, but her mind wandered and she thought first about Walters and then about the errant Holly. All at once she decided to leave the theatre. In less than half an hour she could be in Hammersmith, and there would be plenty of time for a chat while Holly dressed, and they returned to the West End.

It was a relief to be out in the air again, and she took the tube to Hammersmith, and then walked quickly down the Broadway and along the road to Holly's flat. As she turned the corner a taxi wheeled about in the middle of the road and drove off. If she's in that, Katherine thought, my luck's dead out. She hurried down the road and turned up the little garden path. As she rang the bell she noticed that the front door was open, and after waiting a moment she went in and tried the door leading upstairs. She was not surprised to find this was unlatched; it would be like Holly to leave it open—it would save the trouble of coming down to let anyone in. Katherine ran upstairs. It was quiet and dark in the little hall, and as she groped for the switch she called Holly loudly.

"Is anyone there?" For a moment Katherine stood still. In the silence she thought she had heard a light footfall; was it possible that Holly was not going to answer?

"Is anyone there? Holly! Where are you?" She repeated the question in a loud voice, and then her fingers found the switch and turned it on. She stood where she was, looking round her uncomfortably. It struck her as odd that the blinds should still be drawn so late in the day; but then she remembered that if Holly had been out late the night before it was not improbable that she might still be asleep, in spite of the noise and the calling. Katherine was almost tempted to go away again—the thought of an irate figure emerging from the bedroom to demand what all the noise was about was not a pleasing prospect—but then she remembered why she had come, and calling Holly's name again she opened the door nearest to her. It was the bedroom. The curtains were drawn back from the windows and the satin counterpane was rumpled and dirty, but apart from this the room was tidy enough—the only sign of disorder a piece of brown, tweedy material protruding from a cupboard which had been left slightly open. A film of powder covered the dressing-table, and a powder jar stood open, a grubby swansdown puff lying by the side. There was a slightly perfumed atmosphere... Katherine sniffed... and then sniffed the powder. She looked around for a bottle which might contain the essence which was so familiar, and yet to which she could give no name. But the little bottles on Holly's table held no clue. Katherine sighed and went out. The door opposite opened on to the sitting-room; here it was dark, and the lights revealed the curtains still drawn and the remains of a meal on a table in the centre of the room. She crossed the room and drew back the curtains; then she turned back into the room. Holly lay stretched out on the sofa, her head on a cushion, her hands tucked under her cheek. One foot, the slipper dangling, was poised limply over the edge of the couch, the other was drawn up under her, as if she had settled herself to sleep in the most comfortable position. Katherine caught her breath for a moment.

"Holly!" she said sharply. "Wake up! Holly!"

But the figure on the couch did not stir. Holly's eyes remained closed, her lashes sweeping her cheek, her mouth slightly open, and not by the quiver of a breath did she appear to have heard Katherine.

"Holly!" Katherine ran to the couch and put a tentative finger to that rosy cheek... it was cold. Katherine fumbled in her bag and fished out a mirror; she held it to the girl's mouth and waited, but the surface was unclouded and the unformulated suspicion that had begun to work in her mind ever since she had entered the flat now began to take definite shape. Holly was dead... Katherine stood up and looked about her; there must be a telephone... she found it on a table at the back of the sofa, and as she picked it up and pulled it towards her a length of dangling wire showed her that the phone, at least, would be of no use to her. Standing there for a moment, she tried to pull herself together—to plan what she should do—and once again she fancied she heard that light footfall... so slight a sound that she thought it must be pure imagination. And then, without any warning at all she found herself in the grip of hysteria; it became necessary to fight for self-control, to master the ever-mounting feeling of dread. For an instant she turned away from the still figure on the couch and went towards the window—and in that minute the door closed smartly, as if blown to by a puff of wind. Only—there was no wind. A sound of footsteps running lightly downstairs and the front door slamming.

There is no doubt that on certain occasions all events seem to tend towards an unequal balance of good and evil, and it would seem that for a time, at least, the evil will predominate. That the dice were loaded against her Katherine felt certain—the window gave on to the back of the house, and a dingy cat-run bounded by a high wall was all that she could see. Whoever had locked her into the sitting-room with the dead girl had planned on leaving by the front door, and now they were probably strolling comfortably down the Broadway.

Averting her eyes so as to avoid the form on the sofa, Katherine went over to the door and tried the handle—but she had not been mistaken. The door was locked. She sat down on the nearest chair and considered the two courses open to her: to try to break down the door—or to shout from the window in the hope of attracting the attention of someone in the next house. This last seemed to her the best way, and she threw open the window and leant out.

II

Henry Brown held up a slim hand. "One moment, please," he said, and his voice was curt. "I am not aware that I had arranged to skip scenes in this unusual fashion. May I ask…"

The artists on the stage exchanged a swift look, and a young man stepped forward. "I'm afraid it was my idea," he said. "You see—"

Henry frowned. "We'll take the scenes in their proper sequence," he said.

"But Holly isn't here yet," the young man explained.

"Oh…?" Henry's voice was cold.

"So I thought—" the young man began lamely.

Someone stepped forward from the darkness of the stalls and put their arm through Henry's. He turned to find Frederica at his side. "Darling," she said quietly, "why not let's go and have lunch? She's probably gone to get her hair done—she's sure to be back later."

Henry shrugged and consulted his watch, "Break for lunch," he announced. "Everybody back at two-thirty, please." With Frederica at his side he went up to the stage manager. "Do you know anything about Miss Temple?" he asked.

"She always tells me if she's getting her hair done. As a matter of fact a Miss Mickey was in this morning asking for her. I believe she went down to Hammersmith…"

"Let's go!" said Frederica impatiently, "she'll turn up after lunch, Henry. She probably had a date, or something. Anyway, if Katherine's gone down to find her they may turn up together."

Henry rolled up his copy of the script and slipped an elastic band round the cylinder. "I shall be back at two-thirty," he said. "If Miss Temple isn't in by then, you'll have to send someone down there… I suppose you've tried to get her on the phone?"

The stage manager nodded. "Her phone seems to be out of order," he said, "but I can try the exchange again."

"Well, we'll give her till two-thirty," Henry said, "then, if she isn't here, we'll send down for her, that's all." He followed Frederica out into the cold grey morning, buttoning his coat as he went.

"Have you got the car?" he asked.

She shook her head. "Let's go across the road to Medtners," she suggested. "I booked a table."

Henry faced his wife across the table and noted, with some surprise, that she looked pale, there were shadows under her lovely eyes.

"You look tired," he said.

"Do I?" she smiled at him, but he noticed the smile didn't reach her eyes. "I'd like to get some sun, Henry. I wish we could get away."

"We'll go to Madeira," he said absently, "once the play is going well." He studied the menu and gave the order briefly to the head waiter.

Frederica leaned back in her chair, and let her furs slip from her shoulders. "I should love that," she said. She unbuttoned her jacket to reveal a cream sweater embroidered with tiny pink elephants.

"Funny," Henry said. "I wonder whether that child really *has* gone to the hairdresser…"

"You're not still fussing about Holly are you?" asked Frederica sharply. "Good heavens! anyone would think something had happened to her the way you're going on! She's all right, I tell you. Anyway, if she wasn't, you'd soon have heard it."

But Henry wasn't listening. His eyes were watching a young woman who crossed the room with long steps, and who came straight to his table.

"Hello," she said, "I thought I'd find you here."

Frederica stared. "Why, Katherine," she said at last, "how nice to see you!"

III

Detective-Inspector Smith watched Mr. Tittop across the desk. He noticed how Mr. Tittop's hand trembled as he picked up the glass of water and how eagerly he drank it, as if he were parched with thirst. It seemed as if Mr. Tittop must be very nervous.

"I understand that Mr. McCabe had a great many friends," he repeated, "and I believe he was extremely well-informed about most of them."

Archie Tittop lit a cigarette and flicked the match into an ash-tray before replying. "Of course he had a lot of friends," he said, "and a wide circle of acquaintances. It's quite usual to know something about one's intimate friends, I believe," he said at last.

Mr. Smith smiled gently. "Oh, quite usual," he agreed. "Quite. I grant you that. But hardly usual to act on that knowledge."

"Are you insinuating—?" Archie gripped the edge of the desk.

Mr. Smith shook his head. "I am not insinuating anything," he said, "but I am suggesting that Mr. McCabe might have had some special knowledge about a certain friend... I could not say whom... which might account for his death."

"But I understood it was an accident?"

"Did you? Well—perhaps it was. I should like to feel quite certain about that," Mr. Smith said quietly. "I believe that you, as Mr. McCabe's literary Agent, are in possession of certain note-books and other data which might be helpful to me…"

Archie pursed his mouth. "I am not at liberty to disclose any private papers," he said primly.

"Quite so," Mr. Smith agreed. "But this little piece of paper here—" he held it out for Mr. Tittop to see—"I could insist, but I feel sure that it won't be necessary. If you would just tell me what you can about Mr. McCabe's friends, both here and abroad…"

But Mr. Tittop stared at him. "Dimpson knew hundreds of people," he said. "I can't give you the family history of every one of his friends. What is it you want to know?"

Mr. Smith was silent. For some moments he sat there, tapping his finger gently on the desk and thinking deeply. At last, when Archie felt that his nerves would give way and he would scream with annoyance, the Inspector broke the silence.

"Did Mr. McCabe ever mention anyone called Benenberg?" he asked, "Krasnya Benenberg?"

Archie Tittop's eyes narrowed. "Benenberg?" he repeated. "Would he be something to do with the circus? I seem to have heard that name…"

"Yes. He's a circus performer. He came over here to see his sister," said Mr. Smith.

Archie looked up. "His sister? I didn't know he had one."

"No. Well, he hasn't," said Mr. Smith. "She's dead now."

Archie Tittop leaned back in his chair. "Who was she?" he asked.

"She was known as Gallia Karmanskaya," said Mr. Smith. "It was rather a shock to her brother to find she had been murdered. She was a very old friend of McCabe's, I believe, and Benenberg seemed to think there was some connection between the two."

"I believe she hoped he was going to marry her," said Mr. Tittop. "Actually, I doubt whether he would ever have done so. But I think he was very attached to Madame Karmanskaya... I never knew she had a brother," he mused. "How strange!"

Mr. Smith watched him without speaking. Archie pulled open a drawer in his desk and drew out a file. Under K were several letters, listed in their correct order. He read through these and replaced them, shutting the drawer carefully.

"No," he said again, "I never knew she had a brother. But then, they probably were not very friendly. Dimpsie must have met Benenberg when he went over to Paris a couple of years ago. He was mad on circuses and circus folk, you know, and he had stacks of posters and photographs that he'd collected for years. He left the entire collection to Katherine Mickey." He paused, and looked at the Inspector hopefully. "Now, if you went to see her..." he suggested.

Mr. Smith nodded. "Oh yes—I know about the collection," he said. "It occurred to me that you might be able to enlighten me. Miss Mickey had no idea why he left it to her."

"I expect he thought it might come in handy in her profession," said Mr. Tittop. "There must be hundreds of photographs... there's probably some very interesting stuff, if she took the trouble to look for it."

It seemed to Mr. Smith that behind Archie's words lay a hidden meaning, and he stared across the desk into the Agent's watery blue eyes, trying to probe the truth from behind the veil of half-truths and prevarications.

"Did it ever occur to you," he asked, "that Mr. McCabe had made a serious enemy?"

Archie shook his head. "Good heavens, no!" he said. "Of course, I know he said the most outrageous things to people... he's called me the most incredible names before now. But one just never took any notice. I mean to say—that was Dimpsie! He was impossible! But his friends adored him. It was pretty good to be a friend of his, you know... and as for his enemies, I don't really think he had any."

"Oh, come now," Mr. Smith tried to keep the vexation out of his voice, "don't tell me a man as popular as Mr. McCabe never made any enemies! It stands to reason that he must have offended people—and we know that he liked to have a hold on them."

Archie Tittop shook his head. "You're barking up the wrong tree," he said wearily. "All wrong! It didn't matter what Dimpsie said; the only trouble was if he didn't say anything! And even then..." He pressed the tips of his fingers together.

"Then you do not think that Mr. Walters, for instance, resented his dismissal?"

"I haven't any idea," Archie said. "I don't suppose he was over pleased. After all—he'd been with Dimpsie for more than ten years and he'd had a pretty easy time of it."

"Then you do agree that he had been dismissed?" asked the Inspector interestedly.

Archie raised his shaggy eyebrows. "Of course! Dimpsie had a blazing row with him and threw him out! It was only a couple of days before he died, too. Bad luck on Walters—he'd have come in for a bit of money otherwise. But there you are! Dimpsie always was insanely jealous—and Walters had been extremely indiscreet."

Mr. Smith smiled gently. "Mr. McCabe must have been quite a difficult client?" he suggested.

"Oh, well!" Archie shrugged eloquent shoulders. "All clients are difficult sometimes. Dimpsie was one of my greatest friends, you know, and we got along very well. If all my authors were as charming..." he left the sentence unfinished and the Inspector received the impression that to Mr. Tittop his clients were a lot of agreeable but wayward babies.

"You see," Archie went on, his manner becoming almost confidential, "although Dimpsie used to argue a good deal over one thing and another, he was a perfect fiend over money, he left everything in my hands and I always knew where I was with him. He left absolutely everything to me."

"Quite." Mr. Smith nodded thoughtfully. "Of course, he would have invited only his most intimate friends up to Possett Island... so that one can rule out the possibility that any of the guests might have quarrelled with him?"

"How can one tell? There were always quarrels on the Island—but Dimpsie never took them seriously. It was the breath of life to him..."

The Inspector raised his eyebrows. "I wonder..." he said.

14

THE PART IS FILLED

I

DOCTOR HARLEY SLAMMED THE DOOR OF HIS CAR, LOCKED it, and put the key carefully in his pocket. Then he hurried into the house and ran up the stairs without troubling to wait for the lift. He rapped loudly on the door and then rang the bell, without giving anyone time to answer. After a minute the door opened and Katherine was there. Doctor Harley smiled his relief.

"What on earth is the matter, Bill?" she asked. "You seem to be in a terrible hurry."

He followed her into the sitting-room, throwing his hat on to a chair in the hall, and peeling off his gloves as he went.

"I've been in a bit of a panic about you," he admitted. "I tried to ring you several times during the day—and you were never in."

Katherine sat down in the chair opposite him. She wore a green woollen housecoat, a scarlet girdle coiled round her waist like a flame, her hair was loose on her shoulders, and her feet thrust into velvet slippers.

"I'm tired!" she said with a grimace. "It's been a hell of a day, Bill." She told him the events of the morning, of how she had been to Holly's flat and what she had found there. Bill whistled and raised his eyebrows.

"You were taking a bit of a chance, weren't you?" he asked.

"I don't think so... after all, I never supposed that Holly—" She bit her lip. "She died from an overdose of luminal, Bill."

"Did she? And how do you know?" he asked grimly.

"Well—it was obvious she'd taken something. The doctor seemed to think it was something like that. They haven't had the analyst's report yet; but my guess is that it was some kind of sleeping draught. But Bill... I had the most extraordinary feeling while I was there... I simply *had* to get back to the theatre—I felt I wanted to see Henry. I had the devil's own job getting away. I managed to get hold of a woman next door and she got the police to open the door... Of course they wanted me to stay and answer a million questions—but thank God they believed what I told them. I promised faithfully to go back to the station in the afternoon if they would let me go straight down to the theatre. I wanted to see Henry..."

"And was he there?"

"No. I found him at Medtners, having lunch with Frederica. Bill—I swear he didn't know a thing about Holly. And he'd been at the theatre all the morning."

Bill Harley flicked the ash from his cigarette into a wide brass bowl at his elbow. "You don't—didn't," he corrected himself, "seriously imagine that Henry had anything to do with it, did you?"

"I don't *know*, Bill. He was having an affair with her... everyone knew about it. I don't think he cared whether people knew—he never seemed to make any attempt to hide it."

"You're exaggerating, my poppet," Bill said. "I doubt whether Frederica realized what he was up to."

"Of course she knew. She had her own fish to fry... she was only too glad to let Henry go his own way."

"I always thought," he said, "that Henry was devoted to Frederica.

I don't believe he would ever have considered anyone else other than very, very lightly indeed."

"All right. All right," she broke in impatiently, "have it your own way. I don't care whether he was in love with Holly or not—I just had the feeling that he knew something about it... I may be entirely wrong."

"Yes, my poppet, you may be," Bill said. "Whoever wanted Holly out of the way must have had a very good reason... I wonder whether she knew anything? or whether someone thought she knew..."

"Perhaps she knew who Faustine was?" Katherine said, a slight edge to her voice.

"Faustine?... Oh, the lady who married Benenberg, you mean? Well, is she important?"

"Not really. Only Benenberg was married and his wife ran away and left him. Gallia would have known who she was, wouldn't she?"

Bill cocked his head on one side as if listening to something.

"Would she?" he repeated. "No... I don't see why. And, anyway, Faustine hasn't anything to do with Holly—or Gallia—or even poor old Dimpsie, if it comes to that."

"Of course," Katherine considered, "it might have been suicide?"

"You don't sound very sure of it," Bill said.

"I'm not... I just thought—it *could* have been... only I didn't see any bottle of stuff—or pills—or anything like that. I don't know how the stuff was administered. She might have taken something—and thrown the bottle away."

Bill shook his head. "Holly wasn't the type who commits suicide," he said decidedly. "Besides—why should she want to? She had a part in the new play... Henry was making a good deal of fuss over her... It strikes me she had everything to live for."

"I suppose you're right," Katherine said. "Poor Holly..." she sniffed, and then said miserably, "I can't help feeling dreadful about it all… Dimpsie—and then Gallia—and now Holly." The tears welled up in her eyes and she fumbled ineffectually for a handkerchief.

"Here!" Bill held out his large linen square. "Blow!"

Katherine lifted her face obediently, like a little child, It was so reassuring to have Bill there… the dumpy plain little man who was goodness personified. "You *are* good!" she said impulsively.

Doctor Harley threw back his head and laughed; a rich chuckle that seemed to come from the depths of his being. Speechless, he held out his hand for the handkerchief, and wiped his streaming eyes.

"Kate, my angel!" he said, when he could speak. "You'll be the death of me! Good, indeed!" He stuffed the handkerchief into his pocket and his eyes twinkled at her. "No, Kate, I'm not good. But—" He broke off and went over to the window. "Listen!" he said, throwing it open.

Far below them, in the busy street, the newsboy's raucous voice floated up to them… "Evening Star! Big Game Hunter detained. Glen Hemingway leaves Channel steamer at last minute. Evening Star!"

"Did you hear that?" Bill asked. He hurried over to the door. "I'll run down and get a paper… it couldn't possibly be what I thought I heard…" He disappeared from the room, and Katherine remained at the window, gazing down on to the lighted street below.

II

Glen Hemingway's feelings, on leaving the steamer, had been a mixture of indignation and ironical amusement. Not that there was anything amusing in being arrested; during the journey to London he wondered several times whether he had not been too easy-going and acquiescent. After all, surely the Inspector could have been made to see reason… Suppose he, Hemingway, had insisted on continuing his journey. His lips twisted in a grim smile as he pictured himself darting away from the Inspector and hurrying below in an effort to escape, running through the narrow corridors and sliding through doorways, racing in and out of cabins with the dapper and melancholy Mr. Smith always a few yards behind. He grinned to himself and pulled a packet of cigarettes from his pocket.

"Fag?" he offered the Inspector.

Mr. Smith shook his head. "Thanks all the same," he said. He glanced out of the window. "Another ten minutes," he said, "and we'll be there."

"And might I ask where you are taking me?" Glen said sarcastically.

"New Scotland Yard," Mr. Smith said quietly. (That's the first question he's asked me, he thought—a rum chap, this.)

Glen smoked his cigarette calmly. So far he congratulated himself on having kept his temper remarkably well, and above the astonishment over the turn events had taken rose the incredible fact that he was not in the least worried. You're innocent till they prove you guilty, he reminded himself; and it occurred to him that the police force have a strong dislike of making an arrest unless conviction is almost a certainty. It was impossible, he thought, for the police to have any evidence against him—ergo, why worry? And with commendable restraint he refrained from asking the Inspector any questions, nor did he volunteer any remarks. He could see, in his mind's eye, the dread words written in enormous black letters: I HAVE TO WARN YOU THAT ANY STATEMENT YOU MAKE WILL BE TAKEN DOWN AND MAY BE USED IN EVIDENCE AGAINST YOU. Oh no, Glen thought, they don't catch me that way. But he could not help remembering the urgency with which he had packed up all his things and hurried out of London. It was typical of the Fates to let him get so near to complete freedom, only to jerk him back like a puppet on the end of a string. It was ironical, when you came to think of it, that he should have had this feeling of impending disaster, for that undoubtedly had been the reason for his decision to leave for Paris two weeks before it was strictly necessary. Kismet, he murmured, and bowed to the inevitable.

The train snorted into Victoria Station, and from it poured an assortment of people, while porters clambered into the carriages, lifting suit-cases from racks, and hurled trunks and luggage on to the platform. Glen followed Mr. Smith out of the station and sat beside him in the taxi without speaking.

The short drive from Victoria to Westminster was soon over, and Glen realized with grim amusement that they were about to drive under the archway of New Scotland Yard. So far his acquaintance with this building had been confined to detective novels, and now he looked about him interestedly. A dreary place, he decided, following the Inspector down several dingy corridors and turning at last into a small room in which a fire burnt brightly.

At a desk sat a plump little man; his mouth a tight bunch under the sandy moustache; his eyes small and piercing beneath heavy sandy eyebrows. Glen, looking quickly at his hands, noticed that they were well-kept, the nails shapely and the fingers strong though stubby.

"This is Mr. Hemingway," said Mr. Smith.

The little man smiled. "Won't you sit down, Mr. Hemingway," he said. "My name is Buller…" He waited while Glen seated himself in a chair facing him. "We're very sorry to have to ask you to come back to London, Mr. Hemingway—but—we think you may be able to help us."

III

Henry Brown was profoundly shocked to hear of Holly's death. He announced the grim news to an incredulous cast and, although Holly had not been a particular favourite, the theatre was plunged into gloom. Rehearsals were stopped for the time being, and Henry was faced with the necessity of engaging a new ingénue; a task which filled him with disgust. The thought of Holly was constantly in his mind, and he retired to his office, where he sat dejectedly at his desk, refusing to see the gay young things who cluttered the outer office. Holly's baby face with the twinkling eyes and saucy curls haunted him, and he remembered the satin-smooth texture of her skin and the engaging way she had of nestling up to him; the knowledge that all these fascinating and endearing charms were now cold clay hurt unbearably. Miss Tonkins, her hair raven-black and coiled silkily into the nape of her neck, consulted files briskly, answered the phone and repelled the too-insistent applicants for the now vacant part.

"Mr. Brown isn't casting yet," she repeated again and again. "There isn't any point in your waiting... Mr. Brown isn't at the office to-day."

Unfortunately, the full effect of this was spoilt in one instance by the arrival of Frederica, elegant in black wool, an enormous diamond brooch sparkling at her throat, her hair shining gold and an aura of french perfume that lingered tantalizingly in the air. Smiling brilliantly at Miss Tonkins she pushed through the little swing door that protected the secretary from the ravening hordes and disappeared into the inner office, leaving the atmosphere charged with electric waves of sheer fury.

"So Mr. Brown isn't in!" said a little blonde quietly. "Well—I might as well wait here as out in the street. My dogs are tired!" She lifted a silken leg; a plump foot bulged out of a patent shoe with its three-inch heel. "My!" the blonde said, "it's good to have a place to rest!"

Miss Tonkins borrowed a smile from Hedy Lamarr. "Make yourself comfortable," she invited. "Mr. Brown isn't in the office. I shall be locking up at five—but till then you're welcome..." she glanced round the room, "all of you!" The other girls shifted in their seats but decided to stick it out. No one spoke.

In the inner office Mr. Brown, sunk deep into an armchair, watched his wife languidly. Frederica, her coat draped over a chair, sat on the edge of the desk facing her husband. Her voice was warm and seductive, but her eyes were cold, and to a keen observer she would have appeared slightly nervous and unsure of herself. Mr. Brown was almost too languid to pay attention to what she was saying.

"...of course it's terribly sad," she went on, "but you've got to think of the play, Henry. It's a very selfish course you're taking, running away like this. All those people down at the theatre are worried to death. No one knows what you are planning..."

"I'm not planning anything," Henry said wearily. "I wish you'd leave me alone, Freddie. I'm miserable. When I think..."

"Darling!" she was all sympathy, "I know you are... and I am, too. But it won't do any good, will it, just to sit here and gloom. You'll have to get someone to take her place..."

"You don't know what you're saying," Henry said. "That girl... a mere child she was, is dead, Freddie, dead! Perhaps it was *my* fault!" He buried his face in his hands and rocked backwards and forwards in his misery.

"How could it be your fault?" his wife said. "You're indulging in self-pity, Henry, and that's the truth. You know perfectly well that it could not possibly have been anything to do with you... Why, you were giving Holly her big chance—"

Henry looked up at her, his eyes wet. "I was, wasn't I?" he said miserably. "She couldn't have been unhappy; so what was it, then?"

"The police seem to think that it was murder, Henry."

Her husband stared at her. "Didn't you know?" she asked softly. "How was it you didn't know?"

Henry shrugged. "I haven't read the papers," he said. "I couldn't."

"Well, that's what the Coroner said," Frederica told him. "Of course, it's terrible, I quite realize, and I understand how you feel, Henry. Because I know you were in love with Holly..." She paused, waiting for Henry's denial.

"I suppose I was," he admitted, "in a way... not in the way I love you, my Freddie, but in a way that one is with young things... She was so charming and gay... If she had a bad side she hid it from me." He smiled a little. "I know that she did not really care for me... I am not really so foolish as to suppose that she could have been in love with me... but she was very sweet—a little kitten..."

Frederica shrugged. "You make things more difficult," she said.

"What do you mean?" He looked up from the depths of the chair.

"The solution is obvious. Why not let me play the part?"

"You? My dear Freddie! What an idea!"

Frederica smiled at him. "Not such a foolish one, really. It will save a lot of trouble—and besides, I am a quick study, you know."

Henry tapped the fingers of one hand against the other; it struck him that there was a good deal to be said for Frederica's plan. The thought of having to choose someone to take Holly's place filled him with disgust, and there was no real reason why Frederica should not have the part. Of course, there was always the fact that Dimpsie had definitely refused to allow her any part in his plays, but Dimpsie was no longer there... he felt too tired to argue. The shock of Holly's death had affected him more than he realized. He gave in without a struggle.

"All right," he said, "if that is what you want."

Frederica bent over him and kissed him lightly. "You won't be sorry, darling," she said. "Now rest—and I shall go and get a copy of the script."

She went out; the outer office had not changed, the same girls lined the walls and Miss Tonkins sat at her desk typing. Frederica whispered a word in her ear and was gone. The perfumed air seemed to swirl and sway as she closed the door firmly behind her.

Miss Tonkins ripped a sheet of paper out of the typewriter and let her glance drift round the room. "That's all for to-day, ladies," she said. "It's five o'clock and I'm going home."

One by one the waiting girls rose languidly from their seats along the wall. "See you to-morrow, dearie!" said the baby blonde who had complained about her feet.

Miss Tonkins dropped Hedy Lamarr and became Bette Davis, the more-than-efficient secretary. "I think not," she said quietly. "The part has been filled."

The blonde raised over-emphasized eyebrows. "Has it?" she inquired sarcastically. "I'll say it has—and how!" Scornfully she swept to the door and paused, one hand on the knob, to turn and throw a last remark to the waiting Tonkins. "That circus horse!" she threw out.

Miss Tonkins paid no more attention than she would have done to an obstreperous child. Walking to the door she held it open for the girls to pass out, then she shut it firmly. And locked it.

IV

Archie Tittop picked up the telephone and dialled a number thought-fully; with his left hand he poured himself a glass of water, and drank it hastily. A voice on the end of the line repeated a number brightly and asked who was there. Archie gulped the water and asked to speak to Mr. Brown.

"He's just leaving," the voice said. "Is it important?"

"Certainly it is," said Archie indignantly.

"I think I may be able to catch him… Will you hold on, please?" The voice trailed away and Archie waited. Presently he heard Henry's voice. "Yes? What is it, Tittop?"

"I'm sending the contract," Archie said easily. "There's no change in it… I think you'll find it quite satisfactory, Henry."

"I don't know what you're talking about," Henry said. "What contract?"

"For the play," Archie explained, "the usual contract, you know."

"Quite unnecessary," Henry said. "Everything was arranged with McCabe before he died, Tittop. There is no need for a contract. I had accepted the play—McCabe's money will be paid in to you, of course."

"I'm afraid you won't get away with that, Henry," Archie said. "You see, I have an arrangement with Dimpsie by which I am bound to draw up the contract for any play of his which is presented. I think you'll find that it's all correct." He waited, smiling a little.

"And what about Walters?" inquired a cold voice from Henry's end.

"What about him?" Archie echoed.

"Are you admitting his claim?" Henry inquired.

"Not for a moment," Archie said. "I know perfectly well that he never wrote a line of the play. It's simply a try-on, that's all."

"You think so?"

"Certainly I do. By the way, Dimpsie left you his cat… do you remember Simkin? I'm having him sent round to the flat."

"Oh." Henry was taken aback. "It's going to be a little difficult, you know… we live on the top floor… Frederica may not be pleased…"

Archie chuckled. "You'll have to arrange a little lift for him… I can't see Simkin walking down all those stairs. Well, good-bye, Henry. Good luck!" He hung up without waiting for an answer and poured himself another glass of water. If Henry thought he was going to pull a fast one he was mistaken. He rang the bell for his secretary, and gave instructions for the sending of the contract. Then

he reached down beside his desk and pulled up a roomy basket…
"Is Simkin with you?" he asked the woman. "Good! Then pop him
in here and one of the boys can take him round to Berkeley Square
on their way home."

When his secretary had left the room he lifted the water-jug
and poured the last few drops into his glass. If I have to drink much
more water, he told himself, it'll be the end of me.

15

I

MR. SMITH SURVEYED THE WATER FROM THE DECK OF THE Channel steamer. The sea was choppy and a school of porpoises following in the tumbling wash of the ship lifted their slippery brown bodies high out of the water; Mr. Smith watched them interestedly. If it were a little warmer, now, he would have liked to join them, but as it was… he shivered and turned away from the rails. He was looking forward to this trip—he had never been abroad before, and though this would be a very short visit, he intended to make the most of it. He strolled round the deck, fascinated by everything and everyone; the journey would be over all too soon for him. He enjoyed the crossing; he enjoyed the train journey to Paris; and most of all he enjoyed the meal in the dining-car, which was so completely different from its English cousin on the Southern Railway. Once in Paris, however, there was no time to lose. He took a room at the Hotel du Nord; parked his valise, and took a taxi up to Montmartre. He found Krasnya Benenberg without any difficulty. The Cirque d'Hiver was closing down, preparatory to its spring tour, and Krasnya, like the other members of the troupe, was packing and sorting out clothes, props, and a hundred things that were of vital importance to him. The circus itself was dark; the ring empty and the surrounding booths shut and locked; but in the quarters at the back of the booths there was plenty going on. The smell from the animals in their cages struck the Inspector as unusually strong, and he clapped a handkerchief to his nose while passing the lions and tigers who were being fed with lumps of raw meat and tremendous bones, hung about with scraps of yellow fat. The dressing-rooms were in a line at right-angles to the cages, and Krasnya shared one with his partner, a fair-haired girl, with long shapely legs and dimpled cheeks. Mr. Smith tapped on the door and waited. Krasnya poked his head out.

"Come in," he invited, a smile breaking on his pudgy face, "come in, Mister Smitt, I am most pleased to see you." He opened the door, and waved a hand at the crowded interior. "You will not mind that we are crowded, no? We pack, you see, and, then we go South…" he made a grimace, as if to indicate sunshine and warmth. "I am glad, you see, and Faustine is, too."

Faustine smiled at the Inspector and pulled a chair from under a heap of clothes. The clothes toppled to the floor and she kicked them aside carelessly. "Sit, please," she said quietly.

Mr. Smith sat down; he put his hat under the chair and produced a cigarette-case which he handed round. After some time he said: "I am so pleased to have an opportunity of meeting your wife."

Krasnya laughed. "She is good wife, you think? You are right I show you photograph…" He fumbled in an old valise and brought out a pile of glossy press photographs; the kind that are pinned up outside the show. "See"—he pointed with a slim finger—"she is good, na?"

Mr. Smith examined a photograph of Krasnya crossing a slack wire on a bicycle, Faustine standing on his shoulders; in another, they crossed on a tandem, Faustine, balanced with her head upside-down on the seat, working the pedals with her hands, while Krasnya worked a front set of pedals, with no seat on his part of the cycle. A third photograph showed Krasnya alone on the wire; this time the means of locomotion was a scooter. Mr. Smith raised his eyebrows. "They're good," he said, "very good!"

Krasnya looked pleased. "I am not ashamed of them no," he said, "only I am sorry you do not see me when I am in America." He smiled lovingly at Faustine, "You do not mind that I tell, no?" She nodded and said something rapidly in Polish. Then she turned to the Inspector. "You excuse me, please, I must go out... I have to buy things." She smiled at him and, taking a coat from a crowded peg on the wall, she went out.

Krasnya was down on his knees, turning things out of the valise.

"Ah!" he said in triumph, "is here!" He passed the photographs to Mr. Smith. The first was a picture of Krasnya himself, crossing the wire by means of two wheels fixed on to his shoes; the second showed a girl standing on a wheel which she turned with both feet so that it revolved the wire; the third showed the same girl with Krasnya, but this time it was he who was crossing the wire, while she was balanced upside down on his head. Mr. Smith whistled expressively.

"Difficult!" he suggested.

Monsieur Benenberg rolled up his eyes. "Never I found anyone else could do it," he mourned. "Ah! Faustine, she had perfect balance. Beautiful, it was!" He closed his eyes comically.

"She was your first wife, wasn't she?" asked Mr. Smith.

Krasnya nodded. "My only. How I get divorce when I not able to find her? No—poor little Faustine, we are very happy, but we don't can get married, you see. Never mind, perhaps after ten years we can do something—I don't know." He dismissed the matter airily.

But Mr. Smith had one or two questions to ask.

"A strange coincidence that this young lady should be called Faustine," he remarked.

Krasnya smiled and shrugged. "I call her Faustine—the act it

has always been Faustine and Krasnya. I do not want to change it...
that is silly. So Manya does not mind to be call Faustine. Easy for
everyone, you see."

"Did your wife speak English?" he asked.

"Oh yes. Very well—not at all like me. She was very clever—very
intelligent. I think she married to me so to come to Paris... A few
weeks, and then—Kaput! I never see her again."

"Did you go to the police?"

Krasnya smiled pityingly. "What for? They laugh at me. 'So your
wife leaves you, Monsieur, and you come to us. Well—what you
think we can do, eh? Bring her back?'" He laughed sardonically. "No,
Mister Smitt, I do not go to police to make them a big joke. Faustine,
she found herself another man—very handsome, very rich."

"Did she have any admirers?" Mr. Smith asked.

"Oh yes... plenty. She not bother with them at all. No, Faustine
very clever... she know what she want. I think she got."

"What did she want?"

Krasnya stared. "I told you. Big house, rich mans, handsome, big
car... everything. I bet she got it, too."

"You've never seen her since?"

Krasnya shrugged. "At first I was sad... couldn't work. All the
time I walk in Champs-Élysées, in Grands Boulevardes to see her if
she come along." He spread his hands in a gesture of hopelessness.
"Never seen her... never once. Oh!" he paused, his eyebrows raised,
"once, in London, I think perhaps I see her in big car. But..." he
grinned, "better not look too close, I think."

"I'm sorry to bother you like this, Mister Benenberg," the
Inspector said apologetically. "Just one more question. Did she
have her passport, *carte d'identité*, you know?"

"A girl so clever as Faustine don't want passport," he said. "But
she have it, I suppose... I never think to look. I guess she have it."

"How long did you say she had been gone?"

Krasnya counted solemnly on his finger. "Ha! must be seven years. Is a long time!"

Mr. Smith agreed. A lot could happen in seven years, he said, and there was no doubt that one lost track of people very easily. "I doubt whether you'll ever see her again," he remarked casually, and was glad to notice that it seemed to mean very little to Krasnya. Mr. Smith said good-bye, and left the circus hurriedly. Even if he had been tempted to linger, the sawdust and the animal smell, the lights and the crowded dressing-room, the hurry and bustle were not conducive to intensive thinking. Mr. Smith had a lot of thinking to do.

II

It was not only Mr. Smith who was busy with his thoughts. Glen Hemingway had had far too much time on his hands, and his thoughts had been very far from pleasant. However nicely Buller had put it, the fact remained that he had been detained for questioning—and there were certain questions which he had not cared to answer. He left New Scotland Yard and wandered down on to the Embankment; now that Buller had asked him to remain in London for the next two or three days he felt completely at a loss. It was impossible to think of going back to his flat, and there was the question of his gear to be attended to. He had marched off the steamer quite forgetting his luggage—now, he supposed, he would have to rush around, finding out what had happened to it. It was too cold to sit down, and he drifted along by the river, watching the laden barges with unseeing eyes. His mind, busy first with one thing and then another, darted from the question of where he was to stay to the questions that Buller had put to him. Glen, who had always thought of himself as something of a Pukka Sahib found it extremely disconcerting to be asked to give information regarding friends and neighbours. As far as he himself was concerned, that was another matter. His own private reasons for leaving London could not possibly interest anyone, and he had been reluctant to explain why he was in such a hurry to get away. And the explanation he had given had not sounded in the least convincing. He had stolen a glance at Mr. Smith, who had been studiously avoiding his eye, and he was uneasily aware that the Inspector did not look as if he believed him. It occurred to him that perhaps, after all, Superintendent Buller was trying to trap him; perhaps, even now, he was being followed. He turned sharply on his heel and stared at the people walking behind him; a messenger boy sauntering along, a woman in a black hat and a dingy green coat, carrying a paper hold-all, two nurses in uniform, a man in a morning coat and striped trousers, no—none of those could be following him. Glen retraced his steps in the direction of Whitehall. He would check up on his luggage, get some food, and take a room at the nearest hotel. He had promised to let Buller know where he was staying. Outside Lyons he stopped and bought a paper. The sight of his own face grinning at him from the centre of the page startled him considerably. "Big Game Hunter leaves Channel Steamer at Last Moment," he read. For a moment he stood still, furious at the unwanted publicity. Then he grinned; after all, what the hell? He walked on up Whitehall, immersed in reading his own adventures.

III

Both Katherine and Doctor Harley had been astonished to read how Glen had been taken off the Channel Steamer. The newspapers, knowing very little of what had actually occurred, had allowed their imagination to run riot, and the result was a hotchpotch of non-sense. But to Katherine and Bill, trying vainly to read between the lines, there was a sinister implication behind this. The little doctor admitted freely that he didn't know what it was all about.

"You see," he said, "I am no psychologist, that is, in the true sense of the word, but I would say that Glen was far from being the type to get mixed up with the police."

"I hope to heaven it's nothing to do with poor Gallia," Katherine said. "I know they had a few words—he was annoyed with her over something she said. I don't know how serious it was."

"But even so——" Bill said, "where do the police come in. Surely they can't possibly imagine that he had anything to do with the murder? It's too ridiculous!"

Katherine crumpled the papers and threw them in a bunch to the other side of the room.

"Poor Glen!" she said. "Of course there's some idiotic mistake! He must be going through hell!"

"None of the papers say that he was arrested," Bill reminded her.

"Well, what does it matter? Detained for questioning or whatever it is—it's all the same. I wish there was something I could do about it." She stood up and walked about the room purposefully. "I must try to think, Bill."

Bill Harley fingered a pencil and tapped it on the window sill. "I wish you wouldn't get all mixed up in this, Kate," he said. "I really don't like it at all… do chuck it up, there's a dear."

Katherine raised her eyebrows. "Do you mean you want me to throw up my job?" she inquired calmly.

Bill looked quickly at her and then looked away. "No," he said slowly, "I don't mean that… only—I think it's rather foolish of you to get mixed up in all this business—these deaths and murders and what not."

"I'm glad," she said sarcastically, "that you don't want me to throw the job up. Of course, I'll go to H.B. and ask him to put me on to something else... I'll tell him you don't like me ferreting into murder cases."

Doctor Harley chuckled. "Touché!" he said quietly.

Katherine giggled. "Oh well," she said, "that sort of talk gets under my skin, Bill. Of course I can't give it up... what are you frightened of, anyway?"

"I don't know," he said, "it's something I can't put a name to. I just feel there's something going on that we don't know about—and there's someone ready to commit murder to get what they want. Frankly, Kate, I'd prefer you not to get in their way... they probably wouldn't stop at anything at all." His tone was serious and his eyes grave. Katherine could not help feeling touched by the little man's anxiety on her behalf.

"I don't want to get myself in any trouble," she said, "and I do think you're sweet, Bill, to bother about me."

"You're a nice kid," he told her, "and I can say this. I'm older than you are. But to go back—if only one could see the connecting link between these murders... but I can't fathom it."

"If it really begins with Dimpsie," Katherine said, "it's even odder. I can't think of anyone who could benefit by his death... or Gallia's or Holly's for that matter. Unless—" she paused, biting her lip.

"Unless—?" he prompted.

"I was only thinking—unless they knew something. But then—that doesn't get us any further. Oh, Bill," she turned impulsively to the man beside her, "what do *you* think?"

"I think I'd like to get you out of all this," Bill said, "Kate—this isn't the time I would have chosen, but... look here, you know how I feel about you, don't you?" He looked seriously at her, and took her hands in both of his. "Kate, I know I'm an ugly little man, and

I'm older than you—years older—but I do love you. Do you think you could love me a little?"

Katherine's eyes filled with tears. "You're a funny little man," she said tremulously, "but I do love you, strangely enough. I can't think why…"

"In that case," he said firmly, "we're going to be married. And you're going to give up that job. Agreed?"

"Yes, sir," she said meekly. "Anything you say."

Taking her in his arms he kissed her rapturously. "I feel ten years younger," he said. "Oh, Kate! how long I've wanted to do that!"

She giggled. "How long I've wanted you to!"

"Really?" he said, kissing her again. "You concealed your feelings very effectively. I was terrified of you."

"I can see that," she said. "Oh, Bill… I'm so happy!"

And so the two lovers, absorbed in their own affairs, were content to shelve temporarily the question of the murders, and of Glen Hemingway.

IV

If Frederica was horrified to read about Glen in the evening papers she did not show it, nor did she mention the matter to her husband. Her time was fully taken up by rehearsals; choosing and fitting the dresses and having photographs taken. Now that she had achieved her ambition—a part in a McCabe play—she seemed determined to refute the critics who had, so she thought, ruined her chances both with Henry and Dimpsie. Her appearance in the theatre had not surprised the cast inordinately.

"My dear," a young man was heard to say to a friend, "our Freddie was ready to commit murder to get into this. I couldn't be less surprised."

His friend raised expressive eyebrows. "Better not let anyone hear you making remarks like that," he warned, "particularly under the circumstances…"

"I wasn't being serious, hang it all," the young man said.

"Well—there's such a thing as libel, you know."

"Who's talking about libel?" one of the young women, a pert creature in navy slacks and a tweed jacket, put an arm round the two young men.

"No one. I merely remarked that our Freddie had made up her mind to get into the show—by hook or by crook."

The young woman giggled. "I'm not buying," she said. "See you later, chaps." She sauntered off, the jacket hanging from her shoulders, a cigarette stuck between her lips.

Although Holly had shared a dressing-room with Mary Webb, Frederica had insisted on a room to herself. It would hardly do, she pointed out, for the producer's wife to share dressing-room with a minor member of the cast—most unsuitable. Henry was glad enough to agree with her; he liked to be able to drop into the dressing-room occasionally for a chat and a cup of tea; with other people there he would be unable to relax, or to speak his mind, should he so desire. He came along there on this particular afternoon at the end of the rehearsal; the play was going well, and he felt relaxed and at ease. Frederica, who had left the stage the instant the rehearsal was over, indicated Detective-Inspector Smith who, hat in hand, sat gingerly on the edge of a Victorian armchair.

"Did you wish to see me?" Henry asked.

The Inspector stood up. "Actually it was Mrs. Brown that I came to see," he said gently. "It's just a small matter." He turned to Frederica. "I wonder if you could remember what you were doing on the afternoon of January the fifth?"

Frederica stared at him. "January the fifth? I've no idea, I'm afraid." She undid the sports jacket she was wearing and threw it over the back of a chair. "I don't want the brown tweed," she said to the dresser, "you'd better send it to the cleaners. I'll wear the blue crepe."

Henry stood uncertainly in the centre of the tiny room. Taking his cigarette-case from his pocket he passed it to Mr. Smith, who shook his head. Henry took one himself and lit it; then he sat down on a chair opposite the Inspector.

"January the fifth," he repeated. "Why the fifth, specially?"

"It was the day on which Madame Karmanskaya was found murdered," said Mr. Smith deprecatingly.

"You're not suggesting that my wife had anything to do with that…?" Henry stood up, brandishing his cigarette angrily.

"I'm not suggesting anything at all," said Mr. Smith mildly. "I would just like to know if Mrs. Brown can remember what she was doing on that day. We have to check up on these things." His tone was apologetic.

"Well, I can't possibly tell you off-hand," Frederica said casually. "But I can look in my engagement book… I dare say I shall have put it down. Perhaps you'll call in to-morrow?"

"You haven't your engagement book handy?" asked Mr. Smith persuasively. "Or perhaps we could go and find it? It's so much easier to get these little matters cleared up right away, isn't it?"

"Look here," Henry said, "I can't see what my wife can have to do with any of this. Can't you leave her alone! She's had a very tiring day, and now you come round here, pestering and nosing into matters which don't concern you at all. *Do* go away!"

"Henry!" Frederica was profoundly shocked. "Mr. Smith is only doing his duty. He has to ask questions—you know that. That's what policemen are for, isn't it, Mr. Smith?" she flashed a dazzling smile.

"Well, not entirely, ma'am," said Mr. Smith. "I assure you I don't want to pry in the least. I'm sure Mr. Brown knows that, really."

"I suppose I do," agreed Henry wearily, "but really I'm so tired of it all. Ever since we went up to Possett Island there's been trouble. It isn't your fault, Inspector, but I can assure you that neither my wife nor I have anything to do with this dreadful business. Frederica, can't you try and remember what you were doing on that day?"

"I believe," she answered slowly, "that I was at the hairdresser... I can't say for certain till I look in my engagement book. You'd better come back to the flat, Inspector, and I'll look it up for you."

"You won't want me, will you, Inspector?" Henry asked. "I have a thousand things to see to... Freddie, be sure to give the Inspector a cocktail—I shall try and be along later."

Sitting in the Browns' luxurious lounge a cocktail untasted on a table at his side, Mr. Smith waited for Frederica to find her engagement book. A large tabby cat, its brilliant yellow eyes bisected by narrow black slits, jumped heavily off a chair by the window and came and rubbed itself against his leg. Mr. Smith liked cats. He put his hand down and the animal rolled obligingly on to its back, displaying a stomach covered in curly, cream-coloured silk. Mr. Smith tickled the cat and it purred happily, stretching out first one paw and then another covered in long, black velvet gloves.

"Nice pussy," said the Inspector. "Pretty pussy, then!"

Engrossed in the cat he did not see Frederica enter the room; but as soon as she approached the cat jumped to its feet, arching its back and spitting angrily.

"What's the matter, pussy?" inquired Mr. Smith. "Nice pussy!"

But the cat, after spitting in Frederica's direction, ran to the door and vanished. Mr. Smith looked at Frederica and raised his eyebrows.

"What's the matter with the cat?"

Frederica shrugged. "Heaven knows!" she said indifferently. "We've only had it a day or two. It's been sent down from Scotland. Probably it doesn't care for London!" She had changed her dress for a housecoat of silver brocade, fastened at the waist by a jewelled band. Her hair was combed out on her shoulders and around her was a subtle perfume that caused Mr. Smith to sniff the air surreptitiously. She held out a book bound in red morocco.

"Here it is," she said. "There isn't any entry for the morning. Probably I had a massage and lunch at home. We can check that with the masseur... In the afternoon I went to Phillippe's, for my hair, you know—and then..." She came and drew up a chair so that she was facing the Inspector. "As a matter of fact, I didn't really want to mention this in front of my husband. Not that there was anything wrong, you understand, only sometimes Henry is so jealous... I went to tea with an old friend of ours... Mr. Glen Hemingway, the big-game hunter."

"I see," said Mr. Smith, "and you just didn't trouble to tell your husband?"

"Well," Frederica smiled deprecatingly, "one doesn't always want to make a discussion of every little thing... I am sure you understand, Inspector. I'm devoted to my husband, I wouldn't do a thing to hurt him..."

Except deceive him, thought Mr. Smith to himself. Aloud, he said: "You have heard that Mr. Hemingway has been arrested?"

Frederica raised her eyebrows. "Really?" she said.

Mr. Smith was not quite sure whether she had intended that to be an answer to his question. "I expect he will be released," he said, "there is no evidence against him... now."

Frederica stood up. "I'm so glad," she said. "I haven't seen him for some time. I think he was disappointed—" She broke off suddenly and ran to the door. "Why—there's Henry!"

Mr. Smith waited. There was no sound in the hall and presently Frederica came back. "There was no one there," she said. "I must have been imagining things."

"You were saying…" Mr. Smith prompted.

"Oh—about Mr. Hemingway… I think perhaps he was getting a little too fond of me." She looked down modestly. "That is why I haven't seen him lately."

Mr. Smith stood up. "I mustn't keep you," he said. "Thank you so much, Mrs. Brown, you have been most helpful."

"Oh, but you haven't drunk your cocktail," Frederica exclaimed.

The Inspector smiled, but his eyes were melancholy. "I never drink when I'm on duty," he said quietly.

16

GRIM VISITOR

I

HENRY WALTERS LOOKED ROUND THE DISMANTLED APART-
ment; now that he was actually leaving, and everything was
packed up, he could not find it in his heart to be sorry. For the last
time he went through the rooms methodically, making sure that
everything was packed, and that nothing remained of either his
belongings or Dimpsie's. The actual packing had not been so difficult as he had feared; Dimpsie had left minute instructions as to
what was to be done with his things in the event of his death, and
Walters had written innumerable letters and posted endless parcels
until at last everything had been attended to. For himself, he felt he
deserved a holiday; the hot anger that had consumed him during
the few days when he had tried to make Archie Tittop believe in his
collaboration had died down, and now he felt mentally and physi-
cally exhausted. A friend had offered the loan of a tiny cottage in
the wilds of Cornwall, and Walters had accepted gratefully. He
would dig himself in and start work on the biography of Dimpsie,
commissioned by the publishers with whom Dimpsie had published
for the past ten years. He had collected a vast amount of material;
photographs, old scripts and MSS; letters, documents and ancient
diaries; data which would be useless to anybody else but which

would be of untold value to him. And at least, he thought thankfully, Dimpsie had been an extrovert if ever there was one. There was no hidden side to his character; he had always been only too eager to talk about himself and this verbosity had had no sinister meaning that Walters could find; Dimpsie had not felt the need to discuss himself in one aspect only that he might hide another side of his character. He had been what he had never attempted to hide; a thoroughly selfish individual, tempestuous and greedy; and at the same time a mixture of kindliness and generosity, thoughtfulness and sweetness, and downright bad-temper flavoured with malice. It was impossible to assess his character without, Walters thought, making a balance sheet of the good and bad facets. There was no doubt that as an employer he had been easy to work for; for ten years their lives had run smoothly together. Walters was happy enough to be with such a celebrity, and when he said that he wrote a good deal of Dimpsie's work he was not as far from the truth as Archie Tittop imagined. Dimpsie, for all his brilliance, was a careless and shoddy workman; he would dictate his work and then correct; but the final corrections and polishings, the substitution for a well-worn phrase of another fresher and more apt, would be Walters' job, and one that he filled to perfection. He had a complete command of Dimpsie's idiom, and could turn out a neat paragraph that was a perfect copy of the master's work. Dimpsie himself had been deceived on more than one occasion, and had frequently complimented Walters on his writing. Tittop must have realized just how much Dimpsie relied on his secretary, and this made his denial of Walters' right to a collaboration fee even more galling. Of course, Walters knew that had Dimpsie been alive there would have been no question of his collaborating, but now that he was no longer there to insist on every jealously-guarded penny surely his secretary was entitled to some compensation for all the work he had done on the play. That was how Walters himself figured it—and if it wasn't for Archie Tittop, he thought, he would be getting his just dues. Angrily he cleared the last few papers out of the desk drawers and shoved them into a suit-case, snapping the locks and banging the case on to the floor. At least, he consoled himself, he had the note-books, and no one, not even Archie Tittop, knew of their existence. After the biography he would have work to last him for years. The thought cheered him, and he began to calm down, and to consider paying a farewell call on Tittop before leaving for Cornwall. It might be amusing to see how he would react to the idea that perhaps, somewhere hidden away in Possett Castle, he might find Dimpsie's private journals and diaries; not for worlds would Walters tell him that *he* had been commissioned to do the biography—that should come as a surprise. Possibly even as a shock. Walters chuckled wickedly... yes, there were some surprises in store for *some* people.

Two by two he carried the suit-cases out into the hall; the trunks would be fetched later, and as for the furniture, that was nothing to do with him. Most of it was left to be divided between Katherine and Jeffery, he believed, and they would just have to fight it out between themselves. A pity about Jeffery—Walters curled his lip contemptuously—a young man who would not stand up for a friend! Done him out of £100, Jeffery had. He was still engaged in carrying out the suit-cases when a taxi drew up in front of the house. Watching from the window Walters saw an elegant figure descend and run up the steps. Hurrying out into the hall he smiled broadly.

"Well, this *is* nice! Won't you come in?"

II

Mr. Smith sat at the desk in his hotel bedroom and spread out his notes happily. Now that he began to see the case in black and white it looked as if some very interesting data were likely to be forthcoming. He had said to Superintendent Buller before leaving for Paris that it would be forty-eight hours well spent. Buller had chuckled; and had had no comment to make. Mr. Smith, assembling his notes and copying them into a little black book looked forward to surprising the Superintendent quite a lot. There was no doubt, he thought, that the trouble had begun up at Possett Island. Sitting back in his chair he lit his pipe and bit on it grimly; that corpse, hanging on the Christmas Tree... as if it could have been an accident! It seemed to Mr. Smith that the stage had been altogether too well set. The empty house extravagantly lit—everyone out in the woods—and the dead body of their host left for the two latecomers to find. No, decided the Inspector, it was all far too theatrical. He reconstructed the case to his own liking: first—McCabe had intended to spend the afternoon alone, that was obvious. But someone had returned to the house—someone who wished to see the playwright, and who did not wish to be disturbed. Most likely that had been Madame Karmanskaya; she would have made the excuse that she wished to fetch her little dog, and then, while everyone else was out of the way she would have had her chance to find McCabe alone in the studio. But then... what reason would she have had for wishing his death? On the contrary, she had everything to gain by his being alive.

Mr. Smith leapt from his chair and paced up and down the room: of course! for a moment he had almost forgotten the sodden moccasins on Dimpsie's feet. The moccasins that had actually been the cause of his death. Dimpson McCabe had gone out into the snow wearing his moccasins... Mr. Smith took a firm grip on his pipe. Somewhere in the back of his mind a faint memory was stirring. Something to do with Beatrix Potter... stories for children... he went through the titles mechanically: Peter Rabbit, Benjamin Bunny, The Tailor of Gloucester. That was it! Simkin—the cat from the Tailor of

Gloucester—the cat whose portrait Dimpsie's cat had so resembled. The cat who was now in the Browns' apartment.

Mr. Smith went back to his chair and began doodling on a piece of clean white paper. Now, if Dimpsie had seen his pet in any trouble, say if it had been chased by a dog, he would have run out into the snow without thinking. Ergo, someone had staged a little scene of cat being chased by dog, Dimpsie had run out into the snow, and someone had slipped quickly into the studio. It would take less than a minute to connect up the lights which Dimpsie would have been so careful to disconnect, and then, if there were not time to escape, it would have been easy to slip behind the velvet curtains and wait. Mr. Smith doodled vigorously; he could see it all: McCabe returning to the studio, his pet nestling in his arms, to be put down near the fire and made much of. Then back to the tree; he would have lifted the two ends of wire and brought them together to fuse them into one; there would have been a blinding flash—and he would have slumped forward on to the tree. Whoever lay hidden behind the curtain might wait a moment, fearful lest Dimpsie should not be dead but only stunned, and then at last they would creep out… And in the woods, where everyone was engaged in hide-and-seek, they would probably not have been missed. Mr. Smith crumpled the piece of paper now covered with extraordinary signs and portents and returned to his notes.

It was something, he decided, to have got so far. There was the question of Krasnya, and his relationship to Gallia; curious that the brother and sister should have drifted so far apart, but not altogether so improbable as one might think. Krasnya had not really *liked* Dimpsie, he had found him too inquisitive, too interfering. Dimpsie had managed, in some way, to put the little man's back up. But Krasnya had nothing to gain by Dimpsie's death. Indeed, it was difficult to find anyone who benefited more by the playwright's death than by his being alive. Jeffery Gibson came in for a legacy, it was true, but no doubt he would have been happier to know that McCabe was alive and well, there was no reason to suppose that he had not been devoted to his benefactor. The same applied to Katherine Mickey; she gained nothing by McCabe's death; she lost an old and valued friend. Doctor Harley, too, was above suspicion. Certainly he could not hope to gain by losing one of his patients. There remained the Browns, Henry Walters and Archie Tittop, and of these the Agent must be ruled out. It would have been impossible for him to have arrived without the servants being aware of the fact. For a moment Mr. Smith considered the servants—but why should Benson have a grudge against a master who paid him as well as Dimpson had.

The Inspector relit his pipe and went over his notes. Whoever killed Dimpsie also killed Gallia Karmanskaya and Holly Temple; of that much he was certain. He held the match in his fingers, thinking hard, until the flame singed his skin, and he dropped it ruefully. Glen Hemingway... there was nothing really against him except his knowledge of electricity, and almost anyone might know more about things than they cared to say. Glen had been in love with Frederica Brown, she had admitted that much herself, and possibly Dimpsie had found out about this... well, but then why kill Gallia and Holly? What had they got to do with it? Not for the first time Mr. Smith found his tangled threads leading him back to Krasnya Benenberg. Whoever was responsible for these three murders had been someone with nerves of iron; someone who could go about their daily round not showing a sign of what must be passing through their mind, someone... An idea occurred to Mr. Smith—an idea so far-fetched and yet so highly probable that for a moment he was incredulous. But then he reminded himself that murderers are not really ordinary people, even though on the surface they may occasionally appear to be so. Your real murderer will stop at nothing to gain his own ends. If you can find someone who is prepared to go to any lengths to obtain what is necessary for his own personal being—there goes your murderer.

A smile of satisfaction playing on his lips, Mr. Smith lit yet another pipe, slipped his notes into his pocket and hurried down to New Scotland Yard.

III

Archie Tittop was a little uneasy. It had occurred to him that perhaps he had been just a little hard on Henry Walters. It is only fair to admit that this kindly and generous idea had not emanated from Archie himself; it had been suggested by the results of a telephone conversation with McCabe's publisher. Mr. Gross had remarked nonchalantly that he looked forward to publishing a biography of the playwright during the coming year. Archie had risen to the bait like a hungry fish.

"Who do you suggest should write it?" he began. "We shall have to be very careful about this…"

But Mr. Gross broke in quickly. "Oh, that's all fixed. We couldn't get anyone better than Henry."

"Henry?" Archie said, bewildered. "But he doesn't know anything about McCabe as a person. Because he's produced several of the plays that gives him no reason to suppose… why, he didn't know Dimpsie as well as I did, for instance."

"I don't mean Henry Brown," Mr. Gross said. "I was talking of Henry Walters. We couldn't get anyone better. McCabe's confidential secretary for the past ten years… there isn't anything about McCabe that he doesn't know." Mr. Gross rambled on, but Archie was no longer listening. Several rather unpleasant little thoughts

were obtruding themselves into his consciousness. It looked as if
he had been a little hasty in his treatment of Mr. Walters. He got
rid of the tiresome Mr. Gross somehow, and replaced the receiver.
He would have to think.

Pouring himself a glass of water he drank it slowly, remembering
the last time he had seen the secretary. Of course, there could not be
any question about the collaboration; he would stake his professional
integrity on Dimpsie's honesty, and it would be impossible for him
to accept Walters' assertions without overwhelming proof. No, there
would have to be some other way in which he could gloss over the
harsh way he had spoken; he must retract his words to some extent
at least. He imagined Walters writing Dimpsie's biography; it would
be impossible for him to avoid mentioning the Agent's name; Archie
shuddered in anticipation at the possibilities that might occur to a
disgruntled secretary. There was no doubt that he would take the
opportunity to get back at anyone who had annoyed him. Archie
filled his glass again and sipped the water. Of course, it had really
been a mistake to insist on the fact that Dimpsie had sacked his
secretary before his death. The amount involved was small enough,
considering the vast estates the playwright had left, and the money
would no doubt have been a godsend to Walters. Probably Dimpsie
had quarrelled with him a dozen times before; there was no reason to
suppose that they would not have been friends before Christmas was
over. No doubt Walters had been under sentence of death a dozen
times—only to be reprieved at the last minute. It was a pity, Archie
thought, that he had not been told sooner of Mr. Gross' decision.
Well, it was not too late to try and put things right with Walters.

He took up the phone again and dialled Walters' number. He
could hear the ringing tone... ringing, ringing. For a moment he
was tempted to hang up; then someone answered. "Wait a minute,"
the voice said, "I shan't be a minute." Archie could hear two voices

talking; it was impossible to hear what they said, but all at once he heard "Good-bye" quite clearly, and then a strange sound… almost like a muffled shot. It seemed to come from quite near to the telephone. Archie listened, but everything was quiet now. "Hullo!" he said loudly. "Walters, are you there?"

But there was no answer, and then there was a thumping sound, as if someone had dropped something the other end. Archie looked at the receiver doubtfully; he replaced it; and then dialled the operator. But in reply to his query she replied that the line was out of order, and that she would report it to the engineer.

Archie looked at his watch. It was five o'clock. There would be time to hop a taxi to Walters' flat—possibly they could get something settled if they talked things over quietly. Not even to himself would Archie admit his uneasiness concerning what he had overheard on the telephone. In less than ten minutes he was at the flat. He found the front door open and Mr. and Mrs. Smithers anxiously waiting in the hall.

"Oh, sir!" Smithers came forward to meet him. "We're just waiting for the police—there's been a dreadful accident."

Archie followed him into the flat. Walters, the telephone grasped in his right hand, lay sprawled on the floor by the side of the big armchair. He lay face downwards, his head resting on the kerb in front of the fire. From somewhere underneath him came a slow, thick trickle of blood. He was quite dead.

Archie stepped back quickly, and almost fell over Mrs. Smithers, who had followed him in. She had a handkerchief clenched tightly in her hand, and her face was screwed up in an expression of horror.

"What happened?" Archie said. "I was just on the phone to him… and I thought I heard something—that's why I came round. How long has he been like this? Have you sent for the police?" He showered questions on them without waiting for an answer.

Smithers stood at the window looking down the road, and it was Mrs. Smithers who finally spoke.

"I was having a bit of a rest," she explained, "and Smithers was busy downstairs with me, cleaning a bit of silver, he was. We heard a taxi draw up and someone get out... but the bell didn't ring and we never paid no attention. There's always someone popping in and out, you know, and if we had to come upstairs every time we heard the door go we'd never be doing anything else. Of course, I don't know whether it was someone to see Mr. Walters or not—I never saw who it was..."

Smithers looked round angrily. "Now, we don't want to be mixed up in anything," he said, "we've always kept the house respectable, sir, and you understand it's our living we got to think of. We didn't see nothing, Ma, and we didn't hear nothing, neither, so you've no call to be telling Mr. Tittop a long story. Least said soonest mended's *my* motto. You'll excuse her, I'm sure, sir," he said to Archie, "but she's excited—and who would wonder at it!" He turned round to the window again. "Ah, there they are!" he said, with relief. "Taken long enough about it, too."

Archie went out into the hall to meet the Detective-Sergeant, who was accompanied by a constable and the doctor. He introduced himself and followed them back to the flat. Both the Smithers watched while the doctor made his examination; they replied to the sergeant's questions readily enough, but neither of them volunteered the slightest information. As soon as they had retired below stairs, and the constable had telephoned for the photographers, Archie had a few words with the sergeant.

"Could it be suicide?" he asked.

The sergeant and the doctor conferred together for a moment.

"I oughtn't to give you any information, sir," the sergeant said, "but seeing as you were a friend of the gentleman's—well, no, it couldn't have been suicide. You see, he's got hold of the phone in his right hand, and he's been shot right through the heart at a very close range. Whoever did it was able to come right up close to him, and he can't have known they had a gun... must have concealed it in some way..." The sergeant rubbed his chin thoughtfully. "Someone just went right up to him and shot him—and he didn't even back away."

"How do you know?" asked Archie curiously.

"He'd have knocked the table over," the sergeant said. "It would have been right behind him. Gosh! he must have been surprised—if he lived that long."

"There's a Mr. Smith, Detective-Inspector, I think he is, came to see me the other day... he's down from Scotland and he probably came to see Mr. Walters recently. I think perhaps it might be a good thing to get in touch with him." Archie put the suggestion diffidently and the sergeant looked surprised.

"Do you know where to find him, sir?" he asked.

Archie shook his head. "We could try New Scotland Yard."

The arrival of the photographers and the men from the mortuary broke in on them, and Archie wandered back into the hall, wondering what he ought to do. At last he tiptoed to the back of the hall where a door opened on to a dim flight of stairs leading down to the basement. He could hear Mr. and Mrs. Smithers talking in their sitting-room, and he ran down the stairs and peeped round the open door of their private room.

"May I come in?" he asked.

Mr. and Mrs. Smithers were seated one each side of the fire; between them, on a low table covered with a white cloth, were tea-things and a plate of bread and butter. But neither of the Smithers was eating; Mrs. Smithers had her handkerchief up to her eyes, and Smithers was about to light his pipe. He looked up as Archie put his head round the door and nodded briefly. Archie came in and left the door open; it would be as well to keep an ear open for what was taking place upstairs.

Mrs. Smithers got up and brought a chair over to the fire. "Won't you have a cup of tea, sir?" she said. "It's quite fresh—I've just made it." She went out of the room and returned with a cup and saucer. Wiping her eyes, she sat down again and poured Archie a cup of tea.

"It seems just as if we're fated, sir," she said as she passed the cup to him. "First poor Mr. McCabe... and a nicer gentleman I never did know... I said to Smithers if only all our people were like Mr. McCabe, we'd never have no trouble at all. But there—" She sighed, and wiped another tear away. "Mr. Walters was a nice gentleman, I'm sure. Never gave no trouble, and enjoyed his meals... Of course, it's made a lot of work, going all through them papers an' all, but what can you expect? It's got to be done, hasn't it, sir? I said to Smithers, we've been lucky, really. Two houses full of people, and they're all gentlefolk, if you get my meaning. Of course Mr. McCabe was our most *distinguished* tenant... beautiful parties he gave, too." She shook her head reminiscently.

Archie sipped his tea. "I noticed a lot of luggage piled up in the hall," he said. "Whose was that?"

"Why, Mr. Walters was leaving," Mrs. Smithers said. "Didn't you know, sir? He was giving up the flat. As a matter of fact we haven't let it yet. He didn't want people seeing over it until he moved out... and then there are all Mr. McCabe's things—his furniture and his beds and all."

"As a matter of fact," Archie said, "I rather thought the whole of this basement belonged to Mr. McCabe's flat. I don't quite see how it works down here."

Smithers took his pipe out of his mouth. "We've only got this room," he explained. "Mr. McCabe's staircase is inside his own flat—this room faces on to the street, sir, as you can see. Mr. McCabe had the garden rooms, and they're shut off from this part of the house."

"I see…" Archie was thoughtful. "But you can see anyone driving up to the front door from here," he observed; they've got to cross the pavement to get to the steps… Yes, I can see from here quite easily."

"We don't get much time for sitting down, sir," Smithers said smoothly. "There's a lot to do with two houses to run—and when I get my lumbago Mary has to manage it all on her own."

"It must be very hard work," Archie said sympathetically. "I think you said you were cooking for Mr. Walters? How was that?"

"I often did," Mrs. Smithers explained. "I don't cook for many of the tenants, of course, it wouldn't do, but Mr. McCabe was rather privileged, you understand, and I was glad to do for him. And for Mr. Walters too."

"I suppose Walters didn't do much entertaining while he was here," Archie said.

"Oh, he'd people in now and then," Mrs. Smithers said. She was beginning to cheer up a little, and she had put away the handkerchief. "He liked to have a friend in sometimes… he was ever so sorry that young Mr. Gibson wouldn't come and stay with him… it would have been company for him, I thought."

Archie raised his eyebrows. "I didn't know Mr. Walters had asked Mr. Gibson to stay?" he said. "Mr. Gibson never mentioned it to me."

"You talk too much, Mary," said Mr. Smithers. Mrs. Smithers flushed; she twisted her hands in her lap and Archie, observing her, felt distinctly uncomfortable. He replaced his now empty cup on the table and stood up.

"Well, thanks very much for the tea," he said. "I think I'll just trot upstairs and see what's going on." He retreated to the door. "Thanks awfully," he said again, and edged himself out of the room. Once upstairs he heaved a sigh of relief. Sticky, that's what they were, he told himself!

Outside the flat he paused; obviously it was better not to try to go inside. There were policemen everywhere; taking measurements, finger-prints, photographs and going through the drawers and desks that had been so thoroughly emptied by Walters. Archie stood in the doorway and made a sign to the sergeant.

"I shall be at home if you want me," he said, giving his address. "By the way, have you been able to get in touch with Inspector Smith?"

The sergeant smiled. "I've mentioned the matter at headquarters, sir," he said, "and there are some questions I should like to ask you. If you wouldn't mind waiting just a few minutes I'll be disengaged directly." He went back into the flat and Archie wandered to the front door. There was a policeman stationed discreetly in the little alcove where Dimpsie had hung his overcoats. On the other side of the door lay something shiny; it was hardly noticeable on the marble tessellated floor, but Archie, bored to tears, had attempted to while away the time by counting the squares in the conventional design. The metal object was on the fourth square from the door and the third away from the wall. Archie bent down and picked it up—one glance was sufficient and he shoved it hastily into his pocket. The policeman was intent on writing in his note-book and never looked up. Typical, Archie thought, writing away, while clues were lying about under his very nose. He giggled, and the policeman looked up. Archie turned the giggle into a cough; then he sat down on the hall seat to await the sergeant.

IV

Jeffery Gibson pushed his books together, closed the inkwell and finished work for the day. It was curious, he thought, that Henry had never replied to his letter, but perhaps it was just as well. There was really no basis for friendship between them, now, and it was far better to face up to the facts. All the same, he would have liked to have said good-bye to the old boy before he went off into the wilds. Walters might have realized, Jeffery reflected, that now he was back at the university he had very little time to himself. He fished the secretary's letter out of a drawer and read it again. It was impossible to take Walters seriously, he thought, he was getting a terrific sense of his own importance.

"My dear boy," (he read)

"I have, of course, long since forgiven you for your extremely inconsiderate behaviour. This letter is to tell you that I am about to leave London for Cornwall, where I am going to write a biography of our much loved Dimpsie. I suggest we bury the hatchet in the best way possible—by having a party. What about doing a show, a little supper and then back here to finish off? Of course, if this means that you will be too late back at the university, I should be delighted to put you up here.

"Let me know, dear boy, what show you would prefer to see.
"DEVOTEDLY,
"HENRY."

Jeffery folded the letter and put it back in the drawer. Well, he had written the nicest letter he could—firmly declining the invitation, but suggesting tea the following afternoon. This afternoon, in fact. But Walters had not troubled to answer his letter, and Jeffery, in spite of feeling sorry, was conscious of a great feeling of relief. He didn't want to offend Walters—but if he had done so, well, it was probably for the best.

Jeffery stacked his books together in a neat pile and pushed his chair back from the desk. He took off his coat, washed his hands, and brushed his hair. Then he replaced his coat and prepared to go out. A light tap on the door surprised him; he was not expecting anyone at this hour.

"Come in," he called, tidying away his washing things.

"May I?" A tall, melancholy gentleman stood in the doorway, his hat in his hand. There was something vaguely familiar about him, Jeffery thought.

"My name is Smith," the gentleman said. "Detective-Inspector— we met at Possett Island. You may remember?"

"I do," said Jeffery. "Did you want to see me?"

"That was the idea," said Mr. Smith. "I'm afraid I've interrupted you... you were going out?"

"Only to get some food," Jeffery said. "It can wait. What did you want to see me about?"

"Mmn..." the Inspector pursed his lips. "One thing and another... Tell me—how are you getting on?"

"Much as usual," Jeffery said. "I shan't sit for my degree until the end of next year, you know. There's a lot of work to be done before then."

"Yes—of course... And you don't get much chance to go out and about, I imagine?"

"Well, not very much," Jeffery answered.

"Mr. McCabe left you well provided for, I take it?" asked Mr. Smith.

"Yes." Jeffery was beginning to wonder what the Inspector was driving at.

"So of course you feel obliged to work very hard—stick at it, and all that sort of thing."

"I shan't get my degree unless I work for it," Jeffery said.

"But you were not working this afternoon?" the Inspector hazarded.

Jeffery grinned. "I certainly was."

Mr. Smith looked sad. "Really? But you promised to go to tea with Mr. Walters, didn't you?"

"I offered to go, if that's what you mean. But as it happens I was working. Mr. Walters never answered my letter."

"He didn't, didn't he? So you never went to see him, of course. No—you wouldn't... By the way, I suppose you have some kind of proof that you were working all the afternoon?"

"Proof... I don't know what you mean. Why should I want to prove I've been working? I should think my word is sufficient." Jeffery tried hard to keep a note of annoyance from his voice.

"You didn't attend any classes—lectures? Did anyone see you since lunch-time?"

Jeffery lost his temper. "I don't suppose they did. And I'd just like to know why you're asking me these ridiculous questions. I don't have to answer to you for what I do with my time."

"I'm afraid you do," said Mr. Smith sadly. "You see, Henry Walters was shot this afternoon—and a letter from you offering to go and see him was found on his writing-desk."

Jeffery sat down in the nearest chair. "Shot," he repeated. "Phew!" He looked up to find Mr. Smith watching him. "Please, sir, it wasn't me," he said. "Sorry to disappoint you and all that, but it really wasn't. If it'll be any help to you I'll show you the work I was doing... and I'm afraid that it's going to be my only alibi."

I 7

DEATH SCENE

THE DAY OF THE DRESS REHEARSAL FOUND HENRY BROWN exceedingly depressed. If only, he told himself for the thousandth time, he had been firm; if only he had remembered Dimpsie's words. And it was perhaps because he knew in his heart that he had broken faith with the dead playwright that he felt so utterly miserable. There was nothing that he could do. No amount of directing and producing could cover up the fact that Frederica was hopelessly unsuitable for the part, that she was very bad indeed. Where she should have been light and gay she was wooden and mechanical, and where the part called for understanding and sympathy she as ill-at-ease and jerky. How, thought Henry despondently, could I ever have thought she was any good? And he came to the reluctant but inevitable conclusion that he must have been very much in love to have imagined that Frederica could ever amount to anything more than a third-rate artist. Even her glamour did not seem to get across; she needed depth where she was unmistakably shallow; she reminded Henry of a cardboard cut-out.

In the stalls beside him sat Katherine and Doctor Harley. Their engagement had come as a great surprise to Henry, and he was delighted by the news. He had planned a party for them to-night, as the opening night would be taken up by the Press and theatrical friends. He had also invited Glen Hemingway and Jeffery Gibson, but Hemingway, for some reason, had declined the invitation. He was leaving for Paris almost immediately, he explained, otherwise he would have been delighted to accept. Jeffery, also, had refused, but for a different reason. Henry Walters' death had been a shock to him; and now, for some obscure reason, he felt that had he supported Walters in his claim to have collaborated in the play, Walters might yet have been alive. Somehow, Jeffery felt he just couldn't go and see it—when possibly old Walters really *had* written part of it. So he wrote a polite little thank-you note, and tried to put the whole thing out of his head.

Katherine and Bill were chatting in whispers; it was early afternoon and the rehearsal had not yet begun. The cast were still trying on dresses and suits, the stage-manager was wringing his hands over props which were not forthcoming, and the electricians were looping coils of wire all over the stage and getting in the way of the costumiers who were kneeling in prayerful attitudes, their mouths full of pins, taking in a pleat here and giving an inch there, according to Henry's directions. The appearance of Frederica in a tight black suit, crisp white shirt and large black hat created a diversion. She mannequin-minced across the stage, a large muff held up to her cheek, while she peered coyly down at her husband.

"How do you like this, darling?"

Henry raised his eyebrows. "What's it meant to be?" he inquired.

"My suit for the first Act," Frederica said. "Cute, isn't it?"

"Do you mean to tell me," Henry said, his voice rising, in spite of all his efforts to keep calm, "that this is what you have ordered for the first Act? You must be out of your mind!" He sank back into his seat, his hands to his head.

"The script calls for a plain black suit, a white shirt and a large black felt hat," Frederica said coolly. "This is exactly right, Henry."

"You're meant to look like a typist," Henry said bitingly. "You know as well as I do that no typist ever had a suit and a hat like that!"

Frederica's eyes narrowed. "I don't agree," she said. "Tonks always looks exceedingly chic."

"You're not meant to look like Miss Tonkins," Henry groaned. "You're meant to look like a plain little typist who's out of a job. Oh, my God!" he groaned again. "What the hell can I do now... it's too late!"

A little man in a light grey suit jumped down from the stage.

"We can alter the hat easy," he said, "the skirt too. The coat, she is not easy—but by to-morrow I make another, yes? No need to worry, Mr. Brown, Alicia will have it right for you—just the way you want it."

"I shall be a laughing stock," Henry whispered, "if she goes on like that!"

"You don't worry," said Alicia soothingly, "Alicia, he put it right. You will see." He climbed back on to the stage again and began talking earnestly to Frederica.

Henry, watching them, did not notice a tall, slim figure who slipped easily into the chair next to his.

Archie Tittop watched the stage amusedly for a moment and then spoke quietly.

"You know, Henry," he said, "you've broken your contract."

Henry started. "What are you—" He turned and saw Archie seated on his left. "What's this about a contract?" he said. "Am I to have no peace to-day?" he addressed the world at large piteously; but it was Archie who answered him.

"You know perfectly well," he said severely, "that Dimpsie flatly refused to allow Frederica to appear in any of his plays. Under the circumstances, you've broken your contract. I thought it kinder to warn you... we are old friends, after all."

Henry stood up and banged his stick on the floor. "We'll start with the first Act," he ordered. "Freddie, you will wear the blouse and skirt—not the jacket." Then he sat down again. "Now," he said, turning to Archie, "what is it you want me to do?"

Archie smiled gently. "I don't want you to do anything, Henry," he said. "But you *must* understand that I owe a duty to my client. It was Dimpsie's express wish that Frederica should never appear in any play of his. He didn't think she was good enough, to put it quite frankly."

"You know very well the reason she's in this," Henry said grumpily. "I couldn't get anyone else… what was I to do?"

Archie shrugged. "It's your own funeral," he said. "I shall have to take steps…" He broke off to watch the stage. The curtain was lowered and they heard the furniture being pushed into position. The stage hands were busily carting chairs in front of the curtain, and the electricians were removing the coils of wire they had so liberally bestrewn about the stage. For a moment the curtain was raised—then it was hastily lowered again. The chief electrician walked down in front of the footlights.

"Do you want a spot on the lady at the desk, sir?" he asked.

Henry jumped. "Good God, no! What d'you think this is, a pantomime?" he screamed.

The chief electrician retreated hurriedly, and Henry retired grumbling into his seat.

The stage manager hurried down to the stalls.

"All right. Curtain up," he said, watch in hand.

The curtain rose on the first Act. Katherine, her hand in Bill's, settled comfortably in her chair. Please God, she thought, we get through this all right. Doctor Harley was not feeling quite so happy. A conversation he had had with Detective-Inspector Smith kept recurring to his mind and try as he might it was impossible for him to concentrate his attention on the stage. The Inspector had called to see him the day before; Doctor Harley had been busy and the policeman had had to wait some time. At last he had been shown into the doctor's consulting-room.

"I won't keep you long, Doctor," he had said, "but I just want to ask you one or two questions. You knew Miss Temple, did you not?"

Doctor Harley agreed. He had met Miss Temple at Possett Island.

"Did you know that Miss Temple had been found dead in her flat?"

"Yes. Miss Mickey, who found her, told me the story," Doctor Harley explained.

"Quite. Now, did you by any chance prescribe a sleeping-draught for Miss Temple?" the Inspector had asked.

"Definitely not," Doctor Harley said.

"Miss Temple died from an overdose of sulphonal. Apparently this was administered in powder form and mixed into some fish paste sandwiches. There were still three or four of these sandwiches uneaten on the table. I didn't suppose you had actually prescribed sulphonal for Miss Temple—but it occurred to me that you might have, at some time, prescribed it for another patient." Mr. Smith walked over to the window and gazed out on to the busy street.

Doctor Harley sat down at his desk and pulled his prescription book towards him. "One doesn't as a rule prescribe sulphonal in powder form," he said quietly. "I seem to remember a patient lately who told me she could not swallow a pill. I'm afraid it was I who suggested the powder—but actually, that could have nothing to do with Miss Temple." He could hear his own voice, quavering and uncertain. He coughed, and tried to speak more definitely. "I always keep a record of this type of prescription, besides the record of my patients." He turned the pages slowly... yes, there it was. 2 doz. Pwd. Sulphonal. 5 grns.

"Found it?" Mr. Smith was at his elbow.

Doctor Harley held the page open and pointed a finger at the entry.

"Two dozen powders… isn't that rather a lot?"

"Not normally," Doctor Harley said. "If she had bought it by the bottle there would have been thirty tablets… there's nothing much in it, really."

"It never struck you as peculiar that she should have asked for the dose in powder form?" Mr. Smith's voice was noncommittal, but Doctor Harley was not deceived.

"No." He shook his head. "You see, Inspector, a great many of my patients lead completely artificial lives. If a perfectly healthy woman comes to me for a sleeping draught when all she needs is a good brisk walk, how can I be astonished if she cannot exert herself sufficiently to swallow a pill? If these people were to lead normal, healthy lives they wouldn't need me, Inspector."

"I get you." Mr. Smith walked back to the window. "Doctor, did you examine the patient at all?"

"I gave her the routine examination. She told me she couldn't sleep—and it struck me that sulphonal would be the least harmful drug because of its non-tolerant qualities."

"I'm sorry, Doctor," said Mr. Smith, "it was a shot in the dark. There are doctors all over England prescribing sulphonal—and I had to pick on you. I'm very much afraid it was your little powders that accounted for Miss Temple."

Doctor Harley shot to his feet. "No," he said firmly, "I really cannot allow you to say that. There is absolutely no proof at all…"

"Ah," said Mr. Smith gently, "but you see, there is."

It was natural enough that Doctor Harley could not forget this conversation, and in the circumstances it was natural that he did not mention the matter to Katherine. He sat there in the stalls, his attention ostensibly fixed on the stage, but his mind in a turmoil. How long would it be, he thought, before the inevitable happened? How long would he have to sit here—pretending to watch the stage, while every nerve in his body was tremblingly apprehensive of what was bound to be the outcome of that conversation. He felt a tug at his sleeve.

"Do wake up, darling," Katherine was saying. "That was the first Act. Tell Henry it was good, won't you?"

But fortunately before there was time for any chatting the curtain was up again for the second Act. Bill observed with interest that the scene was changed, and that now the stage was set as if for a garden-party. Painted wrought-iron furniture and a flight of white marble steps leading to a Victorian gazebo were an arresting setting. But Henry was not satisfied.

"Lights!" he yelled. "I want an ultramarine and an amber... and where's that moon, for God's sake."

"Sorry, sir," the chief electrician hurried out from the wings, "I've got that Act Two, Scene Two, sir."

"Well, it's wrong. Get it right, will you?" Henry's tone was a little milder.

"Have a cigarette?" Archie offered a handsome gold case.

"Thanks." Henry felt in his pocket for his lighter. "Got a light?"

Archie leant forward. In his hand was a tiny gold cube... the flame flickered—and went out.

"Where did you get that?" Henry said brusquely.

"Do you recognize it?" Archie smiled. "I thought you might do..." He handed it over. "I picked it up on the floor of Dimpsie's flat," he said, not quite truthfully.

"Oh?" Henry stared blankly at him and shoved it into his pocket.

"It doesn't work—wants a new flint or something. Frederica said she'd have it fixed for me."

"I thought there was something funny about it," murmured Archie cryptically; but Henry wasn't listening; all his attention was concentrated on the stage. Frederica, wearing a brilliant scarlet evening gown, its spreading tulle skirts occupying several square feet of the stage, was coming slowly down to the footlights. In the dull blue lighting, against the dead-white of the furniture and the marble steps, the scarlet dress struck a pungent note. Her hair very simply coiled on the nape of her neck shone silver, and her skin was milk-white.

Archie pursed his lips. "Too bad she can't act," he muttered to himself, quietly, so that Henry shouldn't quite hear what he said. But Henry was still concentrating on the stage; he never even noticed Inspector Smith who had come slowly down the aisle and now stood at the side of the row, waiting patiently for a chance to lean across Archie and speak to the producer. In the wings Archie could see two policemen, their sombre uniforms looking strangely out of place. I don't remember any policemen, Archie thought, and then he became aware of Mr. Smith. Now what is it? he thought wearily, and tapped Henry on the arm.

"I think someone wants you," he said quietly.

Henry got up and stepped over Archie's legs into the aisle. He moved back several paces with the Inspector and Archie could no longer hear what they were saying. He strained his ears and caught a phrase here and there:

"… impossible… irrefutable proof… extremely sorry… cannot allow…"

Without wishing to be malicious, Archie couldn't help giggling. Poor old Henry was for it, and no mistake.

Suddenly Henry stepped down to the front of the stalls and banged his stick on the floor. On the stage a dialogue between Frederica and a young man stopped immediately.

Henry cleared his throat. "Freddie," he said loudly and slowly, "Detective-Inspector Smith wishes to speak to you. Will you come down here, my dear?"

For a split second Frederica did not move; then, crossing the stage quickly she went off opposite the two constables and was lost to view. Henry and the Inspector waited patiently for a moment.

"Where is she?" the Inspector asked, after a moment.

"Freddie!" Henry called anxiously. "Hurry up!"

The chief electrician hurried out of the wings and down to the footlights. He shaded his eyes, looking for Henry.

"She's gone up into the flies, sir," he said.

Mr. Smith jumped on to the stage and looked up. "By God, so she has," he murmured. "Come down," he called, and turning to the two constables he gave directions quickly. One of them hurried up the spiral stairway leading to the flies, the other disappeared from view. Henry, his face white, had jumped on to the stage by the Inspector's side.

"It's all right, sir," the constable called. "The lady is up here, sir."

Frederica, in the flies, glanced round her despairingly. Eighty feet below her the stage quivered with light—behind her, at the top of the staircase, the constable stretched out a sweaty hand.

"Come back, madam," he urged.

Frederica kicked off her shoes and started to walk across the slack wire that reached across the poles supporting the drops from one side of the theatre to the other; her arms held out stiffly, her head high, she poised each foot delicately before placing it in front of the other; the scarlet dress hung down below the wire, on each side a frothy semi-circle.

"Freddie!" A shout from Henry shocked her into consciousness of what she was doing, but she did not turn her head. "You'll fall! You'll be killed!"

Mincing, like a doll on a string, Frederica edged along the wire; it stretched in front of her unendingly—fifty feet of it, at least, she reckoned. And the longest wire she'd ever crossed was thirty... once she could have run across, sure-footed as a cat... now, for a second, she allowed her glance to travel down between the drops, down on to the stage. In that second she wavered... and almost fell. Almost—but not quite. With a supreme effort she steadied herself and kept her gaze firmly fixed on the wire... her foot poised elegantly... her arms stiffly outstretched. Slowly, slowly, taking what seemed an age, she raised her eyes and looked across the flies. The tangled ends of rope and wire were swaying back and forth, but she could not notice things like that. Every fibre of her being was concentrated on the effort of balance... and she scarcely saw the fireman's ladder surmounted by a constable with outstretched arm ready to grab her to safety. But it was just the untrained movement of the constable that caught her eye... and for the second time she wavered... and the past flew before her eyes, unfolding like a reel of film. All at once it seemed useless to struggle—it was so much easier to give in. She relaxed, utterly and completely, and dropped like a stone on to the stage.

There was a dead silence... and then Archie's voice was heard crying:

"Bring down the curtain! For God's sake bring down the curtain!"

18

THE ROTTEN CORE

ARCHIE, KATHERINE AND DOCTOR HARLEY, ACCOMPANIED BY Mr. Smith, sat in the lounge at Henry Brown's apartment. Henry, his face ravaged with misery, lay stretched out on a sofa, his hands clenching and unclenching.

"I blame myself," he said again and again. "I blame myself."

Mr. Smith left his chair by the fire and came over to the couch. "I assure you," he said gently, "that nothing you could have done... *nothing*... would have made any ultimate difference."

"But how did you know!" Henry asked again. "What made you suspect?"

"First of all it was the shoes," Mr. Smith said. "When I realized that McCabe had gone out into the snow in his slippers... and I thought that it must be only for the sake of the cat... But really it was not until I knew for certain that Faustine Pravcek was Frederica Brown."

"I don't understand how she ever got into the country," Katherine said. "What about her passport?"

"A day trip from Boulogne," Mr. Smith said. "You'd be surprised how often it's been done. Once she was here the rest was easy. She would never see Krasnya again—why should she? and ultimately she would marry a rich man. With her looks she knew that she had only to be seen in the right environment."

Henry sighed without speaking.

"But how did you get hold of Krasnya," persisted Katherine. "I knew about him, of course, but I never saw him."

"He came down to New Scotland Yard because he was worried and upset about his sister. Then, when he was crossing Trafalgar Square a big car nearly knocked him down. He thought Faustine was driving—but he never saw the number... didn't get a chance."

"But I don't see why she had to go for Dimpsie—it doesn't make sense."

"Dimpsie was very friendly with Gallia—and Gallia told him she had a brother. Dimpsie had been over to the circus and seen Krasnya; Krasnya for some reason gave him the marriage certificate. He wasn't quite sure about Frederica and he made a wisecrack—just to see how the land lay. Frederica couldn't afford to take any chances. She knew she had married Henry bigamously, and she had to preserve that marriage at all costs. If it were ever to be found out, she would be deported—an alien, with nowhere to go. Glen Hemingway was in love with her, and she got him to show her how to fix a fuse. When she did it wrong on purpose, he explained what might happen. That was all she needed to know. She took Gallia's little dog and set it to chasing the cat... Dimpsie rushed out to rescue his pet, and that was her opportunity. As soon as she could she slipped out of the studio again, put the dog back in Gallia's room and rejoined the other guests. Gallia, hoping to have a private chat with Dimpsie, went back to get her little dog, and found his paws were wet. Guessing he'd been out she thought it wiser to leave Dimpsie alone, in case he had been the one to catch Ting and put him to bed. When she realized what had happened she never dared mention that she'd been back to the house. But Holly saw her... and Holly told Walters. It was Holly, too, who found the letter Krasnya had written to his sister. You see, it was when Frederica realized that Gallia was her sister-in-law that she began to get panicky. She felt sure that Gallia must know who she was, and she lost her head completely. I don't believe she ever meant to kill Gallia, but once she was inside the house and Gallia lay asleep in front of her, the temptation was too strong. No one had seen her go in—and no one would see her go out. She had an appointment with Mr. Hemingway—and she kept it. He never noticed anything different in her manner, she was as charming as usual. But it was Holly she was worried about now. Holly knew too much—she knew that Gallia had a brother, and she knew just how friendly Gallia had been with Dimpsie. It was Holly who discovered that Gallia was Polish, and she very foolishly mentioned it to Frederica. And Holly was too friendly with Henry... she wormed her way in everywhere, and Frederica was afraid of her influence. Once she had the sulphonate powders she arranged her plans easily; but she was afraid they might not have time to take full effect and that was why she went back to the flat. You caught her there, Miss Mickey, but she was too quick for you."

"I know," Katherine laughed ruefully, "I'm rather thankful she was. I wouldn't have cared for an encounter in the flat, I must say."

"No. She must have been astonished when you appeared in the restaurant."

"She never turned a hair," Katherine said. "I had had an extraordinary feeling that perhaps Mr. Brown had something to do with it—and I simply *had* to see him. And of course I realized that he didn't—couldn't—know anything about it. It did strike me that Frederica was surprised to see me—but then, she would have been. I wasn't in the habit of barging into people's lunches."

"I don't really get where Walters came in on this," Bill Harley said. "He was a strange individual—I never really understood him."

"I think that Frederica must have wanted to look through Dimpsie's papers," Mr. Smith said. "I imagine it was she who tried to get past Mrs. Smithers shortly after Dimpsie died. When she heard that the flat was being cleared out she couldn't wait any longer. She went to see Walters. We shall never know what he said to her—but he had that unfortunate propensity—he always had to pretend he knew everything, and this time he pretended once too often."

"She must have shot him while he was on the phone," Archie surmised.

Mr. Smith nodded grimly. "I think the phone rang and he went to answer it. Most probably she went up to him to say good-bye, and simply shot him as he stood there."

"But how did she get away?" Henry asked despairingly. "How is it possible that each time, *each time* she got away?"

"Because she had nerves of steel," Mr. Smith told him. Then he turned to Archie. "Mr. Tittop—I have a feeling you suspected something of what was going on?"

Archie looked supremely uncomfortable. "I'm afraid that I guessed what happened about Dimpsie," he admitted. "You see, Dimpsie was certain that Frederica had been married to Krasnya… he'd seen her photograph and he swore he recognized her. He had absolutely refused to allow her to appear in any of his plays, and it is possible that if she taxed him with this he threatened her with exposure. When I heard what had happened up at the castle—well, I'm afraid I guessed the answer."

"And yet you never said anything?" Katherine and Bill spoke together.

"It was only my guess," Archie said. "If Frederica had been down to see me… I rather thought at one time she would come. But she chose Walters."

Mr. Smith stood up. "Miss Mickey—you had a feeling that something was not right. Doctor Harley—were you perfectly satisfied in your own mind about Mr. McCabe's death?"

Bill shook his head. "I did discuss it with Katherine—but there was no proof."

"You see, if only someone had come forward at the inquest, it might have made all the difference."

"But no one knew anything for certain," objected Katherine.

"One has to find out," Mr. Smith said. "That's what we policemen are for." He went over to the couch. "I'm sorry, Mr. Brown," he said, "I wish it hadn't had to be me."

Henry put out his hand. "Please," he said. "I think all the time of how strange it is that one can live with someone, share the same bed and the same everything—and yet"—he made a gesture of resignation—"one can know nothing of the real person that lies hidden beneath a beautiful mask. Frederica was beautiful—and rotten to the core."

Katherine looked at Bill, her eyes full of tears. "Poor Henry," she said, "poor soul!" She went over to the couch and took his hand. "Just remember that she did it because she wanted to live with *you*, Henry," she told him gently.

"I wish I could believe you," he said, "I wish I could."

ALSO AVAILABLE
IN THE BRITISH LIBRARY
CRIME CLASSICS SERIES

Many of our titles are also available
in eBook, large print and audio editions